Victoria is going to the Moon
She'll claim it for
The Empire very soon.
She'll plant a flag for
Sovereignty,
Over her Luna colony:
Victoria is going to the Moon!

# 'THE PERIWINKLE PERSPECTIVE'

## VOLUME ONE

## THE GIANT STEP

# PROLOGUE

'The Moon is not made of cheese!' ~The Times, 24th of June, 1897.'...Neither; as we now know, is it lit from within by some infernal, extra-terrestrial engine. Nor is it populated by a race of green skinned, dust devouring devils, hell bent on the extermination of the human race; as had been predicted by several prominent members of Lord Salisbury's cabinet before the 'Victoria's' celebrated launch from St James' Park on Tuesday evening. These and various other populist presumptions were finally dispelled, earlier today, by Her Majesty's faithful servant: Space Captain Gordon Periwinkle, who proudly conquered that final of all frontiers for Queen and Empire, thus heralding a bold new era of scientific understanding and technological advancement for the benefit of all mankind. It may seem obvious to us now; living, as we do in such enlightened times, but; lest we forget, it is not so very long since our ancestors ceased revering this enigmatic, nocturnal orb as a god in itself: something to be feared and exalted in equal measure; not discounting acts of ritual human sacrifice! How quickly the times are changing! There are those, of course: the ubiquitous Luddites and the naysayers of our times, who would seek to reject Her Majesty's acquisition of the Earth's solitary natural satellite as an outpost for Her ever-expanding Empire; going so far as to decry Her ambition as 'profligate and ungodly'. To Her Majesty; however, the Moon's appropriation represents the very jewel in her crown; prized beyond even the Kohinoor diamond; possessing as it does, peculiar strategic value and thus ensuring her position as, 'Esteemed Empress of all The Earth' for years yet to come. Speaking at an ambassadorial dinner at Buckingham Palace, yesterday; having just been shown the photograph, reprinted on our cover for your delectation, Her Majesty proffered these words on the subject: "On the surface, she may be bleaker than the fantastical imaginings of a penny-chapbook artist: airless; featureless and sterile, and yielding none of the strange

9

minerals nor vacuum resistant vegetation that we had expected of her. Yet, next to the taming of fire and the invention of the wheel, ascendancy over our closest celestial neighbour is, and ever shall be seen as, the single most important venture in the history of our species." And so, what had begun as little more than a testosterone fuelled race between the late Prince Albert and his rocket obsessed kinsmen and those irritating upstart colonials, the Americans: a challenge between two would-be imperialist nations to be the first to build a conveyance capable of breaching our planet's atmosphere and of transporting an intrepid adventurer from the comfort of terra firma, all the way to the turner of the tides herself, had ended with an unforeseen and rather unwelcomed twist. Untold thousands of American dollars and yet more German marks had been invested in the projects of the greatest inventors that those nations could produce, whilst their English counterparts; the hitherto undisputed masters of industrial innovation, had merely scoffed at such ludicrous ambition, ridiculing their foresight with shouts of 'poppycock notion' and 'blasphemous balderdash'. Until, that was, it was brought to Her Majesty's notice, that whosoever could lay claim to ownership of such an unparalleled prize, would, from that moment forth, command control of the entire world. Within a week, the British press were claiming the race null and void as sketches of Victoria's Rocket, as it would become known, began appearing in the dailys across the Empire. The Americans; rather predictably, called foul, whilst their German counterparts proffered a series of barely veiled threats; both nations clearly rattled by Her Majesty's confident allusions; their own iron and steel contraptions appearing ramshackle and unlikely beside Professor Blaise's polished brass, Verneian phallus with her copper riveted portholes and her gleaming, triple fin rudder array, idling atop an enormous lattice scaffold; hissing steam venting from her three industrial boilers.

Space Captain Gordon Periwinkle had been an unlikely choice to command this, the most high-profile and costly endeavour in the entire history of blind pioneering. The real money had been on Fleet Admiral, Sir Archibald Spatchcock; the much-decorated naval frontiersman and trusted advisor to the Crown. He had indeed been the odds-on favourite for the role, right up until a reoccurrence of the gout had put paid to his anticipated appointment, ten days before the expected announcement; Victoria instead offering him the role of 'Mission Commander, Earthside'. Few, it transpired, had even heard of this 'Periwinkle' chap before his sudden elevation to the rank of Space Captain on the very day of The Fleet Admiral's unfortunate withdrawal, but none now would ever forget his name. Within a matter of a few short hours of his touchdown, Captain Periwinkle would achieve a level of immortality, previously known only to monarchs, presidents and serial killers. It was said some years later that everybody alive at that moment could recall their whereabouts at the very instant that Captain Periwinkle left the Earth.

The newly promoted Captain was not a military man, as many had expected to be the minimal qualificational requirement for such a posting. He was but a Gentleman Adventurer: a knight of the noble art of blunder and plunder and an amateur taxidermist on the side, and he had been as flummoxed as the next man to have found himself in the offing for such a plum enterprise, but The Empress herself; on the occasion of his pre-voyage audience, had explained to him that she had seen something in him that she had hitherto not seen in any of the other prospective candidates. He had realised much later, after taking his giant step for mankind, that the 'something' that his patron had been alluding to, had been his ultimate expendability!

And so it had been, that at seven thirty one on the 22nd of June 1897, as an integral part of Victoria's Diamond Jubilee celebrations, Captain Gordon Periwinkle; strapped securely inside the first ever space rocket 'Victoria', was catapulted through the clouds; his destination: the Moon! All across the Empire, street parties were held in his and his Empress' honour; those first few photographs taken of the surface, instantly sparking the imaginations of people the world over.

In America; following a public vote of no confidence, William McKinley: the 25th president of the United States: an office that he had held for a mere one hundred and ten days, was shot and killed on the White House lawn whilst attempting to proffer his resignation, by a disgruntled peanut farmer who had bet his shirt on his countrymen winning the race.

Seizing this unexpected opportunity to assuage his indignation; Kaiser Wilhelm II of Germany, brought forward his plans to destabilise his enemy, by declaring all-out war on the suddenly disorientated America. The 22nd of June 1897 would forever be remembered as the day that changed the course of human history...

\* \* \* \* \* \*

The Captain awoke to the sound of an alarm bell trilling from the dashboard in front of him...or had that been behind him? Or even above? Still harnessed in his pilot's seat, the dazed astronaut found himself hanging upside down, suspended by his own restraints; the strobing beams of a caged, red bulb, slicing through the wisping tendrils of rapidly escaping steam that quickly threatened to fill the cramped confines of the rocket's cabin. He had landed, he realised; though possibly not in the most appropriate of fashions. Releasing himself from the shackles of his bondage, he lowered himself to the ceiling and headed aft to the equipment lockers, there to retrieve his helmet; which he duly donned, screwing it into place by way of the steel thread, bonded to the brass neck and shoulder brace that itself was buckled to the top of his customised canvas diving suit. He connected the copper breathing pipe that protruded from the side of his tinted, tri-windowed diver's helmet, to one of several tanks containing the oxygen that he would need to be able to survive, and clamped it to the housing built into the chest unit of his suit. Twisting the tap on the bottle's neck, he took a deep breath, allowing the clean air to flood his aching lungs. Gathering up his photographic equipment; the flag, wrapped tightly around its pole and the mallet with which he was to hammer it home, he twisted the door's locking wheel widdershins and exposed himself to the bleak and foreboding landscape beyond. He took a deep breath and jumped, landing unceremoniously with a thud in his lead weighted boots. His first thoughts were these: "Hmm; it looks rather like a quarry in South Wales: grey sand, dust and craters full of what appears to be... Dolomite." He had travelled a quarter of a million miles in a highly polished tin can, on a one way ticket to somewhere that; in truth, could have passed for his place of birth; a few miles to the west of Cardiff.

That was not, of course, what he would tell the Queen, in the letter that he later wrote to accompany the photographic plates that he had captured of himself; the upside down Victoria (it's nose cone dented from where it had come to rest against a huge deposit of moon 'slate') and the Union flag... billowing gently in the vacuum of space.

'Hmm...' Again, that was a bit odd, he had to conclude. Physics was not a regular study of his, but even he knew this to be a little on the rum side. He decided not to mention it in his initial missive, though.

Attaching the pod containing the photographic plates; a small sample of local strata and his incipient first observations to a much smaller rocket, he aimed it; as directed: Earthwards, at precisely two twenty GMT and lit the fuse; making sure to stand well back. The firework was then supposed to follow a similar path to his own; he had been assured, before deploying a miniature parachute as it descended toward home soil. The Admiral had attempted to explain the theory to him, involving a series of algebraic equations, but; having never been one for over complicated mathematics either, Gordon had resigned himself to accepting an 'as long as They know what they're doing' attitude and had simply followed his instructions to the letter.

The bulk of his first Luna day was spent hauling various wooden sea chests and tea crates, containing both his questing accoutrements and his general comestible supplies, from the Victoria's hold; out across the dusty plateaux and into a convenient nearby cave, using only his brute strength and a specially weighted market trader's hand cart. He mused as he did so on the executive decision taken to send but a single volunteer on this; the most important voyage of discovery ever mounted in the history of the human race. What if he had been killed on impact or been injured; even only slightly, but in such a way that, without help, the entire mission would have been scuppered? It had made no rational sense to the famed discoverer of the lost city of 'Periwinkle', as he had named it; in his father's honour, of course! Never before had he adventured without a trusted sherpa by his side and he was less than comfortable with the reality of doing so now. The explorer's companion; it had been noted in many a professional adventurer's journal, was most vital in these situations, not solely for morale boosting purposes and the obvious tea and bed making duties, but equally for their uncanny knack for being able to rescue one in the nick of time from potentially life threatening predicaments. It was also useful; it had to be acknowledged, to have somebody at hand to caddy the bally kit. Gordon had argued this point, yet to no avail.

He had been told to expect to find the cave quite close to the rocket's landing site and, whilst to general cynicism he did not consider himself predisposed, he was of the abiding belief that it was both tea and healthy scepticism that had kept him alive thus far and so he had employed the latter to question the Admiral's uncanny foresight during the pre-mission briefing. His concerns, however, had been met; as had every other query that he had raised with the Earthside command team: with a patronising slap on the shoulder from Admiral Spatchcock and a repeat renditioning of his much loved caveat: 'Trust me, Gordon: we're British.' The Captain was not a scientist and he harboured no allusions of his ever becoming one; he had not expected to have understood the minutiae of the mechanics involved in putting a man into space, but then neither was he a simpleton, and he did not appreciate being treated as such, nor dismissed as if he were a mere component in one of Professor Blaise's new-fangled, steam powered devices. He had trekked through some of the least hospitable wilds that planet Earth had to offer; he had fought exotic beasts that no other man had yet encountered and had once even awoken to find himself lightly seasoned and gently stewing in a pot of leeks, over a tribesman's coals! An inventor of steam age marvels he may not have been either, but a man of quick wits and even quicker application he most assuredly was, and so when the Victoria's landing had not gone entirely to plan, he had expected to find the Admiral's plans duly banjaxed and requiring of a last minute rethink. He had therefore been sobered to find that he had yet managed to pitch up exactly as Spatchcock had predicted; such, it seemed, was the precision of the British made telescope!

Once unloaded, his next task had been to remove the Victoria's heavy airlock door and to bolt it into place over the entrance to the cave, sealing any gaps with cement; a small bag of which and a trowel for the application of, could be found amongst his supplies. With the door securely in place, he was finally able to remove his helmet and to slip into something a little more workaday, to make the unpacking of essentials, along with the assembly of the steam powered generator that was to provide his heat; his light and the power to run the Professor's newly patented 'oxygen converter', that much easier. His final proscribed task of the day had been the installation of the Morse transmitter and its accompanying aerial, but before embarking on this, he decided to take a break; to make himself a pot of tea and to break out the sandwiches that command had prepared him for the journey. It had been a long and arduous day thus far and he was quite famished; a few moments quiet contemplation after such a journey was surely every Englishman's prerogative and, after all, who was ever going to discover his tardiness?

And so, pulling his pipe and a tin of rough shag from his tunic pocket, he put his feet up on a large sea chest, sat back and began to consider his lot.

* * * * * *

Gordon had been aware since he had first been summoned to the palace, that the adventure being offered him was likely one of a suicidal nature. Although it had not been so explicit in the advertisement, it had seemed to him to be quite obvious that the facilities and personnel required to put a rocket into space would not be as readily available at the other end for the return trip. He was therefore unsurprised to be informed that, although her illustrious Majesty most confidently believed that they had the means by which to propel him safely Moonward, she was also aware that they did not possess the wherewithal to bring him back down again. But she had insisted that it was the Agency's intention that a second rocket be sent to join him as soon as was humanly possible. It was her abiding hope, she had confessed, that Professor Blaise: the brains behind the British Rocket Programme, would perfect the 'reusable rocket' within a matter of a few weeks, allowing Gordon to be relieved and to return home, though it was by no means a promise.

Gordon Periwinkle was the youngest of four sons. His eldest brother, Virgil was a respected surgeon, specialising in amputations and the fitting of mechanised, prosthetic replacements. Brother number two, Gerald Arthur, was a clergyman with designs on the bishopric: an ambition that; when last they had corresponded, had seemed well within his grasp. His closest sibling, Aubrey, was a member of the bar and making great waves due to a brace of high-profile cases that he had won for a dubious list of clients, against all due expectation.

It was fair, then, to say that Gordon had felt a certain amount of pressure weighing down upon his shoulders; a compulsion; if you will, to live up to the family's exerted standards and to make a proper name for himself in his chosen field of endeavour. Although ultimately requiring him to sacrifice his life for his country, this opportunity had seemed the most sure-fire manner of achieving that goal and so he had signed the legal disclaimer with pride and no delay.

Gordon had left neither wife nor sweetheart, weeping on the gantry; the fairer sex, sadly never having shown the slightest interest in his oft misjudged advances. He carried with him a single lithograph of an unrequited love. It was cruelly ironic, then that; had there been a way for the captain to have returned from his one way mission, he would have been able to have taken his pick from any one of the ten and a half million women resident in Britain at the time; not to mention the millions more inhabiting the further reaches of

Victoria's Glorious Empire and beyond. This particular meditation was not lost on him as he drifted off to sleep.

\* \* \* \* \* \*

On the morning of his second day, he once again donned his space suit and ventured back outside, retrieving the equipment that would enable him to broadcast his discoveries directly. Whilst abroad, he also embarked upon his first proper survey of the scene, collecting further mineral and dust samples; all uncannily similar to the rocks that he used to collect as a child, he noted. He then photographed the landscape from numerous different angles until he noticed the dial on his tank dip into the red zone, indicating that he had only five percent of oxygen left to breathe.

He had been looking forward to this; his first proper survey. He was the first man on the Moon, for heaven's sake and he was lucky enough to be the first human to experience what peculiar fascinations it had to offer. He would also be the first inhabitant of the Earth to view its planet of origin as a celestial body. That evening he confided to his journal the very depth of his disappointment. The tinted glass of his helmet made visibility poor; not that there was that much to see, anyway! The Earth, resplendent in only the night sky, looked eerily similar to the way that the Moon had appeared from the Earth below.

Having unloaded in scrawl in the privacy of his own cave, Gordon felt suitably enough satiated to be able to talk his experiences up as he conversed with mission control, via Samuel Morse's ingenious machine. Tapping out his observations, he was brightened to hear how; owing to his universally acknowledged bravery, the world had changed in his brief absence. The Kaiser; he learned, had succeeded in annexing twelve of the supposedly united states, with two more expected to fall before the weekend. Victoria's own empire had also grown to readmit the states of Idaho and Wisconsin in the north of the country and North Dakota was busily negotiating its own secession as Spatchcock tapped out his reply. The Captain ended his second night in orbit by asking how the proposed plans to send a second rocket with further supplies were proceeding but received only the dots and dashes necessary to spell out the word 'SLOWLY'.

Three weeks passed; each day almost identical to the last and punctuated only by his nightly conversations with the Admiral. The war had been picking up pace: German and British forces were now engaged in a bloody front-line battle, south of California.

It was on the Captain's twenty third day on the Moon, that the Admiral finally admitted that there would be no second mission. Periwinkle's exploits were now old news; 'The Great War', as it was being dubbed, had replaced him in the world's headlines. The Moon had been conquered and what a great day that had been for all, but the only other powers capable of indulging in such frippery were currently financially committed to wiping one another out. 'Besides,' the Admiral had quipped, somewhat caddishly, Gordon had felt, 'what kudos could possibly be gained by being the 'second' man to walk on the Moon, whatever his nationality?'

The race had been won, it seemed: Victoria had her trophy; the space programme was over. He had done a great thing for Queen and Country; doubtless he would never be forgotten, but now all that was left for him was either to starve or to asphyxiate. He felt that he had been let down and idly wondered whether there ever really had been a second rocket in the offing. He thought of his father, losing a son, but gaining a legend and he thought of his brothers, usurped beyond all retort by the very runt of the family litter. He wondered how they would take such forfeiture; whether he might now be recollected with a modicum of respect or whether their ingrained, mutual jealousy of one another might just tip them over the edge.

He had a single tank of oxygen to his name, along with a solitary tin of beans and a thrice brewed pot of Assam. He ate the beans, all the better to fortify himself for the task ahead. He was not going to die cooped up in a cave, like the Neanderthals had done before him; he was going out one last time. He would die the hero he had been painted; treading land that had ne'r been trodden before; for he was Captain Gordon Periwinkle: First Man On The Moon and he would die with the dignity of an English gentleman.

Closing the cave door behind him, Captain Periwinkle trudged out across the plain. He patted the Victoria's distorted nose cone as he passed and smiled at the gently fluttering flag. Over the past three weeks he had described the full diameter of the circle around base camp, up to the limit of half a tank of oxygen. Today he would set off to the very limit of that supply, to see whether there was anything but slate and dolomite to be seen.

He had breached his former perimeter by little more than a quarter of a mile when he thought he caught sight of a movement out of his right-hand panel: fleeting and incorporeal, but... He turned his head toward it, and... saw nothing. He checked his dial and saw that he was in the amber zone and down to his final ten percent, but he continued forward regardless, his resolve never wavering. Some two hundred yards further on, he saw it again; a blur of movement, dark against the littered grey chippings. It stopped; obviously sensing his laboured approach. He also stopped to focus... on a rabbit! Startled, the unlikely rodent bolted behind a grey outcrop and the Captain followed, though the animal had disappeared by the time he reached its anticipated position; a figment of his fading consciousness or proof that there was actually life on this god forsaken rock? Checking his dial, he found that the meter was now touching zero. He took a last look around; took one final dredged breath and... took another. And another. He tapped the dial with his gloved finger, expecting it to flicker, but it remained steadfast against the 'empty' marker. That was when he saw the fence; a long line of it, stretching out ahead of him for as far as his caged eyes could see; barbed wire coils topping its wooden posts. With one final, wary look at his expired oxygen dial, he reached up and began to unscrew his helmet. The air that met his lungs tasted clean and sweet, as opposed to the bitterness of that which he had been breathing for nigh on a month. Finally, freed from the tinted helmet that had made the Luna landscape appear so dull and in permanent twilight, his eyes closed instinctively against the glare of the midday sun. He could hear birdsong, and in the distance, past the boundary of the fence, he could see the trees that they were perched among. He dropped his helmet to the ground; took off his gloves and unclipped the lead weights around his ankles. This was not the Moon! Had he overshot? Was this, in fact Mars, or Venus, perhaps? But then he thought about the cave and how the Admiral had known so precisely where he was going to land. He considered how he had mysteriously blacked out during the voyage, only to regain consciousness upon landing. He had been duped! Moreover, the world had been duped! He pulled out his trusty trowel and began to enlarge what appeared to be a fox hole under the wire. Slipping through, he found himself on a gravel path, which he then cautiously followed along the line of the fence. There was a sign, a little way along it, which he squinted to read, but it seemed to be written in an alien tongue; the same alphabet, he realised, but making use of too many consonants and not enough vowels.

And then it hit him! This was not the Moon and it most definitely was not Mars, nor indeed Venus! The alien script was Welsh. He knew exactly where he was and, more importantly, how to get home...

\* \* \* \* \*

# CHAPTER ONE:

## 'KNOW THY QUARRY'

17th of July, Whitehall, London:

It had been his sole ambition since first the idea had been mooted: to be the first man to step upon the Moon; to be immortalised for an act of noble self-sacrifice that; by its very nature, could ne'er have been superseded. There could be no more befitting a swansong to such a long and distinguished career, and for one humble, but ultimately humiliating moment, that chance had been his; had that perfidious weasel of a Permanent Secretary not lost his nerve at the eleventh hour; striking him from the programme and depositing him here in this dank, subterranean crypt; presumably with the intention of acclimatizing him to the rotting box in which his weary bones would eventually lie.

Two decades of loyal, battlefield service in the name of Queen and Empire and another spent pushing little wooden battle ships across the floor of the admiralty with a broom handle, and they had reduced him to this: a paper shuffler; a 'public relations administrator': a politician, in fewer words; he whose task it now was to make sure that the truth of the matter never came out. A promotion: that was how it had been billed; a privilege, even: Commander of the newly appointed 'Space Agency'; the man in charge of the greatest peacetime bluff since the Empress herself had died and been replaced by a lookalike, back in '62.

He was a man of action, goddammit, not a bally desk jockey! He was a strategist and an order giver; a visible presence on many a campaign, back in his day: hands-on; always there at the back, just behind the big guns; out of range of enemy ordnance, where he could direct the action without fear of distraction.

Up and up the great ladder of command he had climbed; further than any other serving officer of his generation; all the way, in fact, to Fleet Admiral.

It had been the Secretary's opinion that; as such, he had been 'too good a resource to waste'; his experience too valuable to lose and that a more dispensable patsy be found to take his place on the mission.

Admiral Archibald Spatchcock was a living legend: that was how the people of the Empire had always known him, and so he had chosen to bear this insult like he bore the weight of age upon his shoulders, with dignity and quiet revanchist resentment toward any whom he saw as complicit in his usurpment.

The cruellest irony of all, here, was that it had actually been possible to have sent a rocket to the Moon. Dear old professor Blaise had been working on the conundrum for some years before the Secretary had insisted upon bringing the whole misstate shebang forward and; rushed as the Inventor Royal had been in those last few weeks, his specifications had been studied by the most gifted minds in the country; his equations checked and rechecked by the Empire's most eminent mathematicians and all had been in agreement that the theory and, indeed, the mechanics had been sound.

But then the Secretary had presented a revised plan: a scheme ratified by both government and monarch; a strategy designed to excise the possibility of anything going wrong.

He had reasoned it thusly:

"Why take the risk of sending a rocket all the way to the Moon; Spatchy, old boy, when no other nation has it within its power to prove whether we have done so or not? Success shall surely gain us everything, but disaster would be difficult to return from. Why, then, take that chance when we don't have to?"

He had presented his argument in that guilefully insincere way that the Admiral remembered so well from their school days together, his question, as ever, rhetorical.

The Admiral found the words of Lord Palmerston returning to mind; the Prime Minister at the time of the 'Big Switch', who had been of the staunch belief that the proletariat would not have been able to have contained their collective grief so soon after losing Prince Albert:

"Public morale must be maintained at any and all cost," he had insisted, "'tis but a small deception we make for the greater good."

Very few knew of the doppelgänger monarch's existence and just as few would have to be privy to the fact that her much touted claim to the Earth's only natural satellite was as fake as the face on the Penny Lilac stamp.

The Admiral closed the file that he had been reading before his anger had returned him to the path of melancholic reverie and poured himself a drink. Well, so much for the Secretary's fool proof plan, he scoffed, digesting the news that the supposedly gullible Space Captain Gordon Periwinkle had broken the fourth wall; ducked his sacrifice and was now heading back toward civilisation with a treasonous tale to impart. He downed his first Cognac of the day and mustered his bluster; a sudden rapping on his door bringing him back into focus.

\* \* \* \* \* \*

The Moon may very well be made of cheese; such was the opinion of Space Captain Gordon Periwinkle (deceased): former Gentleman Adventurer of international renown and owner of the most famous face never to have graced a coin. Quite frankly, he no longer gave a monkey's what the Moon was made of; he was angry; he was hungry and he wanted to go home. He felt a fool for having been so easily duped; night after night, tapping out his findings to the Admiral and his team at Space Command, all of whom had probably had a jolly hoot at his naive expense! Well, they would be laughing out of the other side of their faces just as soon as he got back home. He would write a memoir: a full exposé; he would make sure that the whole world knew that their glorious Empress was prepared to starve an innocent man to death merely to gain a strategic advantage over her nearest rivals! The world had been cheated that day into believing that Victoria Regina had held all the aces, and so had begun its inexorable transit in a direction that Gordon knew, in his heart of hearts, civilisation had never been destined to travel. He knew this because he had been an unwitting accomplice to these clandestine machinations, as his diary would insist: one but hoodwinked into aiding and abetting this great deception through the exploitation of his own vanity over and against his saner judgement. And whilst none of this had been of his personal orchestration, Gordon was none the less, peculiarly unable to shake the vexing feeling of complicity wracking his soul for his role within this felonious cabal.

Yes, he mused, smiling wanly to himself; that would make an excellent opening gambit for the book!

He stopped for a moment as the track that he had been following suddenly opened onto a wider, more deeply furrowed course, tapering into the distance in both directions. He removed his left boot and; leaning heavily against a sign that read 'CEFNGARW QUARRY. PRIVATE. KEEP OUT!', he pondered his predicament for a moment. If they had been prepared to let him die just to keep their subterfuge safe, then it occurred to him now that they would no doubt also be prepared to kill him to ensure that Victoria's secret remained that way. He would need to be cautious.

* * * * * *

"An 'Agent Z' to see you, Sir," Moneypenny announced; the secretary with the small 's', saluting and keeping her eyes resolutely above his head.

"Well, send him in; send him in!" the Admiral replied, eager to get things started.

"Very good, sir," she replied, ushering the agent in, then leaving and closing the door behind her.

"Shaka... warnoo, is it?" the Admiral attempted, a trifle irritated; presuming the name on the skim-read file in front of him to have been misspelled.

"Shikiwana, Sir. Father was a foreigner."

"Quite. Well come in; come in, Shakta... woony; come in and close the door behind you; careless talk, and all that."

"Thank you, sir; but its-"

"Take a seat," he interrupted, indicating the chair in front of him, "otherwise known as 'agent Z', yes?"

"Yes, Sir."

"Good. Now. Z. You come highly recommended, with an impressive list of... credentials, shall we say. Now, without wishing to cause undue offence, I anticipate your employ here to be brief."

"None taken, Sir, and yes; I expect it shall be."

"Good. Now, other than myself; my secretary and *the* Secretary, of course, does anybody know that you're here?"

"No-one, Sir."

"Good, good. You realise that the, uh... the 'task' that we have 'borrowed' you to perform, is one of the upmost importance for the security of the Empire?"

"Yes, Sir,"

"Also good. Now... it would seem to me that you are, in fact: 'a woman'. Is this correct?"

"Yes, Sir."

"Damnably clever, that; if I may be so bold?"

"Sir?"

"The trick with the trousers, there; remarkable. And the hair. Impossible to tell from this angle."

"I trained under the best, Sir; I can be anything you need me to-"

"Quite, quite. Now. Z. As you are aware, this is a 'Protocol Alpha' mission."

"Yes, Sir."

"Rather delicate question, this, but, well; I'm going to cut to th' chase... Is your... 'femininity' in any way likely to interfere with a Protocol Alpha operation?"

"Are you referring to my need to ablute whilst sitting down, Sir, or to the fact that you believe that I might be too squeamish to slit a man's throat without so much as a by-your-leave?"

"Neither actually. I'm more concerned about the fact that the target in question is a well-known hero of the Empire and; as such, quite probably, the most eligible bachelor in the world, next to the Prince of Wales, of course."

The agent paused before replying: "If I may speak frankly, Sir?"

"You may."

The agent paused, briefly, as if to consider her words, "I have killed more well-known 'heroes of the Empire'; several of whom could also have been considered 'eligible bachelors', than you've had bastard babies... Sir."

"Splendid! Then I do believe that we have an accord. These are your instructions, Z; when you've read them, be sure to eat them."

\* \* \* \* \* \*

Not for the first time since the world's press had witnessed his courageous, cloudward ascent; flung so very boldly, where no man had gone before, had Gordon found himself pining for the aegis of a good sherpa. He was not a man so easily spooked; he was an adventurer; a four square daredevil and hero of the bally Empire, who had proffered his very life; let no-one forget it, to Victoria and her lunatic ambition. Only a true mentalist could accuse him of cowardice; indeed, he would not have endured in his chosen profession for a mere fraction of the time that he had if every breeze to ruffle a tree; every hoot of the startled owl within it and every eerie howl of whatever phantasmagorical beast lay in wait for him in the undergrowth beyond, had made him flinch as it did so presently. A second set of senses was all that he really yearned for; now more than ever: someone to do the flinching for him and to watch his back whilst he gathered his thoughts and pondered his next move. He had been walking for just shy of three hours; having seen dusk surrender to an all too rare, balmy summer's eve; the desperation of his seemingly hopeless situation dogging his thoughts and leading him down the dark path of paranoia, as he trudged the gloomy road back toward civilisation. Over the nine or so miles that he had so far covered, a grim certainty had begun to take root in his mind: the unshakable conviction that Admiral Spatchcock would by now be aware of his unexpected survival and would have neatly deduced that the 'laughing stock of the Empire' would most likely be heading back to the family pile in Sussex; there to relate a tale of political skulduggery; tax payer deceit and international conspiracy for the delectation of his influential kin. For it was unlikely that he had been entirely alone in that quarry; there had to have been someone stationed nearby: guards of some description, whose job it would have been to keep local trespassers out and; presumably, to pronounce his demise when the time had come. Surely they would have noticed and telegraphed his absconsion by now, with the Crown's agents already on route to intercept him? He had therefore convinced himself not to head home just yet: a route that would no doubt be anticipated and duly staked, but instead to make haste for London; the very last destination that a wanted man ought head. Yet, even if they had discovered his escape immediately; dispatching a welcoming party from Whitehall forthwith, he ought still have a reasonable lead, he considered, though he knew that he had to move fast. He would be at his most vulnerable at whichever point he chose to cross the Estuary.

It was at this point that the sudden rhythmic clacking of a nag's brass shoes against the shingle and stone road, rent his internal monologue and sent him vaulting behind a dry stone wall; out of sight and scrabbling in the dirt in search of something with which to defend himself.

"Woah!" he heard, as a heavily laden cart came upon his former position, then stopped, mere feet from where he now lay; his right hand closing around a small chunk of slate. There followed a barrage of words; "Dwylo i fyny! Eich arian neu eich bywyd," none of which meant the slightest jot to him, though their tone gave their meaning away all too readily. Having spent his first five years not far from where he currently cowered, Gordon knew the timbre of the Welsh language well enough to identify it when he heard it ranted, if not the meaning of the individual words themselves. For although educated as a boarder in Cardiff, father had insisted that his boys be taught solely in English: the official language of the British Empire, and so he was at a loss to understand the exact nature of the threat being made toward him now.

"Shoo-my?" said the voice; followed quickly in English with: "hello?"

Gordon's fingers tightened around his makeshift weapon. "I got a rifle b'hyere, m'n," the cart man continued, "an' me an' my boys, see; we-"

"Okay! Okay!" spat Gordon, breaking cover; dropping his rock and raising his arms in humiliating compliance, but the startled cart man merely broke into a soot addled chuckle at the sight of him, and Gordon quickly lowered his hands; once again finding himself the butt of another man's joke.

"Thought y'might've needed a lift, boyo?" the cart man said, once he had contained the chesty cough that had succeeded the laugh, "you's a long way from anywheres, here, m'n; this late in the day... and quite frankly, see, I could do with the company... Dhai, by the way,"

"Gor- Dave," said Gordon, thinking on his feet.

"Pleased t'make yer acquaintance... 'Dave'," said Dhai, helping Gordon up onto the cart beside him, "Nice space suit, by the way; you know, you look just like 'Him'..."

Penarth: the port from where the majority of the area's natural mineral resources were loaded onto ships, bound for export to foreign climes. Gordon's new friend, Dhai, was a coal merchant, making his twice weekly trip to the dock in order to punt his wares. He was also; much to Gordon's irritation, an aspiring comedian. There had been several points during the uncomfortable journey south where he had found himself wishing that Spatchcock's agents might suddenly appear and put them both out of their misery. The only thing worse about the journey than Dhai from Llarffn's ceaseless torrent of excruciatingly predictable puns, had been the rain. Near permanent precipitation was a Welsh phenomenon; something that could outstrip coal as a national export, if only it could have been harnessed and sold to the people of Africa or India, but even here in the land of the bedraggled, a laden cloud still had to begin and end somewhere. Never in all his travels had he crossed into a downpour akin to this one. It had been as if he were walking through a waterfall! One minute it was dry and humid; utterly unlike the summers that he remembered from his youth, and the next; he estimated ten miles travelled from his starting point, the pair had found themselves in a more atypical Welsh summer: drizzle dampened, with a frigid wind whipping at any exposed body parts. It had been uncanny, but; alas, it had not even slowed the cart man's humour free delivery.

On arrival at the port, Dhai had redeemed himself to some extent by introducing Gordon to a friend with a boat, who was heading over to Weston first thing in the morning. It was as good a point as any, Gordon thought, to make the crossing back to Blighty; a fair degree wider than it would have been further along the coast, but in the hands of an experienced mariner, it was unlikely to be a problem...

\* \* \* \* \*

'Know Thy Quarry'. It had been the first lesson that Agent O had taught her when she had landed at the Agency, fresh from her training at the St Barrabus Academy for Stray Girls, all those years ago. It was all very well knowing fifty different ways to kill a man without disturbing his neighbours; so the theory went, but that knowledge was as nought if you had no idea where to find him!

Iggi was a professional assassin and a professional assassin did not even put saddle to horse without having a workable plan in place and this, inevitably, involved research. The way she saw it; having studied her target's file comprehensively over a jar or two in her favourite watering hole, there were three main possibilities to be whittled to one. She chose to consider the most obvious option first.

Ever since Gordon had become the second most famous person in the world, next; of course, to Victoria herself, it had become common knowledge that he and his three brothers had been brought up in a small mining town, just west of Cardiff; not far, as it happened, from his last reported position: headed south toward the coast on the Newport road. In fact, the local council had even renamed the town 'Gordonston' in his honour, putting up a series of little blue plaques on the outside of any building that could lay claim to his having stepped inside.

If Iggi had been in his shoes, then she would have opted to have gone to ground in an area known well to her. It would have made sense for the Captain to have reacquainted himself with the untamed wilds of the Welsh countryside and perhaps attempt to hook up with his late mother's relatives in order to buy himself some time and the contacts necessary to help organise passage to the continent. According to his file, Gordon's mother, Mirabeau, had been the daughter of an heirless local Lord. Following his wife's premature death in '66, Octavian Periwinkle; inheriting his late wife's late father's title, had returned with his brood to his own family's estate in East Sussex; all the easier to reach London in order to make use of his newly elevated position. The Williams side of the family; according to her own sources, had blamed Octavian for Mirabeau's death and had quite publicly severed all ties with their English counterparts; vowing bloody vengeance if their paths were ever to cross again, and so Gordon; it would seem, would have been as welcome back into their bosom as a bag of whelks at a Bar mitzvah.

Option two, then, may have had a few more teeth, but only if one were to presume imbecility on the Captain's part, which she did not. If he was indeed as dim-witted as Crown intelligence insisted on painting him, then his aim would be, as Spatchcock himself had envisaged: to reach the family pile at Pease Pottage, as quickly and as expediently as was humanly possible, working on the presumption that; as a Peer of the realm, his father would have been able to afford him some semblance of protection from those who sought to silence him.

Iggi, however, chose to discount this option too. Having browsed the highlights of a few of his more recent foreign sojourns, she was of the mind that the Admiral had been wrong to discount him so easily. Oh, she knew all about Adventurers and their tenuous relationships with the facts; she had put down a number of them in her time: the profession frequently being abused by those lacking even a shred of Imperial patriotism; those whom; presumably due to the amount of time that they had spent abroad, seemed so often predisposed to pocketing coin from an alien nation in exchange for a little extracurricular espionage activity on the home front. She was well aware that an Adventurer's reported successes were; more often than not, down to the calibre of sherpa that they engaged, rather than their own intrinsic wit and charm, but Gordon Periwinkle did seem to have survived far longer than the average privately educated kleptomaniac in starched jodhpurs; Pith and Saville Row Safari jacket usually did. He was either brighter, she deduced, than a fourth son had any right to be; luckier than any other chinless wonder who thought himself immortal simply by dint of his ancestry, or had made some kind of Mephistophelean pact to keep him from dying until his debt was paid in full. She made a mental note not to underestimate him as she felt that; to his detriment, the Admiral may have done. Which left the third possibility: that Captain Gordon Periwinkle had a hitherto undisclosed bolthole where he could hide whilst petitioning help from his brothers.

It was not unusual for an Adventurer to secure himself a discreet hideaway in this fashion, she knew; in common with the novelist and the playwright who might take lodgings on the coast or rent bothies on the shores of secluded lochs; somewhere to hole up in order to prepare their fiction for public consumption.

Gordon's three brothers were each, in their way, members of London society and Adventurer's retreats were usually within reach of the docks, so it made the greatest sense that London would be his destination of choice. Gordon's relationships with his kin were known to be fractious, to say the least, but at a time of crisis, she thought; if one could not relate to one's family, then who this side of Hades could one relate to?

After careful deliberation, Iggi decided to stake both her reputation and her Early Bird Bonus on option three and hailed the barman for a refill.

\* \* \* \* \*

Six hours was a long time to kill: a stranger after dark in an unfamiliar town; no coat; not even a hat to keep out the insidious Welsh drizzle and without a single shilling to his name with which to barter for a drink and the temporary shelter that came with it. This was not, of course, the first time that Gordon had been in such a position; it did rather come with the territory, after all. If he stopped to add it all up, he had probably spent half his adult life hanging around port towns, waiting for boats and for tides; often trying to avoid whatever locals he had in some way offended or had 'borrowed' something important from and that they wanted back on pain of death. The difference here, though, was that he was alone and; with the might of the British Empire against him rather than behind him, he was unable to call at the local Consulate for either a loan; a bed for the night or help with his onward travel arrangements. Consequently, the imperialist swagger that being a representative of the most powerful political system in the world tended to lend a man, was also gone, replaced by the furtive skulk of the starving and bedraggled fugitive. For that was what he was now: an outlaw on the run; a bounty to be collected; a man whose continued liberty relied upon both his ability to keep moving and his need to keep out of sight, whilst right now he could do neither. He was a rat in a trap, hemmed in on all sides by water. And just to add insult to his soul souring situation, every spare flat of brickwork in the bustling port of Penarth was plastered with a portrait of himself; heroic poses, rather than the 'wanted' posters that he had originally taken them for: stylised paintings of the good 'Space Captain', decked out in the deep purple dress coat of the Imperial Space Agency; gold braid aplenty; chest puffed; jaw jutting; moustache so perfectly rendered that it reminded him of a box privet arch over the entranceway to a rural vicarage. On his head they had chosen to include his favourite Pith; oh, how he wished he had that battered old treasure with him now: the one with the broken Zulu spearhead protruding through the band and around that, those brass rimmed, space farer's goggles that had proved so useless as protective eyewear, but which; for some immediately unfathomable reason, seemed to be the latest fashion accessory to hit industrial South Wales, as everybody that he had passed since his arrival in this smog bound backwater, seemed inclined to sport a pair. In the background of one picture stood the 'Victoria'; penile and glistening beside a great grey Luna crater. In another, she could be seen blasting off, amid a cloud of white steam, whilst in foreground he held a stiff fingered salute and a look so stern that he found himself intimidated by his own paper and ink reflection. In yet another, even less likely pose, he saw himself depicted, hands on hips; knee high booted right foot resting on a three tiered pile of bodies, which included a cowboy; a monocled, spike-helmeted Hun and a green skinned; three eyed, two tentacled 'alien'.

Was it his imagination or did everyone who passed him by look twice at him, convinced that they had seen him somewhere before? Did they think they recognised him from the billboards or the newspapers and what, he wondered, sweating into the converted divers' suit that he had lived in now for nigh on a month, would they be hoping to collect should they decide to dob him in?

"Dhai!" he called, suddenly catching sight of the coal merchant whom an hour ago, he had hoped never to see again. Dhai had just staggered from 'The Moon Beside The Water', a less than salubrious looking inn on the other side of the road and was attempting to use a newspaper as a makeshift umbrella, though failing miserably. He stopped in his tracks, belched; gutturally, and attempted to focus on the figure slinking in the shadows between two imposing wharf side buildings.

"Izzat you, Dave?" he eventually managed to slur.

"Dhai, I need your help," pleaded Gordon, slaloming past two laden coal carts as he crossed the road at a jog.

"Oh, ay?"

"Look, I need to get to London tonight; I'm afraid I can't wait for the tide. My mother is on her last legs," he lied, shamelessly, "I must reach her before the end."

Dhai wobbled forward, appearing to ponder the Englishman's quandary for a moment; apparently oblivious to the fact that his umbrella was in the process of becoming a papier-mâché hat. His eyes narrowed as if in deep thought before suddenly springing open, quickly followed by his mouth, as he spewed the contents of his stomach onto Gordon's moon boots.

"Tha's better, m'n," he said, wiping his lips on the sleeve of his sodden overall and smearing a line of coal dust from ear to ear in the process, making him appear as if he had been run over by one of those new motorised bicycles, "Well, see, if y'could get y'self to Newport, then y'might be able to stow y'self aboard the coal train before it goes through the tunnel."

"There's a tunnel?"

"Oh, ay. Under the Severn an' straight on t'London, see."

"Perfect!" said Gordon, putting an arm around Dhai's shoulder and steering him toward his cart, which was parked outside the inn; his horse still reigned, but snuffling away inside a nose bag, "How quickly can you drive this thing?"

Dhai stopped in his tracks and shrugged off Gordon's arm.

"I'm no' a bloody taxi, m'n," he insisted. He then belched; farted and slowly; as if somebody had tripped the switch that had been powering him, fell flat on his face into a puddle, dead to the world.

\* \* \* \* \* \*

# CHAPTER TWO:

# COMESTABLES, PAPER, SHERPA

'What was it about those damnable Periwinkles?' the Admiral brooded as he strode through the park; newspaper in the crook of his arm; sword stick jabbing the path ahead of him, helping to propel his substantial bulk forward like a punt along the Cam. 'They were a blight,' he concluded; 'had been since first he had come across them: chancers and bottom feeders'; "upstarts, the lot of 'em," he cursed aloud, startling a pigeon who had been minding its own business, scratching around at the edge of the path where the corn vendor had stood the previous evening, "Vermin!" he snapped, a line of spittle lodging in his Dundrearies as he batted the bird away with his cane.

As miffed as he had been to have found himself usurped at all; what had riled him more than anything else about the whole sorry 'Moon Man' situation was that it had been a bally Periwinkle that had done the usurping! Pushing open the doors to his club, he thrust his hat and cane toward Belmore; the doorman, and swept on into the smoky, wood panelled interior as if he owned the place; destination: his favourite chair; the high backed, cracked leather affair by the window. No sooner had he settled himself, but Belmore reappeared; silently and deferentially, to furnish him with his prerequisite cognac: a delicate, club monogrammed napkin between it and the silver tray that it arrived upon.

The Admiral paid him no more heed than he already had and was duly left to his private deliberations. He tried to bury himself in the latest news: casualty figures from the war; territorial losses and gains on the American front; an artist's impression of the 'Enterprise' space rocket on its launch pad at Cape Canaveral from whence they intended to launch the American Moon shot in a week's time. Four man crew...blah blah blah...to include Thomas Edison and his world famous 'movie' camera...blah blah...reusable rocket...blah blah...to disprove the risible British claim...blah blah blah..., but he found it increasingly difficult to concentrate now that his mind had settled on the Periwinkle issue.

He supped at his Cognac and pondered the past, choosing; as ever, to linger longest, on those events that it was outside of his power to do a damn thing about. 'The world turns on a sixpence,' he mused internally; 'decisions made in the moment affecting the path one takes ever after.' It vexed him no end that still; after all these years, he felt that the universe had taken a wrong turn that day back in '44: the day that he had planned to propose to his beloved Beau; the day that he had also received his orders to re-join the fleet and to head to Oregon as part of the British Navy's 'diplomatic' presence in the area. That was the day when the rot had set in; the day when the world had begun its journey along a course that it had never been meant to take.

It was to have been six months before his return to England; six months during which his sweetheart accepted the proposal of another man: one 'Octavian Periwinkle'; infamous gambler; philanderer and all-round cad about town.

He had received her letter on his return to London; indeed, had dashed off an instant reply, urging her not to be so rash; imbuing her with details of all that could be proven about his love rival's crimes, but he had heard not a word more from her. Alas, they had married; Mirabeau and Octavian, and over the ensuing twenty years she had borne him four sons: four shining examples of the Periwinkle pedigree; four fruits, each of which were to fall well within the canopy of the parent tree. Two of whom were rotten enough to warrant around the clock Agency surveillance and one, the subject of a rather hush-hush ecumenical investigation.

The fourth son: the youngest of the set and the one whose life the Admiral actually had both the power and the remit to affect, seemed the least offensive of this incorrigibly corrupt quartet, but the family rot was there, he just knew it! Gordon Periwinkle; on the surface, a patriotic example: a liberator of foreign antiquities; one of a veritable cadre of tomb raiders and relic plunderers, whose role it was to undermine the natives' confidence and leave them vulnerable to Imperial advances, but; as the Admiral well knew, Adventurers were a cunning breed. Although his rank and office afforded him use; upon occasion, of the Crown's most special agents, privy he was not to all that they surveyed. Word did, however, slip out; most often at a dinner party or a social junket of some kind, and so he was keenly aware of the number of Adventuring types who had gone over to the dark side and who had had to be brought to book. Considering the 'Space Captain's' heritage, it seemed sensible to presume that the runt of the Periwinkle litter had at some point been compromised and was in fact, currently working for an alien power. It was a well-known fact in security circles that brother number three had Hun sympathies; he had even gone so far as to have married a bally Helga, for sooth sake! Yes, it was highly probable, the

36

newly instated head of the Imperial Space Agency concluded, that his target took his shilling both ways. It was, therefore, a matter of National Security that he be brought down, rather than it being an unfounded, personal vendetta...

\* \* \* \* \*

It was a peculiarity of his particular trade that the outbound journey tended to be more comfortable than the homeward leg ever was. Outbound he had often made use of such grand conveyances of the age as The Orient Express or The Majestic; depending of course, on who was footing his bills, whereas inbound; having pretty much exhausted any sponsor's advance by this point; mainly on gin cocktails and backgammon, he had often been known to have travelled steerage or to have cadged a lift in a freight car or a guard's waggon and once; having exhausted all other freeloading possibilities, had even begged a berth on a troop carrier, ferrying the wounded home across the channel; pride never having been an indulgence of his, where an expedient return was required. However, by far the most uncomfortable; not to mention demeaning of return journeys that Gordon had ever had the misfortune to have blagged, had been this one: his route from Severn Tunnel Junction, Gwent; non-stop, all the way down to London, hidden for the duration beneath a damp, oil stained tarpaulin in an open cart full of coal. The first four miles of the fuliginous, bone shaking nightmare, had been spent trying to hold his breath, so as not to have been rendered insensible by the smoke that filled the cramped subterranean rail tunnel, whilst the rest had been spent coughing up soot, in tribute to the dawn chorus of Dhai and his ilk, and bracing himself as the train had clattered over an inordinate number of ill-fitting points as it rattled its way southwards.

On the upside, it had at least been quick; contextually speaking, and without death defying incident, and by the time that he was ready to alight at Paddington station, there had been little chance of his being recognised, despite his recent rush of fame; resembling, as he then did, the Golliwogg rag doll that he had so loved as a boy.

If the townsfolk of Penarth could be said to have been keen to worship his noble visage, then they were to be considered as slackers to the good people of the capital. Where a month ago he would have expected to have seen hoardings advertising everything from 'Lifebuoy soap' to 'Bass Ales' and 'Twining's Tea'; to name just those brands whose advertising techniques he had found himself most susceptible to, his own mug shot now rose from pavement to second floor window all the way from Maida Vale to Shoreditch: the remainder of the journey, which he had had to cover on foot.

Just shy of the Bethnal Green road, he came across a new variant on the heroic pin-up theme. Easily twenty foot in height, it portrayed him leering out of the wall, the index finger of his giant right hand pointing forward, with the gently billowing union flag in the background and the words: 'Your Country Needs YOU!' underscoring his portrait.

Gordon's 'bachelor pad' had been a gift from his father for the discreet entertaining of 'other' gentlemen, so as not to impugn the family's good name; Periwinkle senior being of the erroneous, and quite insulting belief; the Captain felt, that his youngest son's failure to win himself a bride alluded to the distinct probability that he therefore preferred his shirts buttoned from the other side!

Never had he been so glad of his father's misjudged disappointment in him.

Carefully; just in case the Crown had done their homework properly before signing off on his death warrant, Gordon slipped his key into the lock of his bolthole's back door; wiggled it about a bit and pushed it aside, in much the same fashion that he imagined Lord Periwinkle might expect him to behave with a pretty-young barrow boy from Spittle Fields market on a balmy summer's eve. It squeaked, irritatingly, as he closed it behind him.

Sticking to the outside edges of the stairs, he ascended cautiously toward his attic bedroom; following a rather queer sound of muffled groaning, interspersed with a rhythmic slapping sound, as if someone were spanking a plucked, but pre stuffed chicken against the wet porcelain wall of a public urinal.

"Begads, man!" he exclaimed, entering the room to find the faces of two men, one directly above and behind the other, staring at him with a mixture of surprise, fear, awe and ecstasy. The higher of the two gurners, and the older by a reasonable twenty years, he recognised instantly as his God-fearing brother, Gerald.

"Ah!" said Gerald, seemingly unwilling to pause in his endeavour, whilst attempting to explain himself to his youngest sibling, though more likely; Gordon decided, on later reflection, quite unable to interrupt what he had started at this inconvenient juncture, "It's not what it looks like, you know; oh! Oh! Oh! Lord, be praised; the devil be banished from this heathen child!"

Gordon; uncertain as to the etiquette in such a situation, raised an eyebrow; pursed his lips and stepped awkwardly from the room, taking up temporary residence on the small landing at the top of the stairs, whilst contemplating this unanticipated turn of events. A few embarrassing moments later, the door swung open again and the younger of the two men came out at such a lick, that he managed to clear the staircase in three strides, disappearing through the pantry and the back door like a rocket fired from a catapult; destination: Moon.

"Would you care to say what it *is* like, then?" Gordon enquired, re-entering the room and instantly regretting the choice of words that he had been practising in his head on the other side of the door.

Gerald, now composed and clothed in full bishop's regalia, frowned and squinted at his brother.

"Pinky! It bally well *is* you! For a moment there y'had me believing you t'be some infernal apparition sent to damn me soul, but no, blast it; Gordon's alive! But tell me, pray: how the very buggery did you get home?"

"I walked," Gordon replied, unflinching; moving toward the room's only window and risking a peek through the curtain, down into the street below, "for the last part, anyway."

Turning back to the window he continued: "I had hoped for a bath and a bite to eat before falling betwixt the crisp white sheets of my own bed, but, as I can see quite clearly from here, they are neither crisp nor are they white."

"Nor are they 'your own'," replied Gerald, defensively, explaining: "They told us you were dead, dear Pinky: starved to death, they said. Sorry t'hear it; rum do, an'all, but in y'r absence, his Lordship turned the place over t'me. He thought I might need a bolthole, meself; somewhere away from the bustle of public life'n all; what with me promotion, don't y'know?"

"Did he," a statement rather than a question from the wounded party.

"But, what with reports of your demise being somewhat... premature, perhaps you and I could come to some... arrangement?"

"Gerald, you disgust me," Gordon began, after a deep and thoughtful breath, "I ought to report you to a magistrate and then, as head of the church, to the Queen herself, but I shan't, as I don't believe th't that would be of benefit to either one of us at this moment in time."

Gerald hooked his staff over the bed's headboard and slunk around its edge to sit on the end. He removed his Mitre, resting it in his lap; revealing a ring of sweaty curls encircling a fallow, pink pate; damp and glistening in the candlelight from his previous exertions.

"So, father was correct in his assumptions," he said, unable to keep the rapture from his tone, "you too like to walk on the Wilde side!"

"Begads! I most certainly do not, Sir!"

"Then y'have me flummoxed, dear boy," said whilst rebalancing his mitre atop his head once more, "perhaps y'would like me to hear y'confession anyway?"

Gordon had confessions aplenty; revelations that would startle clergymen and heathen alike! One came to mind instantly: the image of his loading of poor Dhai into the back of the man's own cart, then abandoning both cart and its inebriate owner outside the terminus for the Severn Tunnel, but he swatted it aside. There would be time for recriminations later. He was tired. His mind had not been entirely his own, these past hours: plots of a malignant nature clashed with his pious programming. Ungodly thoughts; cruel and unseemly conceptions; provoked in part by fatigue and dehydration, he knew, but complicated further by the frustration that he felt at his unfair predicament and the loneliness of his singular plight, raged in the churning mire of his cerebrum. His journey had been arduous, but in all fairness, it had been a doddle if he were to compare it to some of the tight escapes that he had endured, many of which had been life threatening in ways far grislier than death by inhalation.

He was reminded of the time that he had discovered a tribe of cannibal pygmies, east of Limpopo back in ninety four. They had taken exception to his making off with their god and had vowed to make a midmorning snack of him at their earliest convenience. He had been lucky enough that day to have survived the encounter with only a few minor scratches and a single bite to the left ankle; thanks in the main to the bravery and refined wits of his trusty sherpa, Andho, who had graciously lain down his own life so that Gordon might make good his return to London, thereby ensuring the little crystal idol's permanent safe keeping in The British Museum. Damn their insistence that the Moon mission be but a solo jaunt; he always worked better as part of a team!

He felt certain that; with a little qualified assistance in his employ, they would have uncovered the Admiral's dastardly plot that much sooner and had the time to hatch a more sensible counter than simply run.

He swung a chair from its place beneath his desk, placing it to face himself directly opposite his brother. He sat down heavily; legs astride its back rest; hands still clutching at its wooden top: an ungainly and deliberately rebellious posture, intended to remind his cassock-bothering kin just who had the upper hand in this situation. It had been a long and weary day covering those last few miles and with an end point to his hellish journey finally in view, both his mind and his body had begun to flag in sympathy with his spirit. He was tired, hungry and no less irritable that events had taken this unexpected turn. None except himself and his father had known of his connection to this place, or so he had thought. He rarely visited it himself, using it more as a place to store his trophies and as a writing retreat when the family home became too crowded with siblings and their damned offspring. It should have been his safest haven: a place to rest and to plan his next move. Could Gerald's involvement make for yet a further unnecessary complication, he pondered, as he prepared to answer the question that had been proffered, or was there yet the possibility that his presence might prove fortuitous and advantageous?

"My confession?" he said eventually, forcing a sarcastic smile through his evident exhaustion and meandering thought train, "Oh, I have a confession, Gerald, but it is nothing that I ought be hanged for; though I fear my end may be none too far away, regardless."

He paused in his delivery, watching for a reaction from the salty bishop before him, "I hold the distinction, Sir," he intoned gravely; eyes fixed on his brother's, "of being the bearer of a secret that; once revealed, may well form the catalyst that topples the British Empire; a concealment," he added, melodramatically, "that could, even yet, end the reign of Victoria herself!"

"Oh, Pinky: confess; confess!"

"Oh, I shall Gerald; believe me I shall, but first I will need to secure a promise from yourself."

"No need, brother dear; my silence is implied! I have taken an oath-"

"You forget, 'brother dear', that I have witnessed the apparent gay quietude with which you are able to 'interpret' your oaths-"

"On my life, Sir! If y'would be kind enough not to 'interpret' what you've witnessed here t'night in such a way that I would appear less than the paragon that me station requires, then to the very grave shall I take whatever woeful tale y'have to impart."

And so Gordon told him, all about the Moon mission, the homeward trek that followed and the probability of his imminent assassination.

\* \* \* \* \* \*

As with so many of the country's finer drinking establishments; 'The White Rabbit'; since last Iggi had been a patron, had been renamed in honour of the Empress' prized acquisition. Inside, however, 'The Moon Under Water' had changed barely a jot; It remained, she was uplifted to discover, the very hive of scum and villainy that it had earned its reputation for being, these past sixty years. The only immediately discernible difference was that, from the serving staff, all the way down to the very scum and villainy that regularly frequented the premises, all now wore a pair of space farer's goggles, as a tribute to the supposedly late Captain Periwinkle; as had become the fashion of the moment; either over the eyes themselves; hung around the neck like a councillor's chain of office or clamped around the band of whichever style of titfer that particular individual believed suited them best.

Iggi was no follower of fleeting sartorial trends. Individuality tended to play against the discretion required in her particular line of work. Nondescript was her byword; bland and unremarkable, her motto. With her close cropped hair of the shittiest brown; her tight leather chaps tucked into black docker's boots; black blouson and matching Westcott arrangement, topped and tailed with an ankle length duster and a bowler hat, the assassin's assassin found that she could move through the Empire with total impunity, raising only the rarest of glances, and then only from perverts and fetishists.

It is said that, in times of war and turmoil, human technology advances at a pace unrivalled during the intervening years of peace and prosperity. Great leaps of ingenuity are seen to be made to counter such requirements that may otherwise not have presented themselves, possibly for years yet to come.

This had certainly been the case with the war currently being fought on the American front between the invading Hun and the colonists, backed by the might of Victoria's Imperial Army and the allies that she had so far rallied: Ferdinand Von Zeppelin's great behemoth airships, for instance; a flight of fancy, until recently; according to the Empire's latest organ of propaganda, The Daily Mail. Almost a decade on their namesake's drawing board, they now blotted out the Californian sun in their hordes as they massed in the skies above Los Angeles like a pod of airborne whales, preparing to drop their heinous payloads of 'Greckle Bombs' onto the undefended streets below. And the British response: the anti-airship gun; a huge, cart mounted cannon, capable of propelling an arrow-tipped missile skyward, with a velocity and precision deemed impossible only months before, when the necessity for such an exacting weapon had yet to be foreseen.

And Iggi herself had the war to thank for the valuable contraption that her trailing oilskin helped secrete from public view. She had lost her right arm from the elbow joint down; a year previous, during a mission to return a kidnapped Prussian Princess. She had been fitted with a steel hook by the service and sent on a retraining course to learn how to ply her trade left handed, but; due to those same sudden advances in technological thinking, she now wore a veritable 'Swiss army knife' of a prosthetic; at first glance, indistinguishable from the real thing, but at the twist of a dial and the flicking of a few Bakelite switches, capable of transforming into a multitude of specialised armaments, making her the most formidable agent on the Crown's books.

Funny how things turn out, she considered, as she supped her ale from her own pewter tankard. Were it not for this war, she would no doubt have continued in her line of work; she had, after all, a long and distinguished service record behind her, but would probably have found herself relegated to third choice for an assignment such as this, whereas now, she had not a single peer who could match her, either for speed or efficiency in the field.

But whilst gadgetry and ruthlessness were both equally vital components in the executioner's arsenal, it never failed to surprise her how frequently happenstance played an essential role in her missions too. 'When in doubt,' Agent O had taught her, 'step back from the picture and let the world flood over you. Allow yourself to become a part of the background scenery. Watch. Listen. Absorb...'

One conversation began to surface above the general tavern hubbub:

"I'm telling ya', Jack; it was 'im! No doubt about it! Large as life, 'e was; jus' standin' there like you are now."

"You're pullin' my todger, Badger, me ol' son! 'E's dead, I tells ya'; starved t'death, 'e did, an' all f' th'good a the Empire; gawd bless 'im."

"On me dear ol' muvva's life, Jack Winters; I seen 'im, plain as day, I did. 'Ow could I mistake 'im? 'Is bleedin' mug's everywhere! An' anyways, I was servicin' the bishop, at the time, weren't I, an' 'e's 'is bruvva!"

The Service had trained Iggi to be able to pick certain words from the overall gabble and hue of a location and to be able to focus in on them like a barn owl spotting a shrew from the uppermost branches of its roost.

She had committed Periwinkle's file to memory; she knew details of every family member and close associate, from their stated professions to their regular haunts, right down to their secret; often illegal, wants and proclivities.

She continued to watch the pair for the next thirty minutes, eavesdropping as their conversation meandered through a succession of tall tales and debauched assignations, until the younger of the two finally put down his glass, made his excuses and slipped out into the alleyway to relieve himself.

"Mr Badger, isn't it?" she asked, as innocuously as she could, and from close behind his right ear. Her left hand was already around his throat and her right, a little lower as she pulled him in toward her in order to minimise his chances of breaking free.

"Ere, gerroffa me-" but Iggi merely tightened her grip; the sound of whirring cogs and gears presumably adding to the boy's panic.

"The hand currently encasing your plumbs, Mr Badger," she said, "is not; like your plumbs themselves, made of living flesh and blood. I expect you can feel a certain coldness about it; am I right?"

"'Ere, whaddaya' think-"

"'I'm doing', Mr Badger?" she said sarcastically, gently squeezing the snipes testes in her artificial hand to show him that she meant business.

"In a moment, I'm going to ask you a question," she whispered; so close that he ought to have been able to feel the very heat of her breath on his eardrum, "and I am going to need you to think long and hard about the answer that you give me. You see, I'm only going to give you one chance to get that answer right, and if I were to imagine for just one second that you had lied to me, then I would continue to squeeze these torpid tallywags of yours until what you had dangling beneath your rancid sugar stick resembled nothing more than one of the Kaiser's balloons with one of Victoria's spikes poking through its side. Do I make myself clear, Mr Badger?"

She tightened her grip for effect, eliciting a squeal from her victim, not dissimilar in pitch to the sound a rat makes when you poke it with a skewer.

"Y-y-yep; quite clear, miss!"

"Glad to hear it. Now, I need an address, Mr Badger. I need you to tell me where you 'serviced' the good bishop."

There was a pause, broken only by a whirr, a click and her victim's shriek as she squeezed ever tighter.

"Awright, awright!" he said, affecting a falsetto tone, "I'll tell ya'; just don' 'urt me sacks!"

"I'm waiting, Mr Badger-"

"142 Lombard street, Shoreditch!" he snapped, "now let go a' me-!"

"Gladly," she replied, allowing his testicles to drop back into place below his shrivelled member; sore and a little bruised, but essentially intact.

She waited for him to breath a reflexive sigh of relief, then snapped his neck back with her left hand and gently lowered him into the reeking gulley.

\* \* \* \* \* \*

It was an important ritual of his; immediately upon returning from a death defying foreign expedition, to take to his bath; there to remain for an extended period; not solely in order to soak away the accumulated detritus of however many weeks spent without such civil comforts as warm water and carbolic, but also to partake in a relaxing meditation in order that he might mull the events of his trip and begin to formulate in his mind, a more palatable, yet no less riveting narrative, for the divulging of at whatever society dinner parties he found himself invited to, henceforth. He made a point, though, never to commit a single line of these edited anecdotes to paper until he had dictated said adventure at least four times. They improved through the telling, he had always thought and with the addition of the odd minor embellishment, hither and thither; to aide in the tale's ebb and flow, of course and in no way to distort or misrepresent his role in the affairs in question.

A good soak, he had always maintained, did more to clear a man's head and to enliven his mood than any amount of bishop-bashing ever could. Fewer disputes might have ended in gutter brawls if more people recognised the need for a regular steaming of the synapses, he mused, as he lay there wrinkling and absorbing the lavender infused vapours.

It was the ability to appreciate the benefits of a good bath, Gordon had often declaimed, that was what set the British classes apart. He pitied those who shunned such practices; who considered them decadent or unmanly, and would willingly debate with any man who would accuse a 'soaker' of having time on his hands to waste. Time spent alone, naked; and semi-submerged, was not a whimsical luxury of the decorated and the privileged, but a modern necessity and the right of all men, however macho or virile their claim. It was not even just for the cleansing of the body and the rejuvenation of the mind, but equally essential, he felt, for the reinvigoration of the spirit. Thus, Gordon found himself perfectly relaxed and mere seconds from drifting toward his first perfect slumber since departing London all those weeks ago, when he heard the first shot ring out.

He and Gerald had eventually achieved an accord that evening: they would share their Shoreditch digs; neither speaking a word of the other's position, until such time as the most famous man in the Empire could work out a way to show his face abroad without bringing about his own demise. He would stay under house arrest; safe and comfortable there, if not free to enjoy his fame, whilst his brother brought him food and a daily copy of The Times. Gerald had also been given instructions to set forth for 'The Adventurers' Club' at his earliest convenience; there to secure the services of a young and rugged sherpa. Gordon may not have been in the business of embarking upon an exciting foreign quest, just presently, but he felt underdressed without one at his side: insecure; unprotected and like one of those poor Bedlam inmates: locked away for the crime of merely dictating their inner monologue to none but themselves.

Plans for the following morn made, he had disrobed and begun drawing his bath whilst Gerald had gone downstairs with the intention of trying to fathom the workings of a kitchen in the absence of any kind of domestic staff. Gordon estimated the passing of forty five minutes since his brother had gone in search of the means by which to fry an egg and to toast some bread. The sound of the shot had come from the very same direction, meaning that; in all probability, Gerald's gelatinous bulk had stopped a bullet meant for himself. He would find the time to mourn his brother later. In the meantime he had a more pressing matter to attend to: he had left his towel warming in front of the fire in what passed for a drawing room in this godforsaken backstreet hovel, with Gerald tasked with retrieving it on his command. Baths were all well and good, he thought to himself now, as he dripped onto the rug and dabbed at his nethers with a dry flannel, but they did tend to leave one at a temporary disadvantage if an assassin came a calling.

He was good: this assassin, Gordon considered, pulling the spare britches that he always kept; freshly laundered and ready to change into, following a post adventure soak, up and over his still damp legs, before wedging the chair that they had been resting upon, at an angle between the door handle and the slatted boards. It was obvious to him that his erstwhile murderer had judged the staircase's likely propensity for creakage and was even now tiptoeing up, using only the outer edges of the stairs for traction.

Gordon used the time to slip a fresh, white cotton shirt over his head; to tuck it in, then button and buckle the casual, but clean ensemble into place. Pulling up his braces, he then stepped into his awaiting boots; all this within a minute of leaving the water. One learned to dress quickly whilst on safari. Heroic as his litany of deceased sherpas had always been, they could only have held off a rampaging bull elephant for so long!

Still hearing nothing from without, he reached above himself; unhasped the skylight and, clasping its frame with both hands, hauled himself upward in a single fluid movement; none of this a second too soon, it would transpire.

He had expected his stalker; upon finding the bathroom door locked and barred from within, to attempt to shoot out the lock with the pistol that he knew them to be stowing. What he had not anticipated; not even in his most fevered of malarial imaginings, was for a hail of automatic ammunition to pulverise both the door; its withholding frame and a goodly portion of the surrounding brick and mortar work; the remains of which, to rain as a sediment of dust; plaster shards and splinters on top of his recently vacated tub.

It had been his intention to have dallied for a beat; time enough to catch a glimpse of his potential reaper's face, but in his surprise, he had lost his grip and begun to slide gracelessly down the tiled roof; flailing wildly, akin to one of those crackpot hobbyist aviators who occasionally threw themselves from the upper walkways of Tower Bridge, bravely flapping a pair of wooden wings and bellowing "Geronimo."

Boots first; finesse last, he hit the tiles of the outhouse as they would have breached the Thames, and with gravity being the force that it is and inertia its obligatory bedfellow, the pair took him through the slates as easily as had they been a film of winter's morning ice in the toilet bowl that he very narrowly missed putting those self-same boots through.

Above him, the assassin; having reached the open skylight, had estimated his downward trajectory and begun firing random shots into the gloom of the cobbled yard below.

"Oh, Darkness, my old friend," Gordon whispered to himself, pulling his coat from its hook on the back of the door; one that he had obviously left there the last time he had availed himself of the facilities, and; using the cover of the ever present London fog, scarpered down the grime worn alley which linked the rear entrances of the terrace, for the purpose of stringing anti-assassin, low level washing lines, hung with all manner of victim concealing shirts; frocks and bedding requirements from pantry to outhouse.

\* \* \* \* \* \*

The bishop had been no mistake. Much as the nuns who had brought her up had insisted that the murder of a member of the cloth be 'sin of all sins', Gerald Periwinkle had known too much and therefore had needed to be silenced forthwith. If there had been a mistake, then it had been in her shooting the man-mountain at the foot of the stairs, thus impeding her access to the hovel's upper floor. This, Iggi later estimated, had been the few stolen moments that her prey had been able to utilise in order to affect his escape across the roof.

But the exercise had not been wholly wasted. After a short recce of the remaining rooms, she had been able to ascertain that this had indeed been her target's own home: the badly stuffed animal heads and crossed Zulu spears, mounted at regular intervals wherever wall space permitted, was all the evidence she required. This, then, was his safe place and his brother: his ally, and she had successfully dealt with both, making the Captain a more desperate and thus easier duck to flush.

With the star of happenstance still ascending that day, Iggi was unsurprised to find a hand scribbled note on the pantry table, weighted down by a stuffed squirrel, which read: 'COMESTABLES, PAPER, SHERPA'. It was a shopping list, she surmised; an unusual one, fair to say, but it told her everything that she needed to know in order to snare her rabbit once and for all...

\* \* \* \* \* \*

'The Adventurers' Club' was a gentleman's private dining and social establishment, sited just off Piccadilly. It had been in existence for the better part of eighty years, by this point. Its fellowship was exclusive and by invitation only; an invite that was only made available to those who had carved a career from their expeditioning, rather than simply being an après dinner bore. Gordon had been a member since his adventures in Timbuktu in '86, with his accounts being recorded in the annals of 'The Adventurers' Logs' since the following Spring. In between expeditions he had also built himself something of a reputation as the club's go-to 'stuffer'; his skills with needle, thread and sawdust reaping him a tidy extra income. He passed several of his own works as he eased himself in through the store room window: Arnold Wilberforce's Dodo, for one, with its slightly too small, replacement pigeon's feet, along with Sebastian Prendagast's Mammoth's head, which, although working only from pencil sketches; having never personally witnessed a living example of the beast, Gordon still considered one of his best efforts.

It had been necessary for him to enter the club in such a clandestine manner, as he had felt it an odds-on wager that; given the Admiral's zealous need to keep history as it had already been falsely written, the members' entrance would have most likely been under close surveillance by associates of whatever low personages had spoiled his bath, earlier. Also; he knew Mister Rumpole: the club's humourless maître de, to be an absolute stickler for house rules, disavowing deceased members even before the ink had dried on their certificates of death! Once a member had been declared legally dead, all privileges pertaining to such membership were instantly revoked, necessitating a lengthy process of re-evaluation and reapplication if; at some later date, the member in question were to make an unexpectedly miraculous recovery. There was an oft told tale of the 'almost late' Nathanial Trevallion; a man reportedly devoured by piranhas up the Amazon in '81, which had even led on the front page of The Times, but whom; one month later, had attempted to reserve a table for dinner and been given short shrift by Rumpole, regardless of the fact that he was the man's nephew and had known the reportage to be erroneous for an absolute fact. Gordon had neither the time nor the inclination to argue the toss with the man over how he had come to survive his widely advertised death in orbit, any more than he felt obliged to out-run another of Spatchcock's hired killers, so the stock room window it had had to be.

Like everywhere else that he had frequented since his Christ like second coming, things; it appeared, had altered somewhat in his absence. Gone was the statue of the great Charles Darwin, which had dominated the grand vestibule since its erection upon its subject's death in '82; now replaced, it would seem, by a shoddy effigy of himself, sculpted; he could but presume, in something of a hurry and by someone working from the same idealised source materials as the artist who had produced his likeness for the city's billboards. He stayed a moment to admire a portrait too; hung in replacement of Walter Raleigh's famous visgog, just outside the door that led down into the 'Sherpa Suite': the basement taproom patronised by those for whom leading an expedition was beyond both their wit and breeding, but whose natural strength, valour and tendency toward self-sacrifice, meant they would never be short of fulfilled employment.

"Ahem," he said, pulling out a chair and planting his feet atop it.

"Saints preserve us!"

"Gawd bless yer, Uncle!"

"I's a bleedin' miracle, an' no mistake!" sang the motley assortment of carnival freakery that comprised the 'Guild of Sherpas'.

"You recognise me?"

Gordon had been labouring under the naïve misapprehension that; with the addition of a months' worth of beard growth and the lack of either goggles or pith helmet, he looked more like the late Prince Albert than he did himself, and should have been able to travel pretty much incognito at this hour of the night.

"Damn me eyes if it ain't Capt'in Gordon Periwinkle, OBE; returned, unscathed and ready to adventure forth!" pronounced a formidable giant of a man, dressed in pin striped britches with brown braces over a white, collarless shirt; poking out of which was a neck-free pinhead in a bespoke, begoggled bowler hat.

"OBE, you say?" Gordon mused, as the collected throng took up the giant's chant of: "ADVENTURE FORTH! ADVENTURE FORTH!"

"What do they call you, Sir?" Gordon enquired, as the frenzied sherpas began banging their frothing tankards against the sides of one another's heads whilst hastening their crescendoing chant.

"They calls me Tiny, sir; if'n they thinks they c'n get away with it."

"Of course they do," Gordon replied, smirking slightly, "The old ones are always the best, what?"

He proffered a hand which the giant duly accepted, "Consider yourself hired, Tiny; gather your coat; we set forth at once!".

\* \* \* \* \* \*

Iggi hailed a hansom cab and charged its driver with delivering her to 'The Adventurers'. Of course, it was conceivable; she readily accepted, that the Captain could have been heading for any number of backstreet bars; there to secure the services of a low-rent man-at-arms and all round skivvy, but she fancied that the man whom she had been trailing and whose particular quirks and foibles she had been profiling, would have been prepared to risk life and limb in order to retain a sherpa of calibre and distinction. His inherent snobbery, she considered, may yet prove to be his Achilles Heel.

'Protocol Alpha' required not only the termination of a mark; along with any unfortunate witnesses to the event, but also the retrieval and return of the body to the agency who had issued the warrant; in this case Admiral Spatchcock's office. It should have been a simple task, the like of which she had executed many times before and Iggi mentally chastised herself for her apparent ineptitude thus far.

Her years of experience in the field had imbued her with the gift of insight: the ability to be able to second guess her targets; to predict their movements and to anticipate their likely strengths and weaknesses. This one ought have presented her with few problems and certainly nothing that she could not easily have countered. Perhaps she was getting slipshod in her old age, she considered, as the carriage bumped the cobbles and ruts on its way up west. Was it possible, she wondered, that she had become complacent, what with the advantage afforded her by her new, inbuilt armoury?

No. She was tired and in a considerable amount of pain, but she refused to accept that her burden had played any part in his slipping through her net.

She had played it by the book. Upon arrival she had ascertained any viable escape routes and found none that she had considered likely. She had then lain in wait until long after dark; all the better to minimise the chances of being noticed and; once the job done was done, of being seen dragging a corpse through the streets of London. Finally, she had acted only when she had known her target to have been at his most vulnerable: light on in the bathroom; steamy skylight, and the brother alone in the kitchen downstairs.

She had had more than enough time in which to dot the 'I's and to cross any necessary 't's; the fact that the Captain had so far managed to evade her, she put down to serendipity, for the moment, rather than start herself down the path of doubting the validity of her own hard won reputation.

It was not as if he were a particularly hard man to track, for heaven's sake! He was unable to move about in daylight, for a start; giving her the enviable advantage that fewer bystanders were likely to shamble into frame to complicate matters. He was also singularly unaccustomed to acquitting himself unabetted, which made for a more unchoreographed and flailing target, one that she really had no excuse for missing! Perhaps it was this very fact that had caused his luck to hold, she wondered, just as the cabby shouted, "Woah!" and the horse slowed to a stop. Desperate men often made desperate and unpredictable decisions, she knew; more likely to act on a whim than they were a plan. Desperation, though, had also been known to ensure that at some point they were likely to make a serious and fatal error.

Iggi paid the driver; irritating him by demanding a receipt, then stalked confidently toward the club's doors; her coat tails flapping with her stride, to be met; as if by magic, by a fez toting, moustachioed man with slicked black hair and a monocle, wearing a purple velvet Westcott. He would make the perfect foil for her current frustration, she decided.

"Question one," she announced, impudently; whipping her pistol from her belt with her left hand and holding it to Rumpole's temple, "There are two possible answers that you could give me to this poser." she began, "The first, 'yes, madam; step this way', will elicit a smile from yours truly and a penny for your troubles. The second: 'no'; will win you a bullet to the brain. Think very carefully before answering this: 'may I step in and search your establishment for a fugitive that I believe currently to be on the premises, even though, I am, in fact, blatantly and unashamedly, of the female persuasion?"

Iggi fancied that she saw the years of peering down his ski slope of a nose at the determined, but undeserving, who had posed similar questions; though, without the foresight to put a gun to his head whilst doing so, flash before his twitching eyes. He had once; according to his file, even denied entry to the great Sherlock Holmes himself; a man whom he greatly respected, but who; never the less, had not been a member, and so it must have cut him to the very quick to find himself falteringly replying this time in the affirmative.

"Thank you, Rumpole," She said, flipping a coin past him with her prosthetic hand, before: "There. That wasn't too difficult, now, was it?"

Cocking her gun, and pressing in harder, she continued: "Ignoring, for a moment, the ethical dilemma of whether or not it is best practice to admit to a member's presence or not, and concentrating solely on the gun pressed to your head; has, perchance, Captain Gordon Periwinkle passed through these doors today?"

"Captain Periwinkle is no longer a member of this club, Ma'am," Rumpole replied with as much indignation as he could rally, whilst trying really hard to contain his sudden and urgent need to urinate.

"YES OR NO?"

"No," he snivelled.

"Now. One more question, Rumpole and then you may merrily foul yourself. Again, there is a right and a wrong answer."

Iggi smiled as she noted the trickle of sweat as it began to bead from the spot behind where her barrel touched his skin, "In your estimable opinion, would it be possible for a person to enter these premises by any means other than through the front door?"

She could see that Rumpole wanted to say no. He ran a tight club; nothing and no-one got past him. Indeed, what would be the point of him if it were possible to bypass his strict security measures? As it stood, he had already lost enough face as to be lauded a laughing stock at the next 'Guild of Jobsworths' General Annual Meeting, but the girl in the trousers did have a gun to his head.

"Mr Holmes once entered through the stock room window," he blurted, "the catch is a bit dodgy-"

"BANG!" she snapped, lowering her gun to watch a damp patch begin to form in the front of Rumpole's britches,

"Dirty boy." she remarked, adding: Straight through and down the stairs, isn't it?"...

\* \* \* \* \* \*

"Where to then, Guv'nor? Venus? Europa? Or maybe Titan?" enquired Tiny as he shrugged himself into his snake oiled leather long coat and retrieved his blunderbuss from the elephant's foot umbrella stand by the door. He had obviously had a reasonable schooling, thought Gordon; choosing a rifle for himself and checking to see whether or not it was loaded. The best sherpas, in his experience, were those from the privileged end of the social scale; fifth or sixth sons of the gentry: 'the weakest strain'; often the ones with even more in-bred features than usual, such us elephantine ears; wrap-around teeth, or; like poor old Rumpole upstairs: not just imbued with his father's hooter, but his father's before him and his before that! They were often not the shiniest of silver buttons, but were a fiercely loyal breed, he had always found.

"Saturn? Mars?-"

"Battersea." Gordon replied, but seeing his new friend's childlike grin crumple before him, added: "Initially. After that, though, who knows?" and he slapped him on the back for good measure.

"Union rates, Capt'in?"

"Obviously."

"Adventure Forth!"

"Yes, adventure forth!"

The rest of the sherpas; those still conscious, anyway; upon hearing Tiny's hail, began a whole new round of tankard-to-head bashing and hollering of their chant, making so much din that the assassin's bullet-spitting arrival went largely unnoticed, at least until four of their number hit the floor; their bodies cut to ribbons by a strafing barrage of automatic ammunition, fired with gay abandon from a weapon; the likes of which none of them even got to see.

"This way, Capt'in," said Tiny, realising that his employ had begun and using his disintegrating comrades for cover, whilst ushering his new master behind the bar and into the kitchen beyond.

"Dumb waiter!" he shouted above the cacophony, bundling Gordon into the pulley operated food elevator and closing the hatch behind him, "I'll 'old 'em off," he insisted, even though Gordon was making no moves to stop him from doing so, "Bin nice workin' wiv yer, Capt'in" he said, then yanked hard on the rope, sending Gordon racing up to the floor above, just as the assassin burst in behind him...

\*\*\*\*\*

57

# CHAPTER THREE:

# ALABASTER SQUARE

"'Ere, ain't you that-"

"No, I'm his brother."

"Well you look li-"

"I've got a beard, man; a beard! Gordon has a moustache. And goggles."

"Well, yer a dead ringer, guv'nor an' no mist-"

"Just drive, please, cabby,"

"Where to?"

"Battersea."

"Right you are, guv'... Gertchyoucowson!"

Gordon had lost sherpas before. Actually, he reflected numbly; as they sped along the Chelsea Embankment, heading for Battersea Bridge, he had probably lost more than his fair share, over the years; so few of them surviving to enjoy a second adventure. Considering his tally now, so soon after losing Tiny, he was intrigued to discover that it made him feel a trifle guilty; knowing that so many young, fit men had lain down their lives so that his may prosper. That they had all been Guildsmen; trained and certificated in the art and therefore fully aware of the inherent risks unique to their particular trade, should have been enough to have assuaged any belated, unpleasant feelings of culpability on his part. Their families had all been fully compensated, of course; that was, after all, what one paid one's premiums for, and; wherever possible, their remains had been repatriated for right and proper Christian burial. But after recent events, Gordon found himself beginning to wonder just what it had all been about. He had found peace on the Moon, or so he had believed at the time. He had achieved his life's ambition and had whittled a place for himself; not just among his pantheon of high achieving siblings, but above and beyond anyone else of his generation and who knew how many more to come. He had been ready to die, that day, sure in the knowledge that he had acquitted himself respectfully and patriotically and that all who had died in his name along his righteous journey, would forever be a part of the greater story and thus would have been proud to have known that they had been a cog in his fustian machine.

However, his return had denied them that, not to mention the fact that it had claimed yet more lives along the way. He was a bad penny, it seemed and a magnet to death. He had even lost a brother tonight: an unwitting victim in all of this; gunned down in his prime, for the crime of simply helping the youngest of the Periwinkle clan to become the man that nature alone, would have denied him the chance of being. He had wondered then as he wondered now, as the horse rounded a bend at an unnecessary speed and his noggin bounced roundly against the wooden side wall of the carriage, whether he ought not just stop and let fate take its course.

"WOAH!" he heard the cabby command, but his steed singularly failed to obey him, "WOOOAH!" and yet faster the beast would canter on, "Sorry, guv'nor," the cabby gabbled, his upside down face appearing through the curtained gap beneath his perch, "Damned throttle's stuck,"

"Throttle?" Gordon enquired of him, noting that the horse had by now reached a speed unprecedented for a hansom's nag.

"'sa mechanical 'orse, guv'; runs on wheels, she does. Saves me a bomb on hay, but every now'n then the bleedin' peddle jams."

"It's happened before?"

"Oh, yeah."

"Well, what did you do the last time, man?"

"I jus' kept pumpin' 'til it unstuck-"

Gordon became aware of a rising hissing sound, emanating from the direction of the horse's rump, as if something were about to....

'Unstuck', as the cabbie's luck would have it, turned out to be the last word he would ever utter. Gordon; who, in the rear of the vehicle, had been partially shielded from the full force of the exploding 'horse', had managed to survive, yet again; defying now mounting odds: having been thrown from the splintering carriage to land in the shallows of the cold, black river below.

Picking himself up and ringing out his coat whilst trying to unstick his boots from the shoreline filth, he thought back to the train that his mind had been following shortly before the explosion. He had been but a few maudlin moments from throwing in the metaphorical towel; from accepting the rum hand of cards that fate had seen him dealt, when; once again, some omniscient 'hand' had plucked him from the path of danger and set him gently down, as if preserving him for an as yet undisclosed, higher purpose. Was it a sign, he pondered; a marker that he had been 'chosen' and that his story still had a few chapters left to run?

But motorised horses, indeed! Had the world gone mad, this past month? This was not how the future had been meant to unfold! What next, he idly speculated: instant international communications via a Westcott mounted miniaturised Morse code tapper? Mechanised sherpas, perchance, with built in tea making facilities hidden in cubbyholes inside their iron chests? No; all this was wrong. Had great minds not, only recently, concluded that 'everything that had been invented so far was unlikely ever to be surpassed?' That the patent offices be disbanded, as man had reached the very pinnacle of technological innovation and from here on in would be expected to produce nothing bar the refinement of that which had gone before? Mounting the steps to the bridge, he sat for a while to think, emptying his boots of Thames sludge as he did so. He could just vote like a suffragette and commit himself in front of the next steam powered hobby horse to pass his way or head back over to the club to face his gun-toting nemesis, but this was not the Periwinkle way! He alone; outside of Victoria's inner circle, knew that the present had been skewed, and it was his own vanity that had allowed that perversion to happen. It was, therefore, his onerous task to ensure that the world was returned to its original course!

Aubrey was only a year Gordon's senior. As children, they had been inseparable; there being a decade's gap between their selves and their next nearest brother: the dearly departed Gerald Arthur. The pair had always been referred to by their parents; the staff and their eldest brother, Virgil, as 'The Boys', although for some unfathomable reason, Gerald had always insisted on calling them 'The Girls'. (With the benefit of hindsight, he supposed, there had always been something a tad 'off' about Gerald.)

It had been with the onset of puberty that Aubrey and he had begun to diverge: the elder; cannier child, realising that his natural talent for being able to lie through his teeth whilst being believed beyond question, could work to his financial, as well as sibling, advantage; an ability that their father had also been keen to note; advising his son and impelling him toward a career in the legal profession accordingly.

Aubrey was quite probably the last person on Earth to turn to in his hour of need. The boys had not spoken to one another since the 'Bayswater Incident' of '87, when Aubrey had managed to convince both the Metropolitan Police and the presiding Justice of the Peace; along with his wife; her family and the rest of the Periwinkle clan, that it had actually been Gordon who had sourced, booked and paid for the prostitutes in question, regardless of the fact that he had been in Botswana at the time and without his fictional mobile Morse tapper!

It is often said; by people who like to speak in trite clichés that sound as if they ought to make sense, but on closer inspection, are clearly nothing but meaningless drivel, that blood is thicker than water. Gordon had been harangued by this particular trope, more times than he could count over the past ten years, and always by people whom either had no siblings to call their own, or who had never had a sibling like Aubrey! He had vowed to punch the next dining associate who dared to utter that irritating phrase, along with the next man; never to have left his home shores of Blighty, to reply: "Venice? Why, Sir, would one want to venture there; gods-awful smell, don't y'know!"

The hostility between them was well worn and mutual, and he was not anticipating a warm welcome in Alabaster Square. Quite frankly, if there had been any other port available for his storm-lashed vessel that night, then he would most definitely have sailed right into it, but with the way that

Spatchcock's man had seemed to anticipate him thus far this evening, he knew that there was no other choice left open to him. His sister-in-law, Gertrude, had forbad any mention of his name within the household and would not even allow her twin sons to return his correspondences. Never having expected to find himself begging for mercy from the pious pastor's daughter, Gordon had therefore made a point of dispatching postcards to his nephews from every dark corner of the world that he duly visited; provided they could be found to have a compatible and reliable postal service, of course.

He doubted that his recent telegraphed death would have caused much in the way of consternation for her, nor indeed Aubrey, for that matter; not nearly enough, anyway, that on discovering him still to be a paid up member of the human species, he would suddenly have found himself addled with remorse and eager to welcome his younger brother back into the family fold.

Aubrey saw himself as the Periwinkle's 'winner': a race of his own fevered conception; a race between four sons; each eager to prove themselves worthy of their father's title. Not, of course, that this was how things generally worked! A sacrifice such as Gordon's, Aubrey would have found impossible to top, rendering all his efforts from that point forward, mediocre by comparison. For the past month Aubrey must have been a monster to live with and Gordon found himself tending toward pity for Gertrude, until; that was, he recalled her face that day in the court room and he risked a tight, pouting grin at the idea of her suffering now. No. It was more likely, Gordon suspected; finally rounding the corner that led onto the Square, that his 'martyr's death' would have so discombobulated his kin, that they would be happy to receive him, simply in order that Aubrey might gloat his way through a cognac snifter before throwing him back out onto the street for the wolves. And so, to the last place on earth that any well-versed stalker might expect him to go, he went...

\* \* \* \* \* \*

Rumpole's murder had been entirely unprofessional. It had been gratuitous; though gratifying, she grudgingly admitted, but totally unwarranted. Not that she would have phrased it quite like that in her debriefing report, of course! The man had witnessed nothing of the target; she had been quite certain of this, neither had he been particularly obstructive of her passage. She mulled the phrase 'unavoidable collateral damage', but who exactly did she think she was trying to fool? The clean-up squad? The Admiral? Her conscience?

She had walked up to him, quite deliberately; when she could just as easily have bypassed the cowering, damp-crotched coward, and cleaved his head cleanly from his shoulders with the Samurai sword that she had taken from the wall in the vestibule on her way out. She had acted out of sheer, unbridled frustration, which was sloppy; it was inefficient and unethical, she brooded, as she milled around outside the club attempting to attract a passing hansom. She worried that she might have been losing her touch and angrily kicked the maître de's severed head out into the middle of the road in the hope that such an action might help to release some of her pent up aggression, however, sadly it did not.

"Alabaster Square, Battersea," she spat, jumping onto the step and opening the door of a cab that had so rudely failed to stop at her double fingered, foreman's whistle.

"Light's off, guv'; I'm on me way 'ome, 'en I."

"Madam," she corrected, taking her seat as the vehicle jerked to a stop.

"Right, out'a th'cab; c'mon; no freaks after dark. Says so clearly on the sign: look-"

"Alabaster Square, Battersea," Iggi repeated, calmly. She had only just finished self-flagellating for killing one innocent man, and for no greater reason than that of not liking his hat; to kill again so soon and for no more justifiable a reason, would only have confirmed that sinking feeling that she had of somehow having lost her way.

Killing did not come as easily to her as the casual observer might conclude. Catholicism was a hard habit to break. Oh, the disbelieving part was easy, as was the rule breaking and the walking past a church without feeling the compulsion to nip in and spark up a candle, but the guilt, well that had been shagged into all the novices at a very early age.

"South a'the river? At this time a'night; you 'avin' a giraffe?"

"Yes," she said, poking the sword that she had just used to behead poor Rumpole, out through the driver's peephole and up between his knees, "Ha-bleedin'-ha. Now, Alabaster Square, Battersea... Please."

"Right you are Guv'...err, Ma'am."

A retreat to the abode of Aubrey Periwinkle had been of no great surprise to her. It was an established fact that the two brothers did not see eye to eye, but she had already surmised, that; as a desperate man, the Captain was likely to make desperate decisions. His brother Aubrey was also; geographically speaking, the target's nearest known associate and therefore the most likely place that he would attempt to make for, given his circumstances. However, it had been the sherpa whom she had strangled at the club: the portly one with the absurdly small head, who; with his dying breath, had choked the word 'Ba'ersea', thus confirming for her, her next port of call.

Removing her sword from whence it had been resting for the duration of the journey: that being between the driver's knees, where she had been able to wiggle it every time she felt him slowing at a junction, Iggi paid her fare; pocketed her receipt and stepped out into the smarter part of Battersea. The first thing that caught her eye was the billboard poster that had been pasted to a hoarding, behind which, works were in process on behalf of the new subterranean railway company. The picture was of her target, resplendent in his 'Space Captain' regalia, striking an uncomfortable looking, square jawed pose; at once heroic and messianic. The second thing to catch her eye was the target himself: shambling; hunch-shouldered and dishevelled, limping toward his brother's front gate.

Iggi knew nothing of the circumstances by which Britain's greatest patriot had seemingly become Britain's most wanted criminal; nor how he had managed to swap his one-way ticket to oblivion for a second class return. These and other details had been omitted from her briefing, as often they were and, as Father McNulty had taught all his charges, all those years ago: one was never to question those of a higher social status than one's self. 'Accept what you are told and do thy bidding to the best of your abilities': this was The Order's most sacrosanct of tenets. It was also the rule that she found most annoying because; even after all this time working for the Crown, she still found it the hardest rule to break.

She almost pitied him, watching him now: a broken husk of the man whom she had been charged to kill; tattered and torn and reduced to begging sanctuary from the relatives who despised him. She watched him pause; one hand on the gatepost, willing himself to go forward: a respite that he would come to regret, because it ensured her a clear line of sight.

\* \* \* \* \* \*

Gordon ducked instinctively, as a shower of brick dust strafed his left eye; the bullet that had lifted it from the wall not an inch above his head, ricocheting harmlessly into the shadows somewhere off to his right. He heard a muffled yelp behind him and a cussed "Arse!" and turned to witness his would-be assassin, grappling with a large, heavy set man in a long brown coat; a miniature bowler hat crowning a ridiculously undersized head, some fifty yards from where he stood. On the road, abandoned just beyond the gunman's reach, lay the weapon from which he presumed the shot to have just been fired.

"Tiny!"

"Evenin', guv'. You be wantin' me t'brain i'm for ya'?"

With a renewed confidence to his stride, Gordon strutted over to where his newly resurrected sherpa had the villain pinned in a half Nelson. He bent to retrieve the rifle.

"Not just yet," he replied, taking control of the situation as he had done many times in foreign climes too numerous to mention. He looked down at his nemesis and affected his most superior of snarls, knowing fully well that his back was being covered by the circus strongman in the silly hat, "I'd like to know who he is, for starters. By the by, it's good to see you!"

"Likewise, guv'. Speak!" Tiny demanded of his prisoner, tightening his muscle crunching grip on his neck.

The assassin smiled contemptuously back but said nothing.

"Am I to take it that the Admiral sent you?"

That smile only widened as Tiny ratcheted up his hold by another couple of notches.

Feeling more like his usual, dauntless self, Gordon leant in closer to the prisoner and landed a mean right hook squarely to the stomach. His victim winced but refused to show any greater sign of pain.

"That..." he said, stepping back and rolling up his still soggy sleeves, "was for Gerald, and this," he warned, clenching both fists and striking the pose, "This is for-"

"And there we have it!" The assassin eventually said, quite startling both Gordon and Tiny, "There was me thinking you were some kind of modern day folk hero; wondering why on earth the Admiral would want you dead, and now; well... now we get to see your true colours, don't we: beating up a defenceless woman whilst your monkey, here, rubs his stiffy against my back!"

Her words: well-chosen and perfectly timed, Gordon would deliberate upon later; smiling as he considered such audacious aplomb in the face of certain defeat, but for now, he was taken entirely by surprise by this sudden, unexpected revelation. As was Tiny, whose embarrassment caused him to loosen his grip, momentarily, but just enough to give her room to slam her left elbow into his sternum and to kick forward to connect with Gordon's nadgers, winding both men in a single move and freeing herself in the process. Within the second she had a pistol pressed, left handily to Gordon's forehead; the same Gordon currently kneeling before her, his bruised parts sending a spasming and compulsive message to his brain to try to convince him to lay down and go to sleep for a bit.

"Stow it, sunshine," the woman snapped, seeing Tiny reaching for his gun, out of the corner of her eye. She frowned as something else caught her eye; she frowned; pouted and, whipping the gun away from Gordon's head, began shooting wildly up into the sky at it.

A frown, much like a yawn, can be transferred, one person to another. They are infectious. Even Tiny had caught the bug, though with his Lilliputian features, it had the effect of making him look as if someone had belted him over the head with a large wooden mallet. He had stopped trying to wrestle the assassin; had stepped backward and, pulling the blunderbuss from his shoulder, joined their common enemy in taking pot shots at the clouds. The first that Gordon knew of the reason for their oblique behaviour, was when an arm suddenly snaked its way around his chest, and he felt himself lifting sharply from terra firma.

\* \* \* \* \* \*

# CHAPTER FOUR:

## THE BROKER

In Jack's experience, Sundays were generally considered among the capital's quieter nights. He had always presumed that this was due to their being the days farthest from the average worker's next pay day, and were often missed completely by those who had enjoyed that fleeting feeling of having a pocketful of coin just a little too much, the night before and had therefore spent the bulk of the following day at the Metropolitan police force's convenience. Having completed their statutory sixty, those of London's labouring classes often viewed Saturday night as their Sabbath, playing as hard as they felt they had worked, those past six days. There was always a fight of some kind going down; usually somewhere over Dalston way, where one could wager a hard-won shilling on a docker by the name of 'The Mile End Mangler' or 'The Camden Crusher'. Then there were the noble games of Cock Fighting and pauper baiting which; despite having been forced underground by a royal house eager to showcase the Empire's capital as a paragon of nineteenth century sophistication, were both still very much alive and thriving leisure industries; if one knew where to look. Or take a jaunt down Whitechapel way and experience the full gamut of sexual perversions on offer to anyone of any peculiar proclivity or perfidious penchant; for the right price, of course and if; once again, one knew the right man to ask.

Jack Winters was the right man to ask. Jack Winters was a broker; not the 'city' type; he was no toff-pretender, dealing in stocks and shares; bonds and securities and the like, oh no. He was more your 'under city' broker: a dealer in lives and information: a fixer and a pimp, and when times required it of him, a procurer of the kind of merchandise, unavailable to all bar a select few.

This particular Sunday evening had so far proved unpredictably turbulent for a biblically ordained day of rest. Jack's senses had first been prickled when he had witnessed the arrival of an agent of The Crown; one of somewhat notorious temperament, as well, and here in 'The Moon', of all places: Jack's home turf. He had registered Shikiwana's presence as an omen of riotous things to come; her reputation as a spry and clandestine operative not being quite as she no doubt presumed it to be. Naturally, his first instinct had been to assume that she had come for him; though he was at a loss as to imagine exactly why a personage such as himself could be of interest to an agency such as hers. As off-the-record and under-the-counter as his activities usually were, rarely did he stray into realms that may have brought him to the notice of the likes of Shikiwana's paymasters. The Peelers, yes, but; nefarious as his various pursuits might have been considered, he was mere small fry compared to many of the pub's clientele.

Young Badger's arrival, though; following a hasty retreat from one of Jack's more prodigious of regular punters; right under the haughty beak of said purveyor of mayhem and murder, had caused him to emit a slight dribble of urine into his undercrackers: an automatic response to seeing her that he did not doubt for a second to be peculiar to his self! His employee's insistence that he had only recently been in the presence of a man known by the whole world to be deceased, had rung internal alarm bells for Jack, the moment the tale had begun to spew forth; with no amount of persuasion to the contrary able to stow the snipe's wagging tongue on the dubious matter. Jack had cringed and closed his eyes when he had spied the agent attempting a feint of nonchalance, as she followed his most open-minded of gutter boys out into the alley.

Jack had not hung around to become her next victim; slipping out through the side door, just as soon as he had seen her leave by the back; his destination: Mr Vienna.

The name etched into the polished brass plaque beside the door read simply: 'R. VIENNA'. Jack had no idea what the initial stood for, neither did he care; frankly, the less he knew about the mysterious Austrian diplomat to whom he sold the odd snippet of bar room banter, the better. Jack prided himself on his ability to read a man's character within the first few beats of a conversation. The markers were all there: the tone of voice; the eye contact; or lack of it: the visible ticks and tells that people so often failed to realise were the keys to a fellow's conscience. It was an essential skill in his line of work, as was his learned ability to be just as unreadable to his fellow adherents.

He knocked once and was eventually answered by Letterman: Mr Vienna's valet; a man whom Jack had met thrice before that evening, having taken a dislike to him at the very first. The man was smug, and although that was not an unusual trait for someone in his line of work to exhibit, to stifle this particular attribute would be akin to furnishing the man with a backstreet lobotomy. He oozed his smug with the proficiency of a Tory peer, or an American, for that matter, which; unlike his employer, he could quite easily have been. His accent had a certain fluidity to it, which; throughout the course of a three-minute dialogue, would pay homage to the four corners of the English-speaking Empire and be back in time for tea. He was not to be trusted, as far as Jack was concerned.

"Mr Winters for you, sir," announced the servant, in a Manchurian/Devonshire/South African mishmash; showing Jack into the drawing room, following a curt and heavily Austrian accented: "Come," from within.

Mr Vienna was relaxing in the same chair that he had been sat in the last time that Jack had paid him a visit: an imposing, wing backed; ornately carved, red velvet upholstered throne, in front of a roaring log fire.

"Ah, Jack." he said, as the broker strode in, loosening his scarf and divesting himself of both Bowler and goggles, against the sudden onslaught of heat emanating from the grate.

With his slicked back black hair and his red satin kimono; open atop his crossed legs to reveal a little too much depilated thigh, Mr Vienna struck the pose of a rather fey vampire from a penny dreadful.

"Sit." he commanded, "tek ze vate off your lallies." and he smoothed the satin over his knee with the back of his left hand, smiling wryly, the way that Jack imagined a Black Widow might smile following a bout of unbridled passion.

Jack refused the courtesy, preferring to stand. He was not intending to stay for long and, truth be told, the whole Shikiwana experience had rather spooked him. The longer he lingered, the harder he would find it to mask his unease and this, he wagered, would put him at a distinct disadvantage with his current client.

Coming to an undisclosed decision, Mr Vienna pursed his lips, uncrossed his legs and ended the awkward silence with: "I underztand you haf... information for me?"

"Maybe I does; maybe I doesn't." Jack replied cryptically.

"Oh, come now, Mizter Vinterz, you vould not haf come all zis vay on such a... filthy night if you did not believe zat vot you had heard held a certain... significance for your old friend..."

Jack shuddered involuntarily at the way the Austrian emphasised the word 'filthy'. It had not even been raining.

The two men were not friends and even 'associates' would have been a stretch. Jack had not the first clue as to his patron's real identity, nor indeed the line of work in which he dabbled. He knew only that the man paid well for titbits of an 'intriguing' nature; hence his decision to relate Badger's final confession, in light of agent Shikiwana's obvious interest in the tale.

"I'm vaiting.." Mr Vienna shcmoozed.

"Well," Jack began, following a pause, during which he flirted with the notion of adding an extra flourish of detail to his account in order to make the few salient facts that he had ring a little truer, "It'd appear tha' th'man what they sent to th'Moon is both alive 'n well and at large in th'city, and currently being pursued by one a'the Crown's nastiest tracker dogs."

Mr Vienna's left eyebrow raised in conjunction with a mischievous smile, the like of which Jack had not seen him employ before, however, the mark quashed it as quickly as he had formed it, hoping not to show the broker just how intriguing this particular morsel had been to him, but he failed.

"Zankyou, Mr Vinters. I trust you haf not attempted to sell zis information elsevhere?"

"On me muvvers life, guv'na: 'ot off the press, that is; 'app'nin' as we speak."

"Und you haf zis… tittle tattle on good auzority?"

"Oh, th'very bes', Sir. A man died t'night, only moments after tellin' me that, an' I knows th'killer by rep', so I does."

Mr Vienna pouted; apparently considered for a moment, then clicked his finger aloft to alert the attention of his hovering valet.

"Pay za man, Letterman... und be generous. Zankyou, Mr Vinters; you haf been mozt... diverting. I hope ve shall meet again.

\* \* \* \* \* \*

Closing the front door behind the rank smelling ragamuffin, Mr Letterman retired to the basement kitchen. Whilst Mr Vienna waited in his study for a telephonic connection to his superiors in Berlin, the valet knew that he would not be missed. He retrieved his satchel from its peg beside the scullery door; reached inside and withdrew his miniaturised

71

mobile Morse tapper and began hastily dot dashing a message to his own superiors at the American Embassy in Mayfair...

* * * * * *

"A Zeppelin, you say?"

"Yes, Sir."

"Over Battersea?"

"Yes, Sir."

"And nobody saw the bally thing coming?"

"It was one o'clock in the morning, Sir."

"Hmmm... And you say they simply winched him up, right under your nose?"

"Yes, Sir. I had him right there, as close as I am to you now. Hun soldier slides down the rope; nabs the prize and whisks him away before I could even line up the shot."

"Hmmph. Moneypenny?"

"Sir?"

"Take a memo, would you?"

"Sir."

"To the Quartermaster ...ahem... 'Hun musclin' in; need some kind of 'airship alarm' system to give us a heads-up on their arrival; an alert doodad, don't y'know. Earliest convenience, S'. Don't want t'be caught with our britches down again, what? No offence, my dear."

"None taken Sir."

"Now then, Z-"

"Sir?... Sir, if I may?"

"...Well; out with it, Moneypenny. What's on y'noggin?"

"Sir, with respect; we do already have an airship early warning system. We also have anti-airship barrages stationed all along the south and east coasts-"

"Well they're not ballywell working, are they! Big thing t'miss, a Zeppelin. Tell 'em t'get 'em fixed. Pronto! Now, Z,"

"Yes, Sir?"

"Mission parameters have changed. We want him back and we want him back alive, if at all possible. I need to know what that bally traitor's been telling Gerry Hun... Oh, and Z?"

"Sir?"

"See if you can do it without killing so many bystanders, would you? Witnesses: fair play; they made their beds, and all that, but you made quite a mess down at The Adventurers', by all accounts. Poor Rumpole... knew the chap's father, y'know; damn tricky one to explain away, what."

"Yes, Sir. Sorry, Sir."

\* \* \* \* \* \*

She had let him live. He doubted that he would have done the same if their rôles had been reversed. Perhaps it was because she presumed him to know more than he actually did about the Captain and the people who had kidnapped him? It may even have been because; having failed to kill him once already that evening, she had been afraid that to fail a second time might have made her look a bit shit in the assassin stakes? Of course, it may have had a more sentimental reasoning to it. What if; he wondered, she had felt that same sense of patriotic camaraderie that he had when that airship had arrived out of nowhere and, for a few stolen moments, they had fought alongside one another as brothers in arms; well, siblings in arms, he supposed; the assassin had turned out to be a girl, after all! It was even possible, he mused, that she had only intended to stun him, back at the club, rather than actually strangle him to death, but he dismissed this thought quite quickly on recalling how she had growled: "Hurry up'n die, y'freakin' freak; I haven't got time for this!" whilst bouncing his head against the bar's flagstone floor. Who could say? Either way, he was glad to be alive and eager to get on with the job in hand.

It had proved an odd evening so far. She had left him for dead, but he had come to a few seconds later; dazed and gagging, to find himself the only survivor of what, in later years would become known as 'The Sherpa Suite Massacre'. He had followed her up through the club, vowing to avenge his fallen brethren, but had been too late to save old Rumpole. He had watched as the killer had beheaded him, then calmly boarded a hansom. It had stopped momentarily; its driver remonstrating sternly with his potential fare, and in that moment, Tiny had clambered onto the back plate and hitched himself a lift, hoping that she might lead him to his new master. He may only have met the good captain mere minutes earlier, but he had accepted a contract none the less, and a sherpa's contract was a job for life.

The Captain was to be his second master. This would no doubt have come up during his interview, but time having been rather 'of the essence', they had forgone the usual formalities and cut straight to the chase. Quite literally, in fact!

His first master, the redoubtable Major Henry Fanshaw OBE, had died on expedition the year before. Tiny had taken every precaution that could have been expected of him, but the old man had been insistent that the rope bridge in question would not hold the pair of them simultaneously and so had opted to go first; nay, insisted upon it, believing that the weight of Tiny; heavily laden with their tents and expedition equipment, might have been too much for the termite riddled slats to bear. However, sadly for all concerned, the ropes holding said wooden slats in place above the gorge had been too frayed even to hold the Major's wiry frame and the rest; as they say, was history.

There had, of course, been a hearing, following which, Tiny had been fully exonerated of the charge of wilful neglect, levelled at him by the Major's two nieces, and had been returned to the Guild's roster with nought but a slightly uneasy conscience and a resolve to do better next time.

Quite how long she had been standing there; arms folded across her chest, favouring her left hip over her right, he would not like to have guessed, but certainly long enough to have watched him pissing into the bucket in the corner of his cell.

He replaced his hose; wiped his hands on his trousers and doffed his hat with a: "Miss." He was at a loss for any other conversation, given the circumstance.

"Name?"

"Tiny, Miss,"

"Of course it is. Some parents can be quite cruel, can't they."

"Oh, me 'ead wasn't always like this," he said, chuckling, though totally missing her misanthropic wisecrack, "No, no," he continued, limbering up for an anecdote with a deep breath, "We met with a tribe of 'ead shrinkers in Pa'agonia, back in '91. The Major-"

"Yeah, spare me 'til we find ourselves tied to a stake somewhere, about to be burnt as witches-"

"Well, funny y'should mention th-"

"I meant 'shut-the-fornication-up'!" and she paused, as if reciting a mental countdown from ten to minus one, "I've not had a good day; please don't make me regret what I'm about to do."

Tiny frowned. It was his turn to fold his arms whilst he waited for his visitor to compose herself enough to explain.

"You have a contract with Captain Gordon Periwinkle, yes; to keep him safe and to carry his bags, 'til death do you part?"

"I do. Though t'clarify, it is only a 'verbal' at this stage."

"Does that make a difference?"

"Only if you're intendin' t'torture me f'information, really."

"Well, I'm not."

"Well then, no; I 'ave sworn by the code of the Sherpa's Guild t'do everythin' that it is within me power t'do, in order t'keep 'im from 'arm, up to and includin' seein' that 'e don't put 'is back owt by carrying 'eavy loads. I also make the tea." he added, as if that helped.

"Good." she said, "then I have a proposition for you," and she cleared her throat, "I promise; as God is my witness, not to torture or maim you; and definitely not to kill you, if you do so solemnly swear not to attempt to kill me when I open this door."

"You do?"

"I do."

"Then so do I." he replied, considering it a fair offer.

She went on: "I also vow not to attempt to kill, maim or in any way disgruntle Captain Periwinkle in my attempt to rescue him from agents of an enemy power. Do you, Tiny... 'head', vow to stop me from maiming, torturing, murdering and otherwise upsetting your employer, whilst helping me to maim, torture and murder anyone who gets in our way? Oh, except bystanders; you mustn't kill bystanders. Or let me kill them when I get wound up."

"I do," he said, frowning.

"Then; by the temporary powers invested in me, I do declare you deputised in the service of her immortal majesty; empress of all that she surveys, including the Moon. How do you plead?"

"Religious education; am I right?"

\* \* \* \* \* \*

"Zo! Ze great Space Captain Pervy-vinkle, ja? First man to valk on za moon? Ha!"

"HA HA HA HA HA!" from the assembled crew and security detail alike.

"I'm sorry," Gordon interjected, "but all I caught of that was my name, and you got that wrong! It's Periwinkle; Peri-Winkle. Spreck'n ze no English, my her?"

"Ha! Yes, you, I sink, I am going to like! Observe!"

Gordon frowned for the second time that night. He understood the German's hand signals well enough, if not a word that he was trying to say to him, so he stood up and followed his captor's gaze out of the cabin window.

"London." the German officer announced, waving his hand stiffly over the fogbound view below. It could have been anywhere, for all he knew.

"It's pronounced 'LONDON'," Gordon corrected.

"London, ja! Take a good look, Herr Pervy vinkle, at your LON-DON... You vill not be seeing it AGAIN! HA!"

"HA HA HA HA HA HA!" The crew emphasised.

"Lock him in ze brig, soldier!"

Gordon had never ridden an airship before. He had flown over Cairo in a basket, dangling from a hot air balloon back in '92, but had not cared for the experience any more than he had enjoyed his journey to the 'Moon'. If man had been meant to fly, he had remarked to Matsumi, the sherpa who had bravely volunteered to join the falling ballast bags so that Gordon's basket might clear the top of the Great Pyramid of Giza, then he would have evolved wings when he had had the

chance. Unnatural, was what it was and unsteerable t'boot, in his limited experience! The Germans, however, seemed to have got themselves a handle on that age old problem, and if not for the sound of its two howling, fan driven engines one would barely have even noticed that one's feet were not actually            on            the            ground.
He had to admit to a little apprehension though, as he languished, awaiting interrogation in Berlin, or wherever it was that the they were taking him. Those helmets of theirs: why would designers of a dirigible-based transport system absolutely insist on walking around wearing helmets with damned great pointy spikes on the top? It made him feel quite queasy.

\* \* \* \* \* \*

# CHAPTER FIVE:

## WHAT PRICE TITTLE TATTLE?

"Can you ride?"

"'orse; mule; yak or camel, miss?"

"Don't be facetious."

"I once rode a zebra 'cross the plains of-"

"A horse! A bloody horse! Can you ride a horse?"

"Yes I can."

"Good."

"All th'way t'Berlin?"

"We're not going to Berlin, Tiny."

"We're not goin' t'Berlin? Did I miss a bit? I thought we w's goin' to rescue the good capt'in from 'is filthy 'Un kidnappers?"

"We are... but I don't believe the captain is in Berlin. Now, choose your mount... except that one; any one bar that one; Sleuth is mine!"

Tiny tapped his middle fingers against his front teeth as he strolled up and down the line of stables in the Service barracks. He may have been spared death thus far, but his collaborator had not yet earned his trust.

"Hmm," he mused, melodramatically, as he weighed up the relative pros and cons of what was probably the finest assortment of military grade equine he had ever seen collected in one place, "Now, if I was choosin' f'speed," he said, slapping the rump of a lithe looking, all-black mare, "it'd obviously be this fine filly... but f'endurance, well; I might just be tempted t'go with th'stallion, there. O'course," he said, turning to glare at the assassin and raising his eyebrows expectantly, "it'd 'elp if I 'ad an idea of th'plan"

"The mare will do," The assassin-turned-rescuer snapped, "saddle up."

Working with a partner was clearly going to be a new experience for her, Tiny realised, but as he knew well from his own years in the field; not to mention his three at the academy before that, if a sherpa expected to live to see the end of an adventure, then it paid to start out with a thorough working knowledge of both his master's itinerary and his expectations. They needed to be able to work as a team, whether she liked the idea or not. Their lives may yet depend on it. He took a small wooden box from his coat pocket, opened it and took a dried leaf from within, which he duly placed between his teeth.

"Also," he pressed, "I can't keep thinkin' o'yer as me 'assassin-stroke-rescuer'. Wha'dus I call yer?"

His assassin-stroke-rescuer sighed heavily; closed her eyes and rubbed at her forehead as if kneading away a lump beneath her skin. Tiny did the mental countdown with her this time.

"It's Iggi," she said, after an irritated pause, "Iggi Shikiwana."

"Shiki what?"

"My father was foreign; look, it doesn't matter! Just call me Iggi and we'll muddle along."

"Pleased t'fin'lly meet yer, Iggi. Now," and he pulled himself up into the saddle with one hand; like a professional jockey on Derby day, attempting to reassure his wavering backers that; despite appearance to the contrary, he was actually lighter and fitter than he looked, "if yer didn't need me 'elp, I reckons you'd 'ave shot me with that fancy mechanised arm a'yours, back when you 'ad the chance."

It was her turn to raise her eyebrows in expectation of his summery: "but I can only be of any use t'yer if I knows wha's goin' down. So; Iggi: I asks again; wh's y'plan?"

Iggi hoisted herself into her own saddle with equal ease; apparently coming to a decision in the process. She turned her horse and swung in close to Tiny astride his.

"The Admiral believes that your captain is a traitor," she confided; sotto vocco, "I disagree. I saw the look on his face when that Hun agent winched him up: he was as surprised as we were and he fought all the way up. No, there's something odd about this whole shenanigan. For a start he's supposed to be dead. He died on the Moon; we all know that: there's no way back down! When the Crown found out he was alive, they sent me to find him and kill him." Iggi paused, again rubbing at her forehead, as if the verbal divulging of large amounts of clunky exposition physically hurt her. She continued: "Nobody else knew of his return," said whilst leaning in further toward Tiny. An eavesdropper, spying on their early morning stables assignation, may possibly have misinterpreted her actions as those of a beau moving in to steal a kiss, however she was not.

"I was under orders to kill anyone who inadvertently found out that he was back."

"Nice," Tiny butted in.

"And I thought I had," she went on, unabated; ignoring his jibe, "but I missed one."

"Sloppy," he chided, sarcastically. Iggi chose this moment to turn her horse and head for the gate.

"Don't get cocky," she warned him, over her shoulder, "and don't forget that the Admiral ordered 'no witnesses'!"

Digging his mare, Tiny slowly pulled forward until they were back alongside Iggi and Sleuth.

She continued to explain as they trotted toward the sentry post together: "I realised during the Admiral's debriefing; when it was pointed out that our anti airship barrage had missed that bloody great Zeppelin crossing the coast," a pause for effect, "What if it hadn't *crossed* the coast?"

"Well, 'ow else would it 'ave got 'ere?" he enquired, not quite following her line of reasoning.

"Ah! but that's not the whole question, is it?"

Tiny frowned, but said nothing.

"Oh, come on, Tiny; isn't it obvious? How could it have got here that quickly anyway?" she waited for her theory to penetrate, "I let the witness live at approximately 10.45; the Zeppelin shows up, totally undetected and directly on target, two hours later..."

"It was already here!"

"So, you're not as stupid as you look! And as there've been no reported sightings of it since?"

"It's still 'ere!"

"Precisely."

"Any idea where, though?"

"No, but I'm hoping our extraneous witness will be able to lead us to someone who does..."

\* \* \* \* \* \*

There were few places where Jack felt truly comfortable. It came with the lifestyle, he supposed. Having neither scruples nor moral values of any kind, does not tend to win a man a city full of friends to call upon when times got tough. Associates, yes; he had plenty of those, and acquaintances, well they were ten a penny in his line. Jack knew loads of people and loads of people knew Jack; too many, he had often thought and definitely too many of the wrong sort. That was one of the problems that came with being a 'face': everybody felt they knew you and everyone knew where to find you. He found it hard to walk twenty paces in the east end without some lowlife dodger tipping him a wink or doffing him a brim. Of course, if no-one had known him, then he would have found it impossible to have plied his trade these past years; his success did tend to rely quite heavily upon people knowing who to come to and where he was likely to be found. Sadly, this meant that he lived in a permanent state of paranoid vulnerability, but hey: 'you couldn't 'ave everythin'', he always reminded himself! 'The Moon' was his safe place. Alright, it was a pub and so, by definition: a public place; not most people's idea of security, but Jack Winters knew The Moon's layout like the back of his hand and not just in the way that its other regular patrons knew it. If he ever felt so obliged, Jack could tell you exactly how many strides it was from his usual spot at the bar to any of its four exits-cum-entrances. He could also tell you precisely how many seconds it would take a man of his length of stride to clear each of those doors, along with the time needed to disappear after exiting through any one of them. He knew all of this because he had lived in the building's cellar his whole life. The current owners of the establishment had no idea that they had a freeloading lodger, squatting behind their barrels, any more than had their predecessors. He had been born there; his mother having been a barmaid, two decades back, when it had still been 'The White Rabbit'. She had hidden him down there; tending to him between shifts; bringing him scraps from the kitchen and leftovers from the tables. But his mother had vanished mysteriously one night, back in '88; at the height of 'The Ripper Spree', and since then he had been fending for himself; honing his senses and sharpening his act, and making a name for himself among the dregs of society. He rarely strayed too far from home. Tonight had been a rare exception, but he had earned himself a week's wages for making the trip up to Islington. As uncomfortable as both the journey and the oily Mr Vienna always made him feel, it had been well worth the punt!

But now he was home again and, taking a deep breath; a surreptitious scan of the room and a heavy swig of well-earned ale, he allowed himself a moment's relaxation before striking up a conversation with an amiable fellow in a floor length duster and a bowler hat, with a head so small; in comparison to his torso, that he reminded Jack of a spent match...

* * * * * *

He struggled, briefly; reflexively, until he felt the twin barrels of Tiny's pistol nudging against his ribs from his right. Simultaneously, on his left, Iggi had attached a steel clamp around his wrist, in a single, automatic action; connected by way of a retractable, tungsten chain to her prosthetic arm. Jack flinched as she sent a mild electrical charge through the device, to alert the prisoner to the reality of his situation. She saw Tiny flinch too, on the other side, presumably at the memory of her doing a similar thing to him when she had apprehended him during the Zeppelin incident. However, she felt assured that neither of them had seen *her* flinch, as neither of them would have been expecting the charge to shock its giver just as much as it did its receiver!

"Evening, Jack," she said brightly, affecting the leer that had terrified many a mark in her long and illustrious career. Although she and Jack had never met before tonight, they knew each other well enough by reputation. He knew to be scared and she knew to keep her eyes on him at all times; hence the metal clamp.

"I don't know nuffink 'bout nuffink; gawd 'elp me if I don't! It weren't me; I never said nuffink t'no-one; on me muvva's life!"

"Come on, now, Jackie boy; I know you heard something last night; something a bit unusual? I know 'cause I heard poor Badger telling you."

Lowering the voltage by a couple of amps, she reminded him of with whom he was dealing, holding her breath for a beat whilst she did so,

"Now, Jack, I don't want to have to hurt you and neither does Tiny, here,"

For emphasis, Tiny dug his pistol further into Jack's ribs and smiled, rancorously.

"All we need," she pleaded reasonably, "is a name and an address; simple as that," she lied, knowing that she would probably enjoy removing this one, after all the trouble that he had so far caused her.

"M-M-Mungo Jones!" Jack suddenly blurted, spraying beer and spit in an arc encompassing the pair of them; the barmaid's well-presented bosom and three other random drinkers' faces.

"M-M-Mungo Jones?" Iggi parrotted. She did rather enjoy the banter between herself and her victims when she knew for a certainty that she was in possession of the trumping hand,

"What, the M-M-Mungo Jones? The Notorious Eastend gangster, M-M-Mungo Jones?"

"Tha's 'im, yeah! The N-N-Notorious gangster M-M-Mungo Jones, who don't much like being visited by C-C-Crown agents."

"Oh, that M-M-Mungo Jones! Well," and she affected a tone that she anticipated would make him think twice about lying to her further, "why don't we go and pay him a visit? You coming Tiny? Jack?" She gave his arm a painful yank, eliciting a strangled 'yelp' from the broker, along with a:

"Not bloody likely!"

"You sure?" she said, turning toward the front door and dragging sharply on the chain. If Jack had been of the belief that he may have been able to rely upon some of his fellow drinkers to come to his aide in his moment of greatest need; should the bar side altercation that they were trying so desperately not to notice turn nasty, then this single action proved how indifferent to his plight the people who knew him best really were. His knees hit the stone floor with a painful crack, but not a single head looked up from their conversations.

"Popular round here, aren't you, Jack?"

"Alright, alright; maybe it wasn't Mungo. It was dark, weren't it; I mighta' mistook him."

"Well you might!"

Jack rubbed at his knees as he attempted to stand. If he had been planning a retaliatory effort, then he dismissed it quickly, as Tiny wedged the pistol into the nape of his neck and cocked it.

"A-A-Alright; alright! Keep yer wig on; I'll tell ya'!"

Iggi bent down and whispered into his ear:

"Better still, Jack: you'll show me..."

* * * * * *

It took a lot to rattle Space Captain Gordon Periwinkle, OBE: the only man ever to have held such a rank; Hero of The Empire and sole survivor of so many perilous quests that his biographers would have needed four volumes, merely to have listed the most exciting ones!

He doubted that there was a method of torture that had not been tried on him, by one tribe of savages or another, and yet every time; however unlikely the prospect, he had escaped; unscathed and with whatever prize he had sought, tucked lazily under his arm. Luckily, he was as yet unaware that The British Museum had dedicated an entire gallery to his pilfered spoils; luckily, because it was unlikely that his ego had the energy required for the necessary expansion.

His current captors had bound both his hands and his feet and had hung him upside down from the girders of a giant, vaulted hanger. A hundred foot up and dangling, Gordon really ought to have been in a state of panic; any run-of-the-mill hero, no doubt would have been, but Gordon was far from common-or-garden. The more he had seen of his recent deification; coupled with the fact that he honestly appeared impervious to death, the more he felt convinced that he was meant for something greater. They could kidnap him; starve him; deny him access to a clean lavatory; hang him upside down from the rafters and shout incomprehensible gibberish at him through a megaphone until the cows came home, but he would never break. If the genital eating voodoo cult of Kathmandu couldn't scare him, then a bunch of sausage noshing, pointy hats, who could barely keep their own country together, stood even less of a chance!

Now he thought about it, though, he was a tad on the peckish side. It had been days since he had eaten more than a scrumped apple and he could not even recall the last time a sip of water had passed his parched lips. Come to think of it, he could not remember the last time he had so much as dozed; his body running on nothing but adrenalin since leaving the Moon. It was feasible; he fleetingly acknowledged, that his current state of messianic fervour could be attributed to one or more of these deficiencies, but he dismissed this thought out of hand and began whistling the tune to 'Jerusalem'...

\* \* \* \* \* \*

"Weird shit; I dunno. Rumours; gossip'n the like: the gen'ral word on the street."

Iggi and Tiny looked up from their respective rummagings; exchanged a raised brow, then returned their attentions to the job at hand, that of rifling through the personal effects of a Mr 'R. Vienna'.

"Wha'?" Jack responded; apparently offended, "I gots a right t'earn a livin', ain't I? 'Snot as if I'm sellin' state secrets, nor nuffink! It w's bollocks, weren't it; tittle-tattle."

"And you say you've sold to him before?" Iggi prompted, forcing open Mr Vienna's desk drawer with a jiggle of the lockpick attachment on her prosthetic, "what was it last time?"

Jack chuckled as he recalled his luck:

"Ha! One a' me girls tolt me that the 'Victoria' 'ad crashed into th'lake, the night a'th'launch, y'know? Reckoned she w's in th'bushes wiv' a punta' when it 'appened. Said they'd dragged it out with a crane an' put it on a trolley, under a tarpaulin,"

Tiny's top lip began to curl and he took a defiant step toward the broker.

"Thas slander, is wha'tha' is; conspiracy theory claptrap!"

"But tha's jus' it, mister Pin'ead," Jack pleaded, "it don't matter if'n it's true or not; I's what it is. I tells 'em what I 'eard an' if it suits 'em, they pays me rate."

Iggi looked up from the sheaf of papers that she had been indelicately thumbing:

"Tiny?" she asked, lifting the top sheet and waving it toward him, "do you read foreign?"

"Wha' sort of foreign, miss?"

She held up a grey cardboard file in her other hand, surprising Jack, who; still very much attached to it, was forced to raise his own in a stiff armed salute. Stamped across the file in black ink was a stylised 'bird' emblem with the words: 'Deutches Heer'.

"Austrian diplomat, my arse!" Tiny said, pouting over at Jack.

"Wha'? Asked Jack, genuinely nonplussed, it appeared.

"It's a Prussian Eagle, dick brain; symbol of the Imperial German Army!"

"Well, 'ow am I s'posed t'tell an Austrian fr'm a Hun?"

Wordlessly; coolly, one might even have ventured, Iggi pulled her pistol from her belt and blew the broker's brains through the back of his skull. Tiny frowned; his hands on his hips, as he watched his temporary master disengage the wrist cuff and reholster her weapon.

"Tell me honestly," she said, "that he wasn't getting on your tits as well?" She could feel his glare piercing her from across the room: "Think about it for a minute," she went on, tentatively, "what if the conspiracy nuts are right; just this once?" she added, watching his miniature face turn from grey to purple. She knew how tetchy these adventuring types got around the likes of the 'Sun Worshippers' and 'The Flat Earth' theorists. Adventuring had been a much underrated profession prior to The Moon Landing. Those of the landed classes had often been known to ridicule the claims of men like Periwinkle; Darwin and their ilk. It was a populist assumption that many of the age's so called 'pioneers of discovery', simply spent their days hidden away in attic rooms inside nondescript east end slums, writing phantasmagorical stories of their wild quests across undiscovered lands, then once a week, taking a wander down to the docks to buy a crate of nick-nacks from unscrupulous sailors, that they could pass off as ancient relics to the bluffers'n bodgers of The British Museum.

But perceptions had changed since the captain's much lauded mission into the unknown. Adventurers and members of The Sherpa's Guild alike, could now hold up their heads in public without fear of mockery or derision, rather than skulk inside a converted theatre in Piccadilly; there to attempt to outdo one another with fantastical tales of highly unlikely peril and derring do. It was therefore understandable, she reasoned, that her companion might be a little sensitive to the suggestion being mooted.

"It makes sense," she continued, cautiously. Gordon Periwinkle was supposed to have died on the Moon. So what was he doing back in London? Something really didn't tally.

"What if what looked like a slate quarry in South Wales really *was* a slate quarry in South Wales?"

Tiny remained silent; processing her idea, Iggi dearly hoped. She had no idea how much internal damage having his head shrunk to a quarter of its original size may have done to him.

"Come on Tiny; it all fits! What if the agency faked it all and what if a foreign power managed to get their hands on the absolute proof that they'd done so: to whit, one Captain Gordon Periwinkle? What would that do to the Empress' reputation?"

Another silent beat, eventually followed by:

"You shot 'im!"

"And?"

"In cold blood."

"I'm an assassin; it's implied."

"But y' not supposed to be killin' people."

"He was a witness; a very irritating one, at that and he'd served his purpose. Besides," she said, gathering the papers she had discovered back into their file and dropping it into a large, inside pocket of her coat, "If this Vienna bloke is as dodgy as he looks, then this'll send him a message."

Tiny lifted his hat and scratched his head. He took another leaf from his box and began to chew on it.

"We'd better scarper; someone's bound to've 'eard tha' shot an' anyway, 'e could be back any minute."

"I don't think so," Iggi said, smiling and holding aloft a map that she had pilfered from the file, "That carriage we watched leaving: the one with the diplomatic seal on the door? I think I know where it was heading..."

\* \* \* \* \* \*

He had, himself, killed; on occasion, but only as an extreme measure: a means of honest self-defence or in the defence of his previous employer: the late Henry Fanshaw, OBE. Tiny had taken down a total of six individuals during his career, thus far: three head hunters; two cannibals and a Wildman; the last of these being as regrettable as it was accidental. The Wildman in question had taken them by surprise, appearing out of nowhere, on a mountain pass just south of Tibet. The Wildman, wearing nought but a floor length grey beard and a startled expression, had screamed at the sight of them and Tiny had delivered a pre-emptive blow that; when later reconsidered, had been a tad on the excessive side; punching the poor fellow so hard that he had lost his precarious footing and toppled several hundred feet to his death on the valley floor below. Tiny often thought about that Wildman: sat there, high up on his ledge; naked; solitary; minding his own business; meditating peacefully, seemingly without a care in the world, until along came a pair of blundering British explorers, whom; within twenty seconds of disturbing his tranquil idyll, would confirm beyond any doubt for him, the true savage nature of the race that he had chosen to disassociate himself with.

The head-hunters and the cannibals, on the other hand, had had it coming, especially after what the former had attempted to do to him! He felt no remorse for their deaths, and he would do it all again, though he would rather not have killed them if there had been another option.

Iggi, it seemed, saw the taking of lives in an entirely different way. It was something of a compulsion for her, one that she obviously fought to suppress, but; like the gentleman adventurer with a tide to catch; on spying that one last, shiny bauble being worshipped by a tribe of chanting heathens, finds himself torn between a relaxing gin cocktail on the poop deck and yet another brush with the human spit roast and more often than not, lets that demon win.

Tiny wondered how one even got into the assassination game? Was there a college for assassins; did one know from an early age that the killing of strangers for a living was to be your true vocation? Did one start out with a conscience, but gradually de evolve it as one became more and more immured to the sights and sounds of violent death? He could ask her, he supposed, but he did not much fancy his chances if he caught her at the wrong moment!

She was a troubled soul, this one; he ruminated, as the pair of them hunkered down behind a hedge row, some half a mile from where they had parked the horses; he could tell that much from her acerbic demeanour and her blatantly pained; badly disguised, deportment, and he would wager a guess that; whatever ghost from her past she had allowed to cast its gloomy shadow above her, was also; at least in part, responsible for motivating her to do the things that she did.

Psychoanalysis was an essential part of the sherpa's training programme. If he had been intending on staying on in her employ past the job in hand, then he would have made it his business to have got to know the real Iggi Shikiwana and would have done his level best to have helped her to work through her various issues; as he had done with Henry in Peru, but he most assuredly was not! Getting back to the captain was his priority; Iggi, merely his best hope of doing so.

The map that she had produced appeared to show a large area of flat, open space, some twenty miles from the centre of London, with a solitary building marked at its centre. Tiny had spent his last two decades traversing the globe; carving trails where none had bush-beaten before, but like so many others of his noble trade; whilst in Blighty, he had rarely left the confines of the city, so now had no idea where they were, other than to say, 'north'. There was no sign of either habitation, or industrialisation, for several miles around. A single track led from the London road, to the mysterious site; by their rough calculation, two miles in length.

It had been dark by the time that they'd reached the junction. Fresh tracks in the dirt showed that a carriage had swung left from the main road, quite recently and at speed. Iggi and Tiny had ridden past, noting the incongruous hobo sat by the track's now closed gate, grilling a stoat over a small fire. Iggi had flicked him a coin and he, in return had doffed the brim of his cap.

"Don't stare," she had admonished her companion, under her breath, "he's obviously the forward guard."

They had continued for a further quarter mile before taking their steeds off road and tethering them in a small copse. From there they had doubled back on foot until they had the unlikely structure in their sights. It looked to be an enormous hanger, easily large enough to hide a Zeppelin, but built to resemble an oversized hay barn. It had to be over a hundred foot high and all of a generous seven hundred long. The locals would have had to have been pretty dim not to have been a little suspicious, he thought, but then, it had been at least two miles since they had passed even a farmhouse.

"Jackpot." Iggi said, smiling; for all the world appearing to be relishing the idea of the two of them storming a building in the middle of nowhere that was large enough to have been concealing an entire squadron of Hun soldiers...

\* \* \* \* \* \*

# CHAPTER SIX:

## 'THE BARN'

{speech translated from the German}

"Oberst Vienna! It is good to see you again. I trust your journey from London was uneventful?"

The agent smiled tightly at the Sturmbannführer; who held a stiff salute as he waited for his superior to alight his carriage. The pair had met once before; briefly, in Berlin, back in '94, at the outset of the Project. The Oberst recalled voicing his scepticism at the time at Klein's surprising appointment as Head of Operations. It was not that the younger officer's record was not exemplary; of course it was, moreover it was that Vienna would have preferred someone with a little more experience 'in the field' to head up such an important assignment; preferably himself.

Taking a cigarette from its silver case, he placed it between his lips.

Instantly, Klein's face flushed, but it took him a beat longer than Vienna would have liked to 'remind' him of the strict 'RAUCHEN VERBOTEN' policy, in the vicinity of the hanger.

'Good', Vienna thought; noting the man's fear of him and relishing it, but also his adherence to the safety precautions that he himself had designed. Returning his smoke to its case, he lingered momentarily outside the barn's pedestrian entrance: a door that had been cut into a much larger, vehicle sized opening. Craning his neck to look up at the enormous front wall of the structure, he was reminded of a Russian Babushka, as even this door was a door within a door; the entire end wall of the hanger being hinged on either side to allow egress for the airship that the building was intended to conceal. He had seen the plans, of course; in his capacity as Austrian Ambassador to London; he had, in fact, been the agent responsible for scouting and acquiring the site through a benign front company, but this was the first time that he had seen it in the flesh and he had to admit to a flush of patriotic pride at the sheer audacity of it. He removed his black kid-gloves and his heavy opera cape, passing them backwards to Letterman; his valet, who then returned to the carriage to move it around to the side of the building, out of sight of the track.

"The prisoner is safe and well, I trust?" Vienna enquired.

The Sturmbannführer paused again, almost imperceptibly, this time, but the Oberst; an adept in the science of whittling the truth from his subjects, noticed his subordinate's anxious waver and pressed further, "Sturmbannführer?"

"He is... safe, sir, but I fear he is far from being 'well'. He is quite mad, you know; I doubt he will prove of much use to you."

"Has he spoken, at all?"

In reply, Klein pushed open the door a little further and the sound of 'He Who Would Valiant Be' could be heard, sung at the top of an Englishman's voice, but at an echoing distance, some way away from the listeners.

"We shall see."

Inside, and taking up a full four fifths of the bespoke barn, floated the gargantuan LZ X: four hundred and twenty foot of precision German engineering: the prototype of the LZ fleet that were currently in the process of decimating North America. This he had seen before, on its top secret test flight over Lake Constance in '85, shortly before it was dismantled and shipped, piecemeal, to Scotland, there to be transported

91

by rail and inland waterway; to be reconstructed here, within this hanger: an integral part of the invasion plan. Four hundred thousand cubic feet of empire destabilising hydrogen, harnessed within a fabric covered, rigid metal framework: a technology years ahead of its time, he knew and far beyond the people of this complacent nation. He positioned himself directly beneath one of the twin, Daimler engines; the better to admire their workmanship up close; the phrase: 'Deutschland über alles' trilling around inside his head.

Haydn's tune, however, was unable to compete with the off-key caterwauling being produced by the Englishman, whom he could now see swinging by his feet from the barn's eves. Had it not been for this man, Victoria's Empire would have been in tatters by now; with the empress herself hanging here in this dumkopf's stead.

"Onward Christian soldiers..." croaked the Space Captain, flatly, "...marching as to war..."

"Get him down!" barked the Oberst, "NOW!"

At a command from Klein, two Schütze rushed to man the winch that would lower the prisoner to the floor.

"Halt!" ordered the Oberst, as the dangling man's head became level with his own. He waited for the inertia to spin him so that their eyes could meet. Switching to a flawless, though heavily accented English, he announced:

"Space Captain Gordon Perivinkle, I presume? It iz an honour to finally meet you. Your bruzzer haz told me zo much about you!"

"Something about my brother? Really, you Hun ought to at least make an effort with the lingo if you're going to try to interrogate a chap, what."

Oberst Vienna took a step closer so that the two men's noses were barely an inch apart.

"HAFF YOU EATEN?" he shouted.

Gordon screwed up his face against the volume, "Heathen? Calling me names, now, eh? If that counts for intimidation around he-"

"Get him down; feed and water him and put him in the interrogation suite," the Oberst ordered, in his native tongue, then; turning to the Head Of Operations: "Sturmbannführer Klein; a word."

"Oberst?"

Vienna checked his pocket watch as the soldiers unhooked the Captain and led him away, still singing.

"Double the perimeter guard, Sturmbannführer. Admiral Spatchcock will have mobilised his best agents in the hope of neutralising the Captain before we are able to break him. We are at a nexus point, here; nothing can be allowed to go wrong. Is that understood?"

\* \* \* \* \* \*

"Wha's 'appenin'?"

"They seem to be increasing the guard."

"They know we're 'ere?"

"They'd be remiss not to suspect that we might be."

"Should we not be callin' on yer Admiral fella f'some reinforcements?"

"There isn't time," Iggi insisted, passing her spyglass to Tiny, "besides; they may have the numbers, but we have the element of surprise."

Tiny swallowed hard at the thought and focussed in on the carriage that they had last seen leaving Islington, earlier in the evening. Beside it; puffing nonchalantly on a cigarette, was a tall, thin man, dressed in the manner of a gentleman's gentleman, though one who did not appear to have been trained particularly well in the art.

"That'd be this Vienna chap's valet, then," he said, passing the spyglass back to Iggi, "You'd think 'e could afford better, wou'n't yer!"

Iggi said nothing.

"I could've bin a valet, y'know," Tiny went on, "it was a close run thing. Me farver'd bin quite insistent, as i'goes; wan'ed me t'ave a respec'able trade. I got two elda bruvvers, y'see and they both went inta' th'family business,"

A pause, followed by a sigh.

"Am I going to regret enquiring as to the type of business?" asked Iggi, without taking her eyes from the glass.

Frankly, Tiny doubted any genuine interest in his family affairs on her part. Small talk; they had already established, was not a fortè of hers and she seemed only to make even the slightest effort when she was about to end someone's life. He persisted all the same and for two very good reasons: first and foremost, because he was hanging onto the belief that; the better his psychotic companion got to know him, the more likely she was not to want to kill him once her task was complete, and secondly, the less chance there was of her using him as a distraction or a human shield and letting someone *else* kill him for her own gain.

"Den'is'ry, miss." he replied, grinning humourlessly to reveal a line of mismatched; missing and multi coloured choppers that were usually hidden beneath his tufted moustache, 'No'a good advert, apparen'ly; not t'mention th'fact tha' th'sign board over th'door wasn't long enough to accommodate."

Tiny did not add a question demarcation, but left the sentence hanging, none the less. A normal person: one educated in social etiquette; rather than a lunatic with a penchant for cold blooded murder, would generally have taken the bait. To his surprise, and after a pause that left him in little doubt that she could read his mind, Iggi insisted:

"Well, go on, then; get it off your chest."

"Netherwetter," he announced proudly, "Netherwetter, Netherwetter and Netherwetter. 'Toby Netherwetter' would've been a Netherwetter too far."

"Fascinating," she replied, in a tone that redefined the word to mean exactly the opposite of its Standard English dictionary explanation...

\* \* \* \* \* \*

Autophobia is one of the easiest fears to disguise. Show an arachnophobe anything bearing eight legs and their diagnosis becomes transparent, but an autophobe's problems only become readily apparent when the proscribing practitioner is not present. Gordon would have had to have been prepared to admit to his condition for either an enemy or a journalist to have had sufficient suspicions as to have been able to use such a weakness against him and, for all his failings, he was not a man to showcase his vulnerabilities! The youngest of the family; the one with three times as much to live up to as anyone else, Gordon would happily have gone to his grave without breathing a word of his inadequacy to anyone. In fact, he had intended to; not so long ago, when the chance to solve all of his life's problems at a single sitting had been offered him on a silver platter. Sadly, his plans had been thwarted, and he had found himself at the very mercy of his fears from that moment forward.

Now; with the benefit of both a hearty meal and glass of fine German wine inside him, and not forgetting that old chestnut: hindsight, he found himself able to resist the mania that had overcome him these past hours and begin to think more rationally. He would be interrogated; quite probably tortured too, but he could withstand any amount of that. The one thing the only man to have walked on the Moon could not bear was being alone! 'Ha!' he thought, 'the irony!'

\* \* \* \* \* \*

"Zo!" he began, sweeping into the interrogation suite like a villain in a provincial pantomime; stage right; in a puff of smoke, behind a descending orchestral sting and a chorus of 'BOO!' from all assembled.

Of course, that was not how he envisaged his entrance. Oberst Vienna, (not his real name) was the new Unified Germany's 'Inquisitor Prime'. He had both learned from and tutored the best in the ancient arts of information retrieval and baccalaureate level torture.

'It is all in the poise', he had always insisted, before striking said pose and adding: 'The interrogation begins from the moment the interrogator enters the room. Be calm; be cool and, above all else, be confident.' These were the first words that any aspiring pain giver heard at one of his seminars.

His entrance had been choreographed down to the very last beat: every flounce; every sneer, nuanced and calculated; designed to strike fear into the hearts of any who sat before him. 'Intimidation' was his student's watchword: 'Terrify your subject before you utter your first demand and your job is half done.'

Unfortunately, and unbeknownst to the Oberst himself, his more recent students had begun replacing the word 'cool' with the German equivalent of the word 'camp' and this was the reason that he had been stationed in London and not sent to the American front as he had anticipated.

'Englishers,' in the opinion of the Kaiser, 'fear nothing greater than an implied threat to their masculinity.'

And so it was with shiny boots; pointy hats and an enormous floating phallus that the Kaiser expected to overcome the famous English 'stiff upper lip' and win the war.

Vienna smiled, slowly and he imagined, with a sinister leer, as he bore down on the now rested and fully satiated prisoner; a man just ripe; in his experience, for the plucking. The sleep deprived; the starving and the thirsty; in his esteemed opinion, were not to be trusted. A man would say anything if he felt his life was in the balance; anything at all, which was ideal if the objective was to get him to sign a simple document of confession, but useless; he found, for the procurement of vital intelligence.

He clicked his fingers and a guard closed the door behind him. The room; in truth, merely a square steel box, large enough for two human beings; one to sit and one to prowl around, held the basic essential furnishings of an otherwise featureless; soundproofed cell.

"Velcomm, Captain; I trust you are refreshed?" He did not wait for a response, continuing: "I am Oberst Vienna, und I vill be your torturer for today. First, let uz dispenze with za 'shit-of-za-bull'; as you Englisherz say, und accept zat I know zat you underztand me perfectly vell. Zat approach may vork vith za Sturmbannführer, but you und I vill get along zo much better if ve zimply 'cut to ze chase', to use anuzzer of your... colloquialismz."

With this, he unrolled a black leather tool kit on the table between them. "ta-daa!" he said, as if he were a fleapit magician producing a bunch of silk flowers from a suspiciously bulky inside pocket.

The Captain surveyed the tools as a connoisseur of medical apparatus might well have done in his place, nodding; apparently impressed with the collection and ready to proceed to the next stage.

"You vill be glad to hear zat I do not require a great deal from you," the Oberst said, "but I am prepared to go to extra-ordinary lengths to get vot I vont. Now," he said, gesturing toward his tools, "you choose..."

"I'm sorry," the Captain said with a chuckle, "you expect me to choose your torture implement for you?"

The Oberst smiled as he took his seat, flicking out his coat tails behind him as a dry cleaner had once taught him, shortly before she had died in a flat iron incident.

"It iz only polite to let za gezt chooze first."

Quite unexpectedly, the Captain lent forward and chose the last tool that Vienna would have expected of him: the largest, most conspicuous of the twelve on offer; a device that its owner rarely got to utilise before a subject died. Vienna merely shrugged, knowing that his prey would quickly come to regret such misplaced bravery.

"Do your 'vurst'," the Captain said, in an attempt; as far as Vienna could ascertain, to wrong-foot his gaoler.

"Nein, nein; meine Capitan: I alvays do my best. Now, you've made *your* choice; it iz only fair zat I make mine. Bring in ze children!"

The door opened and one of Klein's detail entered, escorting two young boys dressed identically in an approximation of a sailor's outfit; each bound at the wrist and wearing a sackcloth bag over his head.

Vienna stood with a pirouette to peruse the boys, stroking each of their heads in turn.

"Vich should it be, Captain Perivinkle? Do you haf a favourite?"

He whipped away the sacks to reveal Geoffrey and Charles; the prisoner's own estranged nephews.

"I choose zis vun, I zink; Charles, iz it not? Take ze uzzer vun back to hiz muzzer." he ordered, and he laughed: the full Abbenahzer, before leaning forward onto the table to stare into the Captain's eyes, "Yes!" he snapped, "Ve haf your sister-in-law unt your bruzzer, alzo! Now," and he sat back down, the terrified Charles gripped tightly by the stringy bicep, "I am going to ask zum questions of you," he picked up the razor edged tool that the Captain had chosen, "und you... you are going to anzer me. Do I make myzelf clear?"

\* \* \* \* \* \*

'Perhaps', Tiny wondered to himself, as he skulked awkwardly along the hedgerow; keeping low and attempting to move his bulk as lithely and as quietly as possible, so as not to alert the troop of expertly trained soldiers that were even now fanning out in a well drilled arc, on the lookout for highly skilled agents of The Crown; 'Perhaps' he considered, as his foot found a rabbit hole and he all but barrelled straight into one of the highly trained Hun soldiers that he was trying to creep up on; 'Perhaps I should have taken father's advice after all. You never saw a gentleman's gentleman knee deep in cowpat; ditch dirt daubed on his cheeks, chin and forehead by way of a handy, locally sourced camouflage; snooping around the countryside with the express intent of sneaking up on one of the aforementioned, highly trained soldiers and putting a bullet in his head. It certainly was not the kind of thing that qualified sherpas got up to of a normal day, either; come to mention it, but as a validated temporarily deputised agent of The Crown, it was; apparently, all in a day's work!

Iggi had drawn a pair of pistols from their holsters on her back; somewhere beneath that voluminous dusty coat that she always wore. It had crossed Tiny's mind that the pain that he by now felt certain that his comrade in arms lived with on a daily basis, might have had something to do with the sheer amount of weaponry that she had concealed about her person.

"A gun f'ev'ry occasion," he had remarked, as she had handed him a queer looking pistol: longer by a half than the one she had given him to cover Jack, back in 'The Moon', but narrower in the barrel and with a bulbous copper, egg-like protuberance grafted to the business end. Mounted on its top was the kind of crosshair attachment more usually associated with the shank of an elephant gun.

"A silencer," she said, by way of an unhelpful explanation, "get as close to the target as you can before pulling the trigger. The bulb at the front helps to deaden the sound of the shot, but there will still be a spark in this dark. Ideally, you want to use the victim's head to shield the flare, then move onto the next.

"D'yer 'ave any fam'ly, a'all?" Tiny had asked.

"Not anymore."

Tiny guessed that the ambiguity of her answer had been entirely intentional.

He killed his first two soldiers semi-accidentally. Killing soldiers; it seemed, was the entirety of Iggi's plan, but the rabbit hole that his size elevens had discovered had propelled him forward and his trigger finger had fired off his first shot reflexively. The high velocity projectile had entered soldier one, just below the helmet line and exited through his startled mouth, catching the second, who had turned, presumably when he had seen the flare, directly between the eyes.

"Nice work," praised Iggi; appearing as if from nowhere wearing an invigorated smile, having dispatched four herself; if the flares were being counted, within the same timeframe, "On your left," she spat, "Oh, for- DUCK!" and she killed her fifth, in the process saving Tiny's life. "Eyes on the ball, Tiny head; c'mon: five still standing."

\* \* \* \* \* \*

"What do you want t'know?" asked Gordon, alert and all pistons firing, for the first time since The Adventurers' Club debacle.

"Zince you ask zo nicely," his interrogator replied, pulling the quite rightly terrified boy's arm closer and slapping his tiny hand onto the table between them, "I vas vondering vich of hiz teeny tiny fingerz I should cut off first. Vich do you zink, hmm?"

"Ask me a question; dammit, man, and I will answer to the best of my ability; just leave the boy alone!"

The interrogator brought his knife wielding hand down hard and sharp, piercing the wooden tabletop between

Charles' thumb and index finger. The child produced a muffled yelp and began to cry.

"ZA MOON LANDING VOZ FAKED!" the interrogator spat, as if to attempt such a thing had been a personal insult aimed squarely at himself. Gordon neither confirmed nor denied the allegation, waiting to see where his gaoler was going with his spittle spattering rant.

He had been expecting to be quizzed about the mechanics of space travel itself; to have been pumped for information so that the Germans could mount an expedition of their own. Over dinner, he had decided to tell the man nothing; which would not have been difficult, considering how little he actually knew. However, Vienna's advertised intention to torture his nephews in his stead, had instigated an instant change of heart on his part.

"You vill now tell me exactly vair ze outrageous zubterfuge took place."

A little confused by the unexpected path that the inquisitor had taken, but still determined not to see the boys hurt, Gordon told him.

"Cardiff?" mused the interrogator.

"South Wales," Gordon added, just in case the Hun were unaware of the demarcation between the conjoined countries, "although I really don't see of what use that information could be to you. Now release my family, please."

"Zey vill be released in ze fullness of time-"

"I've told you what you want to know: they used an old dolomite quarry just outside Cardiff: Cefngarw."

"Oh, I believe you!" Vienna confirmed, smiling whilst toying with the knife that he had now retrieved from the table, "und zey vill go free vunce you haf helped us viz our own 'Moon landing'."

"Not quite following you, old chap."

"You are going back to ze Moon, Herr Captain, vair you are going to be photographed meeting ze real 'first man on za Moon': a Kaisernought who voz already zair ven you arrived und who vill ask you; everzo nicely, to remove your flag und replace it viz a German vun!"

\* \* \* \* \* \*

Blowing out the brains of an unknown, fellow human being; one who has done nothing specific to invoke one's ire, other than to be prepared to scramble one's own thought grinder, with very little prompting and given half a chance, was one thing, thought Tiny, as he searched his many pockets for a clean handkerchief with which to blot his face, but receiving a man's brains; sprayed across one's own mush, mixed with a concoction of blood; hair, gobbets of skin and whatever other fowl ingredient a Hun soldier kept inside his skull, was entirely another!

"That's the last of them," said Iggi, again saving Tiny's life: a woman; the sherpa imagined, who had no doubt tasted noggin juice aplenty during the course of her career; enough, as to have forgotten how stomach churning such an experience could be for a blood'n guts virgin like himself.

"You've got a bit just there," she pointed out helpfully, flicking a morsel of grey matter from the white-faced sherpa's cheek. "No idea how many might be on the inside, though," she reasoned, "but by my reckoning, we've seriously depleted them."

Tiny's tally had not increased since his initial two accidentals, the carnage all around them being almost entirely attributable to his bloodthirsty partner in death. All was silent as they crept the last few yards toward the barn, then: "My thanks," said a voice, suddenly; in an accent quite undecided, belonging to the bearer of a pair of pistols which they noted were pointed at the pair of them as they rounded the corner of the structure, "I seriously doubt my own agents could have dealt with so many without disturbing the neighbours," he said; a trifle smugly, to Tiny's mind.

It was the valet, Tiny now recognised; he whom, even from a distance and through Iggi's augmented spyglass, had appeared an ill fit for an upper-class servant. Tiny now knew why that had been.

"Drop your weapons, if you please," he demanded with a condescending smirk; the style of which, Tiny instantly associated with that of an American, "I don't wish to have to kill you," he drawled, "after all, we are kinda' on the same side, but my boys'll take it from here in."

Iggi; not an easy personage to disarm, was about to say something glib and probably racist, when the pair were suddenly clobbered from behind and darkness claimed them...

\* \* \* \* \* \*

The steel box containing the Captain; his eight-year-old nephew and the Oberst, shook, momentarily; a reverberation, both men realised, that could only have been caused by one thing.

"Meine Gott! Vot imbecile vould let off a grenade near a Zeppelin? Guard!" Vienna screamed, letting go of the boy and yanking open the cell's door. Instantly, the volume grew, and it became apparent that the secret base was under siege.

"HALT! HAAAALT!" Gordon's erstwhile interrogator screamed, bolting from the cell; presumably, Gordon ruminated, to attempt to reason with whichever liberating force had not properly thought through their strategy.

Grabbing Vienna's discarded tool, he cut through Charles' bindings and removed the gag from his mouth.

"Don't talk," Gordon chided, as the boy immediately attempted to unload a diatribe concerning his unfortunate day so far, "just stick close t'yer uncle,"

\* \* \* \* \* \*

The Oberst grabbed a rifle from a nearby guard, pushing the man to the floor and; positioning himself so that his back was to the airship, began picking off the invaders as they stepped through the ragged hole that they had torn in the barn's side wall. He recognised their uniforms as American, just a second before a bullet tore through his shoulder and another strafed his cheek and he was thrown to the floor to land beside the prone and quite blatantly deceased, Sturmbannführer Klein.

As he teetered on the brink of consciousness, he heard a voice that he recognised; one that he had known well, these past three years that he had languished in Victoria's ignominious capital: the 'Englishman' with the dubious regional accent; his valet, Letterman. "Ah, Vienna!" The voice declared, his former butler now looming over him, "I would thank you for capturing the Englishman for us, but we'll take it from here. Your plan was a good one, but; as usual, lacking in both foresight and ambition. A few more blurry plates would have proved nothing, whereas we; on the other hand, have access to the latest moving picture technology. Shame you won't live to make the premiere."

\* \* \* \* \*

It was Iggi who came to first, to find herself bound: wrist and ankles and lying; foetaly wound, on the velvet upholstered seat of Vienna's carriage. Tiny; still out for the count at this point, had been similarly slumped to sleep off his own concussion, on the bench opposite.

Her first waking thought, as always, was pain. Pain in her head where she had been walloped and pain in her neck and shoulders: that ever present ache that rattled her senses and helped to keep her in a near permanent state of exasperated belligerence. Peering through the window; her head still spinning and her eyes lazy to focus, she caught a glimpse of the man whom she had been following: her quarry, Captain Gordon Periwinkle, being marched; hands cuffed and on top of his head, between a rank of retreating American troopers. Beside him, and similarly trussed, walked two small boys: twins, unless that bump on the head was causing her to see double.

"Tiny!" she shot, "C'mon, wake up, man!"

The sherpa stirred groggily and farted, which woke him with a start.

"W-wha-?"

"Quickly! The Yanks have got the Captain! Untie my wrists!" and she twisted painfully so that he could reach her bindings.

"Yanks? What've they got t'do with it?"

"Buggered if I know, but they're getting away!"

The exact reason for what happened next would forever remain a mystery to the unlikely pair, but it was most likely; a singed and blistered Iggi would later recount to her superior, that a stray bullet had pierced one of the canisters containing the hydrogen required to float the airship, resulting in an explosion that destroyed both the Zeppelin and its hanger, along with pretty much any evidence that either had ever existed. The coach containing the two Crown agents, or at least, what was left of it, was eventually retrieved from the boughs of a nearby oak tree, but no sign of the horses that had been reined to it were ever found...

\* \* \* \* \*

# CHAPTER SEVEN:

## HENCE THE BARRELBOMB

"Facts!" the Admiral had grumbled, tugging on a large, Zeppelin shaped cigar that did not appear to want to stay lit, "That's what interests me, Z: sustainable certainties." He struck another Lucifer and dragged so hard on his stogie, that Iggi should not have been surprised to have seen his bulging eyeballs drop from their sockets and roll across the desk toward her, "Speculation is for scientists; don't y'know, and philosophers," he added tartly; punctuating her scolding with a retching cough, "and those bloody poets, who will keep insisting on sticking their oars in; damn their eyes!" and with one final retch he managed to loosen whatever mucus based clag had been clogging his lungs and denying oxygen to the leaf mould sandwich between his lips.

So she had given him the facts, as they had fallen; as it was her duty to have done, though she was aware that so little of what they had witnessed over the past day could be corroborated by anyone other than her irritatingly conscience led sidekick, Tiny, a man whose word the Admiral seemed disinclined to indulge. She had delivered them regardless; chief among them: a Hun conspiracy on home soil; the existence of, and ultimate destruction of, an actual Zeppelin in the home counties; a second foreign faction (possibly American) also with a keen interest in the Captain, and the two mysterious children that had been captured along with him. Only one of her imparted facts, however, did her superior seem capable of focussing on, and that was the somewhat sobering truth that she had failed. Again.

One simple task: to bring down (and latterly bring in) an unarmed and friendless fugitive. It really should not have been beyond her seasoned talents! Her record showed that a job such as this should have been well beneath her dignity to have even considered, but; to her resigned annoyance, she had really needed the purse.

Iggi was twenty-nine; she would be entering her third decade in a matter of months. Few in her trade ever lived to see such a grand age and none of those who purportedly had, had she ever actually met. Rumour of their existence she put down to wishful thinking on the part of her peers, and hyperbole on behalf of the Service, who struggled to recruit in an area with such high mortality rates.

She was an enigma. She should have died a year ago and she would have done too, had it not been for this damned war and the Service's intention to turn her into a weapon; fitting her with this accursed prosthetic limb. It had made her near invincible, which on the one hand had been a boon, but equally it had proved the bane of her life. Yes, she had exceeded her already flawless reputation as the Empire's 'go-to' assassin, but the six million guineas built-in weapons system had also come at huge personal cost; to whit, the pain that she tried so hard to keep hidden and to control whenever she used the satanic contraption.

But Iggi had an ultimate plan: to save enough lucre to buy herself a retirement; to use the power that they had entrusted in her with this state-of-the-art mechanical adornment, to free herself from the shackles that bound her to the Service, and to disappear, in the hope of living; perhaps as much as another decade, comfortable and far from the Empire's malignant influence. This job, as simple as it had originally appeared, had been offering her enough cash to finally make that break. It was to have been her swansong: an epilogue to the legend that had been created around her.

"...and to that end," she heard the Admiral rumble on, shattering her daydream and dragging her back to the reality of the here and now, "I'm replacing you with agent X; effective immediately."

"What? NO!" she found herself spitting; wishing she had listened to the build up to his unexpected revelation, "No! I can do this!" she insisted, "I can find him; I just need another twenty-four hours!"

"Time's up, I'm afraid, Shoka weeny. X is already on the case. Should've done it sooner. Reckons he can have the Captain under lock'n key before tiffin. Now, if you'll excuse me, I have a meeting with her illustrious empress. We two shan't meet again."

\* \* \* \* \*

"Any good, is 'e: this 'Agent X'?"

"*She's*... adequate," was all she would admit.

"D's tha'mean you won't need t'kill me, now?"

"I wasn't going to kill you anyway."

Tiny let out an audible breath that necessitated in the readjustment of his belt buckle by two notches.

"*She* will, though; you're an inconvenient loose end. As am I."

Tiny sucked back his overhang and retightened his belt.

"What'rewegoin't'do?" he squealed, grabbing her by the shoulders in his panic and in so doing, eliciting a strangled silence from the punters on the tables closest to their booth.

"What are *we* going to do?" she replied, shrugging off his probably inappropriate grip and reaching for her tankard, "*We* aren't going to do anything. *You*, on the other hand, are going to start running and you're not going to stop until you reach Australia; do you hear me? I, however; well, I'm just going to sit here drinking ale until agent X arrives and then I'm going to ignite this barrel of explosives I brought with me and blow the whole fuckin' pub to kingdom come." With this, she lifted the sack cloth on the bench beside her to reveal a waxed wick sticking out of an oak beer barrel that smelled suspiciously gunpowdery.

Tiny sighed. Life had been so simple just two days ago. The case against him; brought by his previous employer's next of kin, had finally been defeated and he had been free to find himself a new master. He had gone straight from the Magistrate's court to the Adventurers' Club; his plan, to lift a few jars with his fellow sherpas, in celebration of his acquittal. But then the Captain had bowled in, followed by the assassin, and a chain of events even more depressing than those of the past nine months had brought him to this moment and the choices laid before him now. He had always quite fancied Australia; it had certainly been high on his bucket list, and the idea of avoiding certain death by running away was definitely an appealing one. But he had taken a tender; even if it had only been a 'verbal', and he was honour bound to the spirit of that contract. He sighed again. What he was about to do could go either way, but; considering the situation that he currently found himself in, he decided it was worth a try. He took a small, wooden box from his coat pocket and placed it on the table between himself and Iggi. He guessed that she would recognise it. He carried it with him always and his use of its contents had hardly been surreptitious. Iggi frowned back at him.

"Take it," he said, "I fink it'll 'elp."

She reached forward; guardedly, unhooked the clasp and lifted the lid. She looked up at him suspiciously, her frown deepening.

"Sneezeweed," he explained, reaching down to extract a piece of chopped, green leaf from the box, "don' worry; I's perfec'ly legal. Now, it doesn't work f'ev'ryone," he explained, taking a piece for himself, "but without' it, I wouldn't be able t'function," and he tapped the side of his semi-shrunken head for emphasis, "yer chew it," he said, "not all the time; just when the pain's at I's wors'. I's quite strong an' it can be addictive, but t'my mind, i's the bes' th't money c'n buy."

He caught a look in her eyes that morphed before his own, switching through surprise; disbelief; anger and vulnerability, before settling on mute acceptance; all within the frame of as many blinks.

Wordlessly, Iggi put the leaf in her mouth and began to chew.

"All th'way fr'm Siberia," he said, "via 'The Doktars Steamfunk Emporium, Paradise Alley.' He watched as she screwed up her face, "I's no' a pleasant taste; does 'ave a bit of a tart bite, b't trust me; it does the job. And if it doesn't work for yer; I don't go nowhere withou' a bottle of Arnica tinc'ure. 'Omeopathy w's a volunt'ry module," he added, "I took tha' instead of 'and-to-'and combat classes back at the Guild; thought it'd be more use. 'Ow wrong can yer be, eh?"

There was a long pause during which a variety of unpleasant scenarios played on through his mind. What seemed like an aeon later, Iggi thanked him. It was delivered as if she had just entered into a Faustian pact from which there could be no escape, this side of death.

Feeling a little more self-assured, Tiny dared to venture further: "I's the arm, I take it?" but he received no reply, instead she remarked: "You're an odd one, Toby Netherwetter," and she smiled, which was disconcerting, as a smile from Iggi usually indicated that she was about to commit bloody murder, "I would've thought you'd have been glad to be rid of me?"

Tiny smiled back. It was his turn to deliver a question instead of an answer: "I take it you're currently unemployed, then?"

Iggi supped her beer, then explained: "I was only on secondment; I'm still an active employee of The Crown. In fact," and she pulled back her sleeve to reveal her mechanical arm, "you could say I'm owned by The bastard Crown."

"So they'll just reassign you to another mission?"

"Hmm... It's more likely they'll send me for re-evaluation; which I'll fail, then some chinless Whitehall pen pusher will skim read the report and stamp 'TERMINATION' on my file and that'll be that."

"Hence th' barra bomb?"

"Hence the barrel bomb"

Tiny leant in closer, "Wha' if I could make you a better offer than certain death?"

"Better than certain death? How much better?"

"Well, surely anything's better than 'certain' death?"

"You haven't *lived!*"

"Well 'ow 'bout 'not quite' certain death?"

"So, 'uncertain' death?"

"Tha's abou' th' size of it, yeah." he admitted, realising that the offer had sounded much better in his head.

"What's the offer?"

"I 'ave savings," he explained, "no' a lot, but I'd like t'offer you a retainer, if you'll 'elp me t'finish th'job."

"Seriously? You'd like to hire me as, what... your minder?"

"If y'wouldn't rather jus' blow yerself up, tha'is."

Iggi smiled again; a smile that became a chuckle. It was quite a nice smile, he considered, when it didn't have to precede a death.

"This stuff isn't bad," she said, reaching forward and pocketing the rest of the Sneezeweed, "Alright, you're on, but let's just get one thing straight before we start. You may be the money, but I'm the boss. We do things my way and you do as I tell you. That clear?"

"Crystal."

"Good. Now get out of here as fast as you can; Agent X has just come through the door to my left and I lit the fuse on the bomb thirty seconds ago."

"You did wha-?"

"Go, Tiny!"

He clocked the agent quickening her pace across the bar as he and Iggi bolted for the nearest exit. They had just reached Micawber Street when the bomb went off; the resulting explosion throwing them to the ground.

The agent, by Tiny's reckoning, would have been directly in line with it as the wick had reached the powder.

"Get up!" Iggi shouted, though he could barely hear her; his ears still ringing from the blast, "Tiny! Get up! Move it!"

He did as he was told, and the pair did not stop running for a mile...

\* \* \* \* \*

"Space Captain Gordon Peri-Winkle, meet Thomas Edison: inventor of the incandescent light bulb; the phonograph and the moving picture camera; along with so many other, startling, American innovations, of course."

A general rumble of sycophantic chuckling and appreciative hand clapping from all present could be heard to herald the man's arrival in the marquee and equally to signify their approval of his introduction by the man, whom Gordon had heard referred to as 'Letterman'.

"Umm... pleased t'meet you, I'm sure." he replied, offering his flattened palm instinctively, rather than because he had a burning desire to ingratiate himself with the unhumbled genius, standing grinning before him.

"Likewise!" the inventor assured him, "likewise," and he proceeded to pump Gordon's hand so vigorously, that he began to wonder if the inventor was hoping to shake it free from its mooring in order to use it as a component in his next invention, "Goddam'it, but y'all had us fooled, there; yessir! Hook, line'n sinker!" Edison raved, "It looked so real! In hindsight, though, the flag shoulda' bin a giveaway."

"You'll have to excuse me," Gordon said, extricating his hand from the knuckle-numbing embrace of one of the most celebrated men of the moment, "but I've been brought here against my will and I need to speak to whoever might be in charge..."

It had been dark when he had been captured whilst escaping from the last bunch of crackpots to have insisted on locking him up, and it had been dark when he had finally awoken to find himself trapped inside a steel animal cage of the type more commonly associated with travelling fairs. It had been raining too, he had noted; he could hear it drumming on the canvas tent that housed his cage, reminding him of those damnable Welsh camping holidays of his youth. He was also starving hungry again and he had pointed this out to Letterman when he had come to collect him.

They had drugged him, in much the same fashion as the Space Agency had during the Moon mission; they had handcuffed him, reminiscent of the Hun's approach to international relations, and then they had put a bag over his head that had stunk of rancid cheese; presumably just for a bit of variation on the prevailing theme. 'Come to think of it', he considered, retrospectively, as he had been led from the cage and into an adjoining tent by his latest captor, it may even have been the cheese that had knocked him out!

If Gordon's adventuring days had taught him anything, then they had shown him how to spot the one man among a crowd of men who considered himself superior to all comers. It was often a larger feather or a more intricate facial tattoo; a more elaborate robe or human rib-bone chest adornment, or simply that he was the one wearing the biggest hat in the room. The American leader fitted this pattern precisely, reminding Gordon very much of King Rammalamma of Dingdong island; an insignificant backwater that he had visited back in '89 during his South African tour. In fact the two men were so similar that they could have been separated at birth; though come to think of it, he was sure that Rammalamma's skin tone had been a shade or three darker than this man's and his nose a little broader too; so not all that like him at all, really. The pomposity was the same, though; that must have been what he had recognised, that and the stentorian boom of the voice; that and the big hat.

Spotting the obvious leader, Gordon had pulled away from the rabbiting inventor; catching Letterman by surprise; still handcuffed to him on his left hand side, and dragging him along for the ride as he strode up to the chief and coughed loudly to alert him and his nodding cronies of his presence.

"Ah!" the 'King' pronounced brashly, "So, you're the Limey explorer who thought he was the first man t'conquer th'Moon, huh?"

At the sound of his voice, the assembled sycophants shifted their allegiance as a man, from the inventor, holding court in the one corner, to the man regaling in the opposite. 'Interesting dynamic', thought Gordon, scouring his memory to try to recall where he had seen such a display of macho jockeying before. Had it been the Punjab in '91? No. Burundi, then; again on that ill-fated, three sherpa, African trek? No, but it would come to him.

"General Pernicous B. Ollyphante, the third," the 'King' spat; morsels of some kind of cheese based finger-food ejaculating from his mouth as he spoke, catching most of his fawning minions in their square jawed faces; though none chose to react in any way, "commanding officer of the fourth battalion; currently stationed in Ingerland on protection dooty to our country's finest minds."

Well, that answered a lot of the questions that Gordon had been about to ask.

"Ah see y'all met our esteemed producer, there?" he stated, but did not await a reply, "Had t'git him out afore those damned invaders took a pot shot. This guy; he's gonna change the world; ya'll see if he don't!"

The Queen's English; in Gordon's opinion, was a perfectly serviceable and accommodating, internationally accepted language, spoken the Empire over and by many a disparate people and Gordon had always found himself able to make colloquial allowances for those for whom it had been a second or even a third tongue. The Americans, however, claimed to be native speakers, yet managed like no other, to mangle the syntax to such a degree as to make themselves less intelligible, even, than a Frenchman; who slurred his way through his sentences, making French, so utterly incomprehensible.

'How,' he despaired, 'could the yanks make such a fist of it?' Their grammar was appalling and inconsistent at best and they so often misused the vocabulary to such ridiculous effect.

"I'm so sorry," he replied to the General, petulantly, "but I'm sure I haven't a damn clue as to what you are talking about."

"Funny man, huh?" the General barked, and the whole room chuckled in agreement, "Well, see here, Limey, 'cause this is how it's gowna' be: Mr Edison here is gowna' make one of his famous movin' pictures an YOU are gowna' be his latest star."

The room erupted on mass, as if this had been a breath-taking surprise to them all; the General's audience rapt by his every proclamation.

Gordon, however, not so much.

"Now, we had our suspicions all along," Ollyphante continued, "but it was thanks to a none too bright German infiltration agent that we learned the full extent a'the British deceit, and to 'Space Captain, Peri Winkle', here's own nephew, Chas, that we gleaned the final part of th'puzzle: the location used for th'faked Moon landing-"

"It's 'Periwinkle,'" Gordon chimed, "and 'Charles'!" only then realising that, up until that moment; so engrossed had he been in his own predicament, he had entirely forgotten about the fates of his kin! "What have you done with my family?" he demanded, threateningly; though fully aware that he was in no position to verbally browbeat anyone.

The General let out a hollow, booming guffaw that was unsurprisingly mimicked by his underlings.

"Oh, th'family man, huh? Don't fret, y'll see botha' y'nephews again, just as soon as y'do as I ask-"

"And my brother, Aubrey and his wife?"

The General looked to Letterman, who Gordon saw shake his head.

"They were also prisoners of the Hun in that blasted hanger-"

"They were prisoners of no-one," Letterman corrected him, "but if it'll put your mind at rest: Oberst Vienna lied to you; they were never at the hanger; only their sons were on site, who we now have safe here with us."

"Whom," Gordon said, half under his breath, but Letterman had heard him.

"Excuse me?"

"It's 'whom' we now have safe ly' with us."

\* \* \* \* \*

The butler coughed; resolutely, though reverentially; in that manner that only a professionally schooled; class and privilege

113

acquiescent Victorian manservant has ever been able to successfully master.

"What is it Wadcliffe; come on, out with it, man?"

"A Mr 'Weener' to see you, sir; says it is imperative that he speak with you as a matter of some urgency."

"Never heard of him; send him away."

"He's most insistent, sir," Radcliffe pressed, firmly, but deftly, "he says it concerns the young masters."

"'Weener', you say?"

"To be perfectly honest, sir, he may have said 'Veirna'; it is so hard to be certain; the gentleman in question is a little... 'worse for wear'; shall we say, and has something of a... foreign accent."

"Weener; Veirna- is there a chance he could have said 'Vienna', Wadcliffe?'

"It is a distinct possibility, sir."

"Well, then, show him in, man; at once! Before the neighbours see him!"

"Very good, sir."

'What the very devil was he doing paying home visits?' the lawyer thought to himself; this was most irregular! Most irregular indeed!'

Radcliffe returned presently to usher a stumbling cadaver of a man into the drawing room of number two Alabaster Square. The skin of the visitor's face was blistered and weeping, as it was on his head, where most of his hair had been burnt away to reveal an excoriated seam that somewhat resembled a lava flow from a recently erupted volcano. His clothes: what remained of a German military uniform; by the looks of them, were scorched; blackened, and in some places, completely burnt away. A blood-soaked tourniquet was tied tightly around his exposed right shoulder.

"Good gwief, man; what in blazes happened to you?"

"Prezizely," the carcass, which had once been R. Vienna; Austrian Ambassador to London, replied. Gingerly, he attempted to lower himself into a chair by the grate, without waiting to be offered.

"Not there!" Aubrey Periwinkle; master of the house, snapped urgently, indicating a small wooden stool instead: the

114

temporary abode of a large stack of heavily thumbed books, which he duly removed to his already book encumbered desk, so that the bleeding man could sit without fear of staining the upholstery, "it's an heirloom" he explained, a little more sympathetically, "worth a fortune; don't y'know. Belonged to my gweat aunt Wamona. Here."

The dishevelled diplomat did as he was bidden; he was in no mood and even worse condition to argue, "Zo," he rattled, obviously in great pain, but attempting a show of tactful civility anyway, whilst forcing a smile that; although it probably felt charming on the inside, actually appeared quite sinister in its rictus leer, "Zis vould be Batterzee, zen? You know, I haf never wentured south of ze river."

"It's pwonounced 'B'tershia'," Aubrey corrected, tersely; having done the same, he felt, a thousand times before. The twentieth century was almost upon them and the smart money was on the South eclipsing the West for property fashionability within a very few years, "Think 'Fitzwovia'," he added, "we're up and coming." He saw the Austrian wince, not at his reprimand; not even at his questionable financial gamble, but clearly from one of his many and varied mortal injuries. Aubrey enquired as to whether or not his associate had seen a doctor.

"Nein," the blistered and bleeding man coughed, "My cover iz blown. I haf not..." punctuated by another hacking coughing fit, "got long to lif. Zey vill... track me down und... punish me." Another wince as he attempted to alter his position on the uncomfortable seat.

Aubrey and the Ambassador's relationship was professional rather than familiar. They had each been of particular use to the other over the past eighteen months. As the husband of a German wife, whose grandfather was a member of the Kaiser's inner circle, the Ambassador had petitioned Aubrey for his help in securing the site and the surrounding land for the building of 'The Barn'. A 'Super Farm', had been how Aubrey had sold the idea: 'a social experiment'; this had been the cover that his old University pal; the right honourable Henry Chaplin: the man currently in the process of formalising some kind of common agricultural department for the government had agreed to. 'A new kind of farming on an industrial, steam driven scale' had been his pitch, and; with a few guineas left in a brown paper bag, underneath a bench in St James' Park, an understanding had been reached. In return, Randolph Vienna had promised to recommend Aubrey to the Kaiser for a position within a German annexed England. Aubrey was neither patriot nor sympathiser: he was merely a pragmatist. He studied the form in all his dealings and took on only the cases that he felt he could win.

And all had been proceeding to plan until his brat brother had helped Victoria to annexe The Moon for her own Empire.

It seemed that few of the world's leaders had been convinced by Gordon's much lauded expedition, though none had been in a position to disavow the Empress' claim. Many of these nations had sent covert agents to London in the wake of the 'landing', each in the hope of unearthing word that might lead to the uncovering of a conspiracy to defraud.

The Ambassador; a man best placed, had been the agent for Berlin, and he had entrusted his intelligence to Aubrey because of the familial connection. Aubrey; seeing his chance to kill two birds with one stone, had offered the Germans his twin sons to use as bait; his German wife, Gertrude going along with them to ensure their comfort.

"I twust that my family are safe and that you were able to deal with my bwother before... whatever befell you?" Aubrey enquired, expecting no less than an affirmative response from his partner in crime, "did he do this to you, by the way?"

The Austrian shook his head slowly, smarting from the agony that any movement; however small, seemed to cause him, "Nein... Ze Americans did zis. Zey haf your bruzzer... und your kinde. Your vife, however... it iz my... sad duty to impart... perished in za fire. I voz lucky to escape mysel-"

"Gertwude? No! You said they would be safe, Wandowlph; a spwatt to catch a mackwell, you said! I twusted you!"

"Ve vere played, Aubrey; zey had... an inzide man."

Aubrey stood and began to pace up and down the length of his room.

"What about the barn; you mentioned a fire-"

"It iz gone, Aubrey; all... gone-"

"And the Zeppelin?"

"Destroyed. Ve are finished, Aubrey."

"Is there anything left; anything at all that could lead them back here?" He was panicking now; not to mention worrying for his sons' safety and grieving for his poor, dead wife, "Where have they taken them; do you have any idea, Wandolph?" He became aware that the Ambassador was screaming, and that the reason for this may have had something to do with the fact that he was shaking the man physically by the shoulders.

"Help me, Aubrey! Find me a doktor und I vill tell you vare zey are!"

Aubrey let go of the German and called for his servant: "Wadcliffe?"

"Sir?"

"Send a telegwam to my bwother, Virgil; tell him his services are wequired post haste!"

"Very good, sir."

\* \* \* \* \*

# CHAPTER EIGHT:

## ENTER THE PROFESSOR

"Why'd th'Yanks want th' Captain?"

"Why would the *Germans* want the Captain."

"Why d's th' *Crown* want th' Captain?" Tiny topped and tailed.

Replacing the billycan over the sputtering campfire; just in case either of them might be desperate enough for a refill later, Iggi stepped back up into the caravan and pulled the door closed behind her. She placed two battered, tin mugs; full almost to the brim with warm, brown liquid, onto the wooden table in front of her guest. His mug's enamel was chipped and peeling and its contents looked less than appealing, but Tiny accepted his offering gratefully and with a jocular: "Gawd bless ya' guv'na, an' no mistake."

Iggi sagged onto the stool opposite him, linking her palms around her own mug in the hope of soaking up some warmth and bringing some life back to her numb fingers. She shivered at the sudden shock to her system.

"It's all I've got," she apologised, ahead of his tasting of her 'nearest equivalent' to tea.

Following her wanton destruction of 'The Moon', the pair had decamped to this rather rickety and ramshackle old Vardo that Iggi had appropriated a few years back from a Romany hit man that she had been contracted to put down. It was a bold move on her part, she acknowledged mentally, but for the first time in as long as she could remember, she felt she had found someone whom she could trust. Besides, she added to her inner monologue; they had had nowhere else to go.

The Vardo was stuck where she had first found it: in the bog of Hackney marshes; wedged fast, halfway up its wheels. With Sleuth's help she could probably have got it out, now that she could count on the added torque of her mechanical arm, but she was worried that the stress of moving it might just have done for her ancient gypsy hovel once and for all.

"The Admiral wanted him back," she explained with a sigh, "because; for some reason, he was convinced he'd defect. God only knows why! I think he was worried he'd tell someone the truth about the Moon landing and maybe give the Germans the idea that they could fake one of their own."

Tiny frowned; his face screwing up like a soggy rag.

"*I'm* still not convinced it w's faked!" he spat.

"Oh, come on, dumblewit; of *course* it was faked! How d'you think he got back home if it wasn't?"

Tiny's features; though diminutive and permanently scrunched; like an autumn apple on the turn, betrayed his disillusionment in no lesser way than would a moon faced; wrinkle free young bride's on realising that she had just been jilted at the altar.

Conceding him a moment to let her assertion sink in, she eventually asked him if he was alright. She took a slug of her tea, wondering if he was actually going to cry on her.

predictin' gizmo," he drawled on, laboriously, "but he's dun gone'n made me a weather cuntrolling' deevice."

The American party; and there did seem to be quite a lot of them, had made camp on a Welsh hillside, overlooking the quarry that Gordon had spent all this time trying to escape from. He was not able to see it for himself; having been kept in his cage since his altercation with the General the night before, but had been reliably informed by Letterman, that Professor Blaise's 'fake' rocket 'Victoria' was still exactly where he had left her.

"We've got one of those," Gordon said, yawning for effect.

"A weather cuntroller?" The General mocked; his cronies joining him in a three-part, harmonised guffaw, "Ah don' think so! If'n y'hadda' dun, then the British weather would be like it is in California, now; would'n it?" and he laughed a bit more, "You Limeys, y'see rain an' you go'n inventorate yerselves the umbrella. Y'know what that says t'me, Gordy?" As usual, he answered his own question: "Lack a'vision's what it says, boy! Now you show'n American a drop'a rain an' he comes up with a doohickey *t'stup* it rainin'. Period!"

Gordon found himself wishing he had kept his wise cracks to himself, but it had got him thinking, all the same: in all the time that he had spent on the 'Moon'; in reality, a rocky hole just outside of Cardiff, it had not rained a single drop! Oh, it had been windy; which should have given the game away sooner, of course, but surely there should have been rain? More than two weeks in Wales without rain was not only unlikely, it was totally unprecedented. He filed this anomalous information for later use.

"So, are y'ready t'make y'screen dayboo?"

Gripping the bars of his cage with both hands, Gordon glared down at the General with unabashed contempt.

"You'll get nothing out of me until I've seen Charles and Geoffrey." he spat, indignantly.

"Why a' course!" the General acquiesced, surprisingly easily, "We're nut animals, Gordy; we're on the same side, here: the side a' progress and freedom. Loourtenant?" The General called, inviting the younger of his cadre to join him in front of the cage.

"Sir?"

"Do th'honours, would you, looutenant?"

"Yessir; right away, sir!"

The young officer stepped around behind the cage and tugged at the tarpaulin that Gordon had considered the back wall of his cell. As it came away, a second animal trailer came into view; this one marked 'CHIMPANZEES', but in the place of its original ape tenants, it now contained two frightened young children dressed in pale blue sailor suits, huddled together on the floor in the far corner.

"Charles! Geoffrey!" Gordon exclaimed; a mixture of surprise and relief in his voice, "Are you both alright? Have they fed you?"

The boys looked across at their uncle; four red eyes staring accusingly back at him.

"They tells me they ain't allowed t'talk t'you, Gordy, on account a' yous bein' a deviant'n all," the General mocked, collecting his cap and his swagger from the map table and leading his men to the flap, "Ah'll leave y'all t'git reacquainted. Don' go nowhere, now: show starts in an hour."

* * * * *

"Ah, Spatchcock! I thought I might find you skulking down here."

"Secretary..."

"Come; walk with me, Spatchy, old boy; we've cud t'chew. Have you spoken to Professor Blaise of late?"

"Got a meeting scheduled for Friday, Sir-"

"Good, good; the dates have been set. Timings are crucial, don't y'know. Wouldn't want t'miss th'tide, what?"

"Absolutely, sir."

To all who found themselves pulled into the Admiral's mighty orbit, deference; as a general rule of thumb, was their survival strategy of choice. One did that which one were bidden do, and one did it to the best of one's abilities, or one paid the going rate for having had the audacity to displease him. For the Admiral was not a happy man; men in his position rarely were. He was; in the truest sense of the word, a bully.

But Spatchcock had a right to bully; he had been born to the rôle; being the son of a son of an Admiral who had fought at Trafalgar, gave a chap a sense of heroic entitlement, that was damn near enshrined in empirical law.

But a bully bullies because a bully has been bullied, and the Admiral was no exception to that rule.

When one lives one's life, slave to the beat of a particular drum, one will find it nigh on impossible to defy the rhythm being set; thus, whilst the bullied continue to mete out their frustration on those who allow themselves to be bullied; the bully, in turn, continues to allow themself to be bullied by those whom they acknowledge as having a more substantial claim to bully than they.

"Heard you lost another of my agents, old man; dashed inconsiderate of you; I say, dashed inconsiderate! One gone AWOL, the other blown to smithereens in a public hostelry. It's a poor show, Spatchy, old chap; a damned poor show."

"If I might interject, sir? Agent X is still holding on; the doctor is with her now. Bit of a pig's ear, by all accounts; lost an arm; an eye and a few other bits'n pieces, but he expects her to make a full recovery in-"

"Word on the ground is it's Fenians," the Secretary whispered, conspiratorially, "dash it all, man: I thought we'd heard the last of those Empire bashin' blighters! We seem to be taking a thrashing on all fronts!"

"It's... nothing you can't handle, Secretary, I'm sure-"

"Now see here, Spatchcock: agents don't grow on trees, y'know! PM's furious with you, and I'd steer well clear of Her Illustrious Majesty for a while; if y'know what's good f'you.

"Don't mind telling you, old man, it's a bloody shambles! A shambles! In fact, I'd venture s'far as t'say it's a bally disaster! A Zeppelin hanger; they tell me, right under our damned noses; half the countryside alight, and now those bloody Yanks have got their hands on your astronaut and gone t'ground. You're a laughing stock upstairs, old boy; a bally laughing stock! I'd laugh myself if it wasn't so damnably serious; now what've you got t'say t'that?"

"I assure you, sir, it's all in han-"

"I shouldn't need to remind you that Periwinkle's retrieval is the Empire's single most important undertaking since we sent the cowardly blighter off t'die in the first place!"

"Mister Secretary-"

"No. This calls f'special measures!"

"...Sir?"

"I've had a word with the Surgeon. As long as she's still breathing, he said he can get her fixed up and back in the trap by the weekend. He's got another of those mechanical contraptions of Blaise's. Similar to Z's; you've seen what she can do with th'thing, I take it? Marvellous the things ol' Blaise can do with a few springs'n sprockets, what? And this one's a step up on the last one! Lighter; they tell me, and leaner, and with a few extra gizmos'n gadgets and, would you credit it: the whole thing's powered by the bally sun!"

"The sun, you say?" The Admiral repeated, trying his damnedest to sound enthusiastic, but realising that he probably sounded more sarcastic than he would have liked, "Be gads; whatever will they think of next?"

"Only problem is," the Secretary expanded, "the cost."

"Going to be a big one, is it?"

"Oh, you can be certain of it!" rapped the Secretary, "and it's coming out of your department's budget!"

\* \* \* \* \*

It was a glorious July morning; not at all as it should have been. The sun was shining like it sometimes did in England and the birds were merrily twittering in the trees in confusion, as the Americans wheeled the two carnival cages through the steel gates and onto the lot, or 'quarry', as Gordon was still insisting on calling it. There was a slight breeze, which had a bitter chill to it, but apparently the eminent Mr Edison could do nothing about that. The sky; thoroughly devoid of cloud, was as blue as a Caribbean sea; much as it would probably have been on the day that Gordon had stepped from the 'Victoria' in his tinted helmet and claimed this old pit in the Empress' honour. The sentry saluted as The General rode past on his silver steed, only to find himself instantly admonished for dropping his façade and using an American salute instead of the standard English protocol that would have completed the deceit, had anybody come a-calling. Not that the average British soldier would have been fooled for a moment, Gordon knew: the uniform was an atrocious fit, for a start, and the actor's 'Cor Blimey' accent had all the veracity of the career of an Adventurer who claimed to have visited the Moon!

Once inside the gates, the accompanying marines fanned out, taking up covering positions among the crumbling slate hillocks, whilst the circus convoy continued to roll forward, churning up grey dust in its wake. In no time at all, Gordon saw the fuzzy outline of his 'rocket', shimmering on the hazy grey horizon ahead. The General; mounted in the lead, raised his ever-present swagger and cried: "HALT!"

Gathering his bearings, Gordon scanned the topography, attempting to re-familiarize himself with his surroundings. He estimated a slight advantage to himself over his captors, whom he presumed; on finding this place, would have had little interest in anything bar the abandoned 'set'. He, however, had studied it in detail.

Letterman, he noticed, had arrived some time before them; as had Edison and his team, a pair of whom were currently sat atop what Gordon could only presume to be the latter's weather controller. It was an unlikely looking contraption, sitting somewhere between a khaki painted 'Stephenson's Rocket' and the slightly more ostentatious design of 'Blaise's Anti-airship Cannon', but then that was Americans for you, he decided. It chugged, contentedly to itself, like a panting puppy after its daily constitutional; short bursts of steam pulsing every few minutes through a jauntily angled exhaust chimney with a hinged cap. The 'cab' consisted of a padded, wooden bench seat; raised from the ground by way of a brass expander, akin to his shaving mirror back in the bathroom of his Lombard Street abode, and a parasol, large enough to envelop the operator's perch and the array of switches; dials and levers in front of it that somehow worked the peculiar machine. The dashboard reminded Gordon of the Victoria's so called 'control panel', except that this one seemed to work.

To his mind, it stood to reason that if the Americans had developed a weather controller, then the British boffins no doubt had one too, and if 'Space Control' had left 'the Moon set'; as the General was calling it, in place after he had escaped, then; not only had they intended to re-use it at a later date, but the British equivalent of Edison's machine must also still be somewhere close by. If he could find it, he pondered, then he might yet manage to scupper the Yankee plot.

\* \* \* \* \*

"COME!"

"Admiral Spatchcock."

"Ah! You must be th'new gal; welcome t'th'bunker, m'dear. No tea today, just a pair of large Cognacs, if y'would; no ice: plays havoc with me system, don't y'know. And sharpish, there's a poppet. Oh, and send th'fellow in, would you? Haven't got all day, what?"

"Professor Blaise."

"Yes, that's the chap; matter of some urgency-"

The visitor coughed, "Professor Blaise... at your service," she insisted, striding into the Admiral's office and availing herself of the seat, obviously intended for those for the berating of.

As patronising scowls shot through brass framed pince nez went, Spatchcock's; in response to such brazen, suffragist effrontery, rated toward the higher end on her misogyny index.

"If this is intended as a jape, young lady," he assured her, his temper simmering; the skin of his be-whiskered jowls reddening to match the permanent russet of his pocked and cratered schnozzle, "then consider your appointment t'this department forfeit with immediate effect!"

"Hamble," she said with a smirk, refusing to rise to his supercilious swagger; instead offering him the back of her satin-gloved hand to kiss. He declined.

They had met before, of course; twice: once when she had delivered and demonstrated the 'Victoria', and then again when she had represented her 'agoraphobic' father at the rocket's launch, but there was no reason that he should be expected to remember that, she considered; she was, after all, 'just a girlie'. 'Shame,' she thought, having hoped that her reputation might have reached the Ministry's bowels by this point, to make her reveal to the Admiral now, a tad easier.

"Professor Blaise," the Admiral blustered; all foaming spittle and peaking blood pressure, "is a....well, he is; he's most definitely a..."

"A professor?" she offered, arching her perfectly manicured eyebrows, "Professor Hamble Blaise," she continued, with a congenial smile, "previously 'daughter of', but latterly the definitive article... and 'By Royal Appointment'... don't y'know."

Hamble had come across the Admiral's type before; far too often, and if experience had taught her anything then it had been that to proclaim indignation; pique or indeed to express exasperation at such an antiquated perspective, would be to put herself at a distinct disadvantage as the conversation progressed.

Confidence and equanimity were key to countering bullies such as Spatchcock, she knew. She had learnt this from her mother, by her own poor example.

"Now see here," the Admiral blundered onward, "Professor Blaise has been inventing for The Crown for a decade or-"

"I'll stop you there," she said, removing her bowler to allow her titian curls to tumble freely onto her lace shrouded shoulders,

"Professor 'Harold' Blaise died two years ago. Everything that Queen Vic' has ordered since then has been designed, built and installed, with; dare I say it: a certain feminine panache, by yours truly."

"But you're-"

"A woman? Come, now, Admiral," she teased, placing her hat on the desk between them and flicking a mote of dust from its brim, "let's not let that unfortunate detail come between us? Surely we live in enlightened times?"

The Admiral harrumphed but allowed the ghost of a smile to play on his lips. He was softening, she felt; ever so slightly: his set relaxing, almost, but not quite imperceptibly. He withdrew a cigar from a mother of pearl inlaid box on his desk; clipped its tip with an overtly fussy cigar clipper that she recognised as her father's handiwork, then reached forward to flick the first in a row of plinth mounted, Bakelite switches to his left. Hamble knew for a fact that this particular switch connected via a wire to a red bulb in his secretary's office, two doors further down the corridor; she knew this to be the case because she had been the one to have both designed and installed all of the electrical systems within the ministry whilst working as her father's unpaid assistant, five years earlier.

There followed an insistent tapping at the door behind her; a bark of 'COME!' from the old man himself, followed by an: "Ah, Moneypenny!" as his timid, militarily uniformed servant appeared in the frame, "A large cognac for meself and a...-"

"Two large cognacs; if it's no trouble, Moneypenny?"

"None at all, ma'am," from the secretary, barely stifling a grin; curtseying politely and shuffling back out of the room before the Admiral could protest.

"Enlightened times," he mused, drawing back in his chair, lighting his cigar and forcing a broader, less beaten smile through gritted teeth as he chugged and exhaled, "Enlightened times-"

Again she interrupted him: "Enlightened enough," she goaded, punctuating her rudeness with a pout, "that you can send a woman out to kill for you, but not enlightened enough that you can accept that a woman built the very weapons that you'd see fitted to her for the purpose?"

The Admiral puffed and glared back at the curiosity before him. Her insolent, feminist manner quite obviously disquieted him, but; she noted, she seemed to be earning herself something of a grudging respect with her brash; 'no prisoners' approach. 'Mummy would be appalled,' she brooded.

"Touché," he conceded, humourlessly, then; regaining something of his earlier bombast, scoffed: "But that, m'dear lady, is an entirely different matter! The Crown enlists the services of convent gals," he explained, as if elucidating to a class of raw recruits, "as it helps to channel their natural anger. Rather have'em on our side than yours, what?" and he guffawed at his own pyrrhic victory, "Now then..."

"Professor,"

"'Professor', yes; quite. Well, 'Professor'; me time's precious: what is it th't I can do for you?"

Awkwardly and somewhat reluctantly, he finally reached out for and gently shook her proffered fingers; wetly, as if in doing so he was somewhat letting the side down.

"It was you who asked to see me?" she reminded him.

"Ah! Yes, it was, wasn't it; what?"

Years of living and working alongside her father had taught Hamble how to deal with decrepit dinosaurs such as Spatchcock. As everybody seemed so keen to point out, Professor Harold Blaise had been 'a famous inventor', though it would not be unfair to say that; although novel and frequently distracting, none of his inventions had ever proved in any way"world altering'. Whilst Harry Blaise had been something of a whiz at taking general household objects and making unnecessarily complicated, and ultimately pointless modifications to them, his only daughter had furthered the family trademark in his wake by identifying real world requirements and finding unique and practical solutions to actual day-to-day problems.

It had not been until he had lain prone on his deathbed that Blaise senior had finally admitted to a modicum of admiration for her skill, drive and imagination, something that; had he have said as much even a few days sooner, may actually have saved his life. Prior to that particular moment, he had professed nought but scorn for her peculiar ambition; ridiculing her proposals and attempting to marry her off to any and every eligible bachelor that he came across: an attitude that had, over time, driven a larger and ever widening chasm of coldness between them. Had he in life have shown anything bar chauvinistic contempt for her work, then she may just have been inspired to have unveiled her steam powered iron lung, which would have extended his life for long enough for him to have appreciated just what it was that he had spawned.

She had slaved under his name those past two years whilst he had been confined to his bed, completing her father's commissions; delivering and demonstrating them: on his death, intending to reveal herself as his successor. However, it had transpired that, despite the recent explosion in technological advancements, the world of the late 1890s was no nearer to accepting female emancipation than had the decade that had preceded it, back when her dear mother had felt the need to padlock herself to the axle of Gladstone's ministerial coach in the hope of convincing him to allow her to vote.

"Am I to deduce then, m'dear-"

"Professor," she reminded him, firmly, but calmly (though in truth, her much vaunted accreditation was more of an honorary, 'on-the-job' title than it was a bonafide academic qualification.

"Professor," he accepted, "that it was y'good self who gave us 'The Victoria' and not your 'namesake?'"

"You are, sir."

"Then let me congratulate you: firstly, on your excellent work and secondly on not revealing to the press that it was not actually y'father's work. The Crown salutes you, m'd-Professor."

The situation requiring recognition; it was therefore fortuitous that Moneypenny chose this moment to return with their drinks,

"Though let it be known that it was the last time," she insisted, accepting a chink of glasses over the desk, "that I intend to do so."

"Hmmm," he said, throwing back his drink and returning his glass to Moneypenny's silver tray. As if to underline her assertion, Hamble followed suit.

"Y'said something about a 'sister ship'," he continued, dismissing his secretary with a wave, "Y'said 'y'father' had another one on the bench, what?"

This she had not expected. She had presumed that she had been summoned to make an adjustment to the 'Blaise 5000'; her latest prosthetic limb design, the one that Virgil had recently fitted to one of their wounded agents.

"We need t'send another rocket, don't y'know, and sharpish, before the Americans beat us to it. We were thinking Mars, this time. Any chance y'can have it on the gantry for Friday?"

# CHAPTER NINE:

## BEELZEBUB'S WHORE

"Well, bwother?"

"He's stable. I've done all I can do without access to specialist equipment," the surgeon replied, rinsing his hands and drying them on the last of the guest towels, "He needs to rest," he implored, removing his blood spattered apron and retrieving his coat from the hook on the back of the door, "I've given him a strong sedative to help with the pain, but he should really be in a hospital, y'know.

"I don't suppose you'd consider telling me who the deuce the man is and how the blazes he came to end up like that?"

Aubrey pursed his lips and shook his head slowly. He could think of no other whom he would tolerate speaking to him in such a way, and in his own home t'boot, but Virgil was different.

"Least said," he said, as cryptically as he could muster; closing the guest room door and ushering his brother silently along the landing; down the stairs and back into the drawing room below. Once inside, he closed that door as well.

"I don't like all this cloak'n dagger business, Aubrey; don't like it at all, and I don't mind telling you! I have a reputation to consider, damn you; I can't be seen t'be sneaking around in the dark, stitchin' up the types of Mafioso ruffian whom you choose to associate y'self with. It won't do-"

"Y'chawity's noted, Virgil," Aubrey acquiesced tightly; trying not to reveal quite how it pained him to do so.

Virgil had changed; he had never seen him so uptight before. These were trying times for all of them, of course; poor Gerald was not even in the ground yet, but Virgil had always been so resolute; so stoic and unflappable. Of his trio of over-reaching siblings, Aubrey had always conceded a certain proud regard for the eldest. Although vexingly virtuous and unimpeachable, Virgil had always been an incredibly hard man to hate. As children, he had been an absolute paragon to the younger three: a steadfast standard toward which to strive. Never smug nor disparaging; though he would have had every right to have been so, Virgil had always gone out of his way to help his less talented kin, even if it had meant causing himself a hardship in the process.

He had excelled at everything he had ever attempted to do, sailing through Eton and Oxford without ever appearing challenged in any way. Their father had foreseen him a doctor, with a Harley Street practice to be bragged about, but Virgil's sights had been higher still and so, in short order, he had become a pioneering surgeon in the field of transplanted organs and prosthetic replacements; years ahead of his time and far beyond anything his brothers were ever likely to attain. He had even managed to bag himself a minor Blue Blood for a wife and; before Aubrey and Gordon had yet dispatched with Nanny's services, Virgil had been busy endowing the Periwinkle clan with its first and only daughters; each with a title and an annual civil list stipend to her name.

Virgil was perfect, and try as he often had, Aubrey could find no fault in him worth highlighting. He had long ago resigned himself to living in his shadow; something he never could have acceded to Gordon or even Gerald, for that matter.

"Have no fear," he assured him now, attempting to placate him, "my... 'fwiend' will wecompense you just as soon as he is able-"

"It isn't about the bally money, old fruit!" Virgil rapped back, helping himself to a healthy tot from the etched crystal decanter on Aubrey's desk; a move that further surprised the receptacle's owner, "I'm in town on a summons from The Crown," he rattled on, "Top secret work, don't y'know. I shouldn't wonder if they haven't had me followed!"

If he had seen his younger brother's eyes widen at the mention of this possibility, then he did not acknowledge it, continuing: "Nipped over here on me way to collect poor Gerald's body from the coroner. Y'know, they still haven't apprehended the blighter who murdered him? I don't suppose with your connections y'might've heard-"

"No. Now, sit,"

Aubrey gestured toward the seat by the grate, dropping into a chair himself and joining his brother in a hefty snifter. It had been a fraught few days. He had lost both a brother and a wife and his sons had been kidnapped by enemy agents; all this, not to mention the fact that if his half dead house guest upstairs were to be discovered on the premises, then his involvement in the foiled German invasion plan would likely come to light and he would no doubt be hanged with him as a traitor! Then there was the matter of his failed attempt to have his other brother killed! Aubrey's head span with the various tangled threads that he had woven for himself; unable to decide a coherent plan for their unravelling. He wanted to unload his troubles; he needed to lay his worries before another, but he knew that to do so now would be to unfairly inveigle his brother in a plot that he doubted even he could walk away from.

He tried a different tack, asking: "How is our father?" summoning all of the acting talents that he had learned at the bar, to make himself appear as if he cared one jot for the cantankerous old duffer's well-being.

"As well as can be expected," came Virgil's terse reply, "considering th't the poor man's lost half his brood in the space of a month. His mind isn't what it was. Y'know," he went on, pouring them each another generous measure of cognac, "It wouldn't kill you t'drop him a line, Aubrey. I take it you'll be travelling down for the funeral?"

Aubrey's reply was drowned out by the unexpected crashing open of the drawing room door and the arrival at their feet of a crumpled and cowed Radcliffe.

Picked out in the door frame; lit to devilish effect by the fire that still blazed in the grate behind them, stood a nightmare in freshly stitched scars and blood sodden bandages. If this had been a gothic novel, then a sudden crack of overhead thunder would have shaken the room, complimented by a rip of forked lightening as seen through the stairwell window behind him, but it was not. Like something that would have given Mary Shelley cheese dreams, the ravaged monster that had once been Oberst Randolph Vienna, stared down at the two brothers through his one remaining eye. The other; the

133

one that Virgil had replaced with a blackened monocle; fused to his slowly reconstituting skin, glinted like a beacon; reflected flames playing across its opaque surface, as if offering a window to the fire that raged within him. His bald head appeared as if someone had taken a cleaver to it; removed any unnecessary components and then sewn it back together to resemble the pucker lipped sneer of a dockyard cutthroat. His nose; admittedly beaky to begin with, had melted and now reset, giving it a distinctly avian appearance and where his left ear should have been, he now had a brass ear trumpet sewn over the hole.

From the neck down he was swaddled in bandages, through which the signs of oozing burns and freshly stitched wounds could be ascertained by the fluids that wept through their gauze coverings. Excluding his head, the only other part of his anatomy not to have been entirely mummified, was his huge German sausage, which hung unshackled between his legs; almost to his knees, singed, like a lightly sautéed boa constrictor. On his feet he wore-

"I say, Wandolph," said Aubrey indignantly, sitting bolt upright, "y'weawing me wife's boots!"

"Be gads, man! I gave y'enough morphine t'scuttle a rhinoc'rous!" exclaimed Virgil.

"K-K-KILL," the monster gargled, stepping stiffly into the room; fused joints refusing to bend, "K-KILL G-GOOR DAN P-PERI VINKLE!"

*******

The principle, Hamble reflected, pulling back the stained and dusty tarp to reveal the polished brass nose cone and shiny stabilizer fins of the reserve rocket, was exactly the same; regardless of one's ultimate destination. One needed to be travelling at a particular velocity in order to be capable of escaping the earth's gravitational pull and thus of breaching the atmosphere and propelling oneself forward; theoretically, into infinity. She had worked it all out before and with that information had achieved what none had done before her. There was no earthly reason why she could not do it again with a rocket to Mars or even beyond! Alright, Mars was farther away; a lot farther away, to be fair, but that just meant that it would take longer to get there, so more than one hamper might need to be packed.

All she had to do was to work out exactly how far Mars was away from St James' Park; calculate how long it would take a rocket travelling at escape velocity to reach it and then work out exactly when Mars would appear in the sky above London; setting the launch day so that the two objects would collide. It was a simple matter of mathematics; not her strongest point, admittedly, but she had been spot on the last time around, so she felt reasonably confident that she could repeat the exercise now.

'The Periwinkle', as she had named it; in honour of the man who had sacrificed his life so that she might go down in history as the designer of the world's first working interstellar craft, had been sat beneath its shroud in the corner of her Chelsea workshop for the past five months. The Crown had ordered and paid for two rockets; this second one: the backup, had been built alongside the first, just in case anything had gone wrong with the 'Victoria'. Oh, she had tinkered with it in the meantime; she had added a few minor tweaks and flourishes as she had thought of them; in between her other commissions, just in case, after the success of the first venture, another idiot could be found to pilot it, but the differences between the pair were purely cosmetic.

"Tea, boss?"

"Hmm?"

"Tea break." said Abdul, delivering a cup of tepid tea to the workbench with such force that the receptacle's surface became tidal and left the chipped china to slop onto the paperwork that she had just been perusing.

"Abdul!" she berated, hastily mopping at the mess with the corner of her apron, "How many times?"

Abdul was her 'assistant', if that was not too optimistic a description. She had found him a couple of years ago, sneaking around her workshop in the dead of night; trying to find something of value to liberate, but he had come a cropper when; like one of her resident rodents on the hunt for meagre morsels, he had inadvertently triggered one of her anti-thieving traps; losing his thieving hand in the process. Whilst they had awaited the arrival of her surgeon friend, Hamble had listened to the vagabond's tale of woe and had found herself feeling sorry for him; so sorry, in fact, that after the surgeon had attached her 'Iron fist' to his bloodied stump, she had found herself offering him a job and the attic room in which to sleep.

Abdul's least favourite chore around the workshop, Hamble had quickly discovered, was the making of tea. He found the job insulting, he said; discriminatory and beneath his many untapped natural attributes; whatever they were, which was why he had failed the entrance paper to the Sherpa's Guild that he had travelled to this country to join.

He blamed his 'Iron Fist' for his clumsiness; he always did, but as Hamble had often noted: give him an intricate task involving awkward to reach screws or tightly sprung springs and he was second to none at their manipulation.

"These were my original launch calculations!" she snapped, holding the papers up by their soggy corners and blowing on them in the vain hope of drying them out.

"Beg pardon, misses, but have you not got spare?"

"No, Abdul, I haven't, got a spare!"

"It is fist. Can I not have sun powered gun arm like you gave to angry bird?"

"No, Abdul, you can't! I haven't got time to build it. You do it; I told you; just follow my plans... Or have you ruined those as well?"

Shooing her helper away, Hamble lifted a notebook from the top of a teetering stack of used ledgers, sat back down at her bench and began scribbling...

\* \* \* \* \*

"Heeeey! So, you're the guy everyone's been tuckin' about?" minced the rather effete young fellow whom Letterman had introduced as 'Chuck', the 'movie' director, "I just love a guy with a powerful mousse-tache!" he cheerfully mispronounced.

Gordon stayed silent. Over the past few days cooped in his cage, being fed and watered through a flap by a succession of American soldiers, he had come to appreciate the futility of challenging their grammatical mistakes.

The colonists had left the shores of Blighty just shy of three centuries back, their aim: to conquer the New World and to grow tobacco for the greedy English market. They had set forth full of hope; righteousness and that British sense of Adventure, taking with them experts in the many fields of British endeavour, along with the English religion and a perfectly sensible and serviceable language; honed to perfection over many thousands of hours of usage, with which to educate any locals that they ran into. It must have been something in the air or possibly even the water, but by the time they had felt confident enough to rise up against their King; declaring their ungrateful independence, some century and a half later, they had managed to corrupt everything that they had started out with!

Gordon had once harboured a penchant for visiting North America: a holiday destination, rather than an expedition, of course; the place had actually been thoroughly charted, after all. He had wanted to visit the Grand Canyon; Niagara Falls; the Everglades and the Rockies, but he had to admit: the more he saw of these now 'natives'; the less he relished the idea of spending a protracted amount of time among them.

Chuck described a full circle of the tiger's cage that had been Gordon's residence for the better part of the past week: the caravan train from Watford and the ensuing incarceration, alternating between surveying him through a rough square made of his two thumbs and two index fingers touched together, and what appeared to be a thick rimmed monocle that he kept on a string around his neck. He punctuated his hop, skip and dance routine with bursts of: "Oh, yes!"; "Oh, yeah, baby!" and "Hit me baby, one more time!"

He was joined by a pair of miserable marines; neither of whom looked entirely comfortable with being paraded as clothes horses for his benefit.

"Now, Gordy, dear, this is Marty. Marty is wearing an exact replica of the customised diving suit that you wore in the prequel; right down to the fact that it was two sizes too big for you. Now, Norm, here; Norm's wearing a more 'fitted' version; note the darts here, here and here. You see here, where it's a little tighter around your biceps and your crotch area? And of course, we've taken the liberty of adding a little padding across the chest and the shoulders, to bulk you out a bit. And you'll have noticed the holster too? Neat, huh? The ray gun's not real, a' course, but it makes you look more heroic, don't you think?"

"Are you offering me a choice?" Gordon asked, not quite believing what was playing out before him.

"Sure, hon'; I like my actors to be happy; it makes for a more natural performance."

"I'll go with the original-"

"Put him in the 'fitted'" said Letterman, reappearing from behind a flat, "General's orders."

Chuck clapped his hands and squealed.

"A word, Chuck." Letterman added, steering the director around the wooden set and out of both sight and earshot of his 'star'.

Gordon had been able to see very little of what his captors had been doing since they had wheeled his and his nephews' cages behind the two huge wooden set pieces; perfectly shielding them, both from view of the camera and the direct, unseasonal, Welsh sunlight. He had heard a great deal of hammering and sawing, though; the general unintelligible hubbub of chattering workers and the occasional barked order from the General himself. With nothing else to do with himself whilst he waited to be humiliated, he had used every moment at his disposal to attempt to win his nephews' trust. Reluctant at first; either to speak or even look at him, he had found himself a hard sell, but by tea on the third day, Geoffrey had finally broken:

"M'ma said you were Beelzebub's whore," he had said, quite innocently.

"Aaaand do you understand what that means, at all?" Gordon had enquired, tentatively; careful not to slander the sister-in-law that he could quite cheerfully have throttled at any point over the past decade, given half a chance.

"It means you like it when the devil puts his winkle into your bottom hole," Charles had responded, sulkily; still refusing to turn to face him.

Geoffrey, on the other hand, had slid his way across the cage floor on his backside, stopping to sit cross legged, facing his uncle at the bars. It had been the first time that uncle and nephew had seen each other up close. Charles he had met quite recently, back in the German cell, as that Oberst Vienna chap had been threatening to kill him in order to make Gordon talk. He had noted that; although incredibly similar, the boys were in no way identical. Geoffrey had something ephemeral about him, that most assuredly recalled the Periwinkle set, whilst Charles was most definitely a Schmidt. He had also noted that neither looked anything like their father. Their mother, he had been able to see quite clearly in them: they both had her hair colouring and her eyes, and… he had stopped himself short of comparing them any further, for fear of drawing to mind that misjudged, but mercifully brief dalliance that he and she had shared, that drunken weekend at the Manor, when she had confided in him the detail of her new husband's impotence, long before the Bayswater incident.

"Is it true?" Geoffrey had enquired.

Gordon had taken a breath before replying: "Whoever translated your mother's vivid description did not lie to you about the meaning of her words," he had begun, "but as to the actual truth behind her depiction of me; no, it is not true."

"Bullshit." Charles had decided, taking Gordon aback.

"Your parents and I," he then attempted to explain, "had something of a falling out; ooh, way back before you were born. You must've had similar at one time or another?"

"Charles persuaded our cousin Gretchen to take off her dress, then when we got caught, he blamed me," Geoffrey had then revealed, "I didn't speak to him for a week!"

"There you go! Well, this was really quite similar! And how did you resolve things between you?"

"I beat him with a horse whip until he confessed,"

"Wish I'd thought of that" Gordon had admitted, looking again for signs of Aubrey in Charles' face...

Something was most assuredly not right.

Escape velocity was a constant, everybody knew that; Isaac Newton had proved as much a century and a half before. She had read about it in one of father's old books. In order to outwit the Earth's gravitational pull, an object had to be travelling at least seven miles per second. Once through the atmosphere, inertia would do the rest; or so the theory went. This had been the basis upon which she had both strung and tightened the catapult that had sent her rocket skyward. She had told Space Command' to expect the journey to the Moon to take seventy two minutes; give or take, and it had done, according to the write up in the following morning's Times.

She remembered how the Germans had scoffed at the time and the Americans had demanded to see her workings, but that had just been a case of sour grapes, she had decided. The proof was there; actual photographic proof of her rocket on the surface of the Moon! But looking at it again now, having just had to work it all out from scratch due to Abdul's accidental destruction of her original calculations, Hamble had come to an altogether different conclusion. No matter how many times she had tried it; at every attempt it came out at seventy two hours! She had put the buggering point in the wrong place!

She had checked it again. She had got Abdul to check it. She went next door to the candlestick maker and got him to check it. All concurred that at that speed, the journey could not be completed any quicker.

On the wall above her desk was a framed copy of The Times dated the 22nd of June 1897. Under the strapline 'VICTORIA CONQUERS THE MOON' was a photograph of Space Captain Gordon Periwinkle, standing proudly; hand on hip in front of her dented rocket, beside a gently fluttering flag.

"If I didn't know better," she said, as Abdul wavered beside her, "I'd say that picture was taken in a Welsh quarry..."

* * * * *

140

"I said don't look round; didn't I? Isn't that what I said? 'Don't look round,' I said, 'but I think we've picked up a tail'; yeah, that was it."

"Sorry, boss, I's just au'oma'ic; in'it ? The moment someone says 'don't do' a fing; y'just can't 'elp y'self doin' it, can yer?"

"Well, *you* can't, obviously."

"Well, I'm not th' trained spy among us, am I!"

Iggi had seen this sort of thing happen to other people, back in her convent days and had avoided it in the same way that she had tried to avoid catching the eye of Father McNulty. Two girls would get talking after Mass and discover that they had a common interest in crochet or butterflies and the like. They would start to spend more and more of their spare time together; begin confiding in each other; trusting one another, and then; once they had become truly comfortable with each other's company, that was when the bickering would start. She had heard this referred to as 'friendship' and; unlike Father McNulty, she had been lucky enough to have managed to avoid its touch for almost thirty years!

There was something vaguely comforting about sharing her time with another, though, she noted; not that she would have admitted as much aloud. She actually quite liked the feeling; it calmed her...made her feel protective; forced her to acknowledge the kind of emotions that she had previously rejected as potential vulnerabilities. But vulnerable was not how she currently felt. If anything, it had sharpened her senses. She decided to run with it, provided it did not begin to interfere with her professional judgement.

"They're hanging well back," she reported, using a mirror to keep tabs on their pursuer, whilst steering Sleuth steadily forward.

It was getting dark. She had tried to convince herself that it could just have been a trick of what was left of the dusk light, but she was certain now that there was someone there, six hundred or so yards behind them, "she's trying to stay low," she said, "but I just led us round in a loop and she's still there-"

141

"But surely you done f'that agent in 'The Moon'?" stated Tiny, sneaking; she noticed, another surreptitious peak behind them.

"There are plenty more where she came from," Iggi assured him.

"Yeah, but surely y' mus' all know each other, right? Don't you 'ave works get t'gethers at Chris'mas?"

"We know each other, yes; of course we do; we sometimes work in pairs, but no; we don't 'socialise'; it's best avoided in this game, and yes, to your unvoiced follow up question: we are prepared to kill each other if the Crown orders us to."

"So yer reckon I's anuvva agent?"

Iggi checked again in her mirror. She would not have staked her life on it, but judging by their pursuer's style, she was almost certain that they were being tracked by the same agent, which made no sense at all. Agent X; or 'Katie Snodgrass', as she had known her when they had been kids, would have been level with the bomb as the powder had ignited. If by some sixth sense she had managed to escape unharmed, then surely she would have been on them much sooner than this! They would be in Chepstow within the hour; over the border and at the place that they had agreed to rest for this second night on the road. No, something was most definitely amiss, here. If it was an agent of The Crown, then her little half mile loop would have alerted her to her discovery. She would be preparing herself for an attack. Iggi would have to act quickly if she were to save her friend.

# CHAPTER TEN:

## FRIENDS AND FAMILY

In the world according to Virgil Periwinkle, its most important occupant had but a single vice and that was that he never could resist the clarion call of his halfwit younger brothers in their hours of direst need. He was similarly predisposed to entreaties from his father and his own daughters too, for that matter, though he had been sure to have instilled a sense of proud independence in both his girls that his own father had singularly failed to bring to his younger sons.

Virgil had never doubted that this incorrigible weakness of his would prove his eventual downfall. He had tried to resist them; god help him, he had tried, but whenever he had imagined simply ignoring their persistent telegrams, he had thought of his mother, prostrate on the lawn; the day of his twenty first birthday: the handle of a croquet mallet, wedged defiantly up her posterior, from where she had tripped and fallen during a friendly with Aunt Maud and Uncle Boothby.

He had done what he had been able to, but sadly, it had been too little, too late and he had been unable to stem the bleeding as; regardless of his being almost a third of his way into a medical degree at the time, he had had to fight both the patriarch of the family and his uncle, to be given clearance to attend his dying mother's nethers. He had vowed that day always to be on hand when his family needed him and was yet to even bend the solemn promise that he had made himself.

He had failed poor Gerald; murdered in his own home, for which he was duly mortified and had thought his youngest brother Gordon lost too until half an hour ago, when; following the unlikely resurrection of his most recent patient, certain details had come to light that had necessitated him removing himself from Alabaster Square forthwith and hailing a cab to Chelsea to impart said news.

"Virgil! What a lovely surprise! Come in; come in! Abdul? Tea! Here, let me take your coat; though I must warn you; my love, that if you've come looking for a bit of extra marital attention, I'm afraid I'm not in the mood. Shit is afoot, my darling, and I have things t'do."

"Hamble, dearest; It is not affection that I have raced here to deliver; rather it is news that I believe you would want to know."

"TEA, Abdul!" Hamble hollered, to which the Egyptian sighed very deeply and very loudly and stomped his way out to the kitchen, "Go on," she implored of her guest, "I have news of my own, but let me hear yours first."

They sat, either side of her workbench; their arms resting on a vice each.

"I don't know quite how to put this, my love, so-"

Virgil broke off suddenly as Abdul finally divested himself of his duty, slamming down two filthy mugs between them. Steaming water ran the length of the not quite level bench to dribble off the end and onto the floor, and only the surgeon's lightning reactions saved the professor's calculations this time.

"Anything else?" Abdul enquired, doffing his fez and smiling sarcastically.

"Go and check the straps on the cargo, then finish making the sandwiches... GO!" she snapped, reaching over her vice to clasp her lover's hands, mid bench, "Tell me, darling; for my news cannot wait."

Virgil cleared his throat and continued: "It would appear," he divulged, dolefully, that the Moon landing... was faked!"

"Oh, tell me something I *don't* know!"

"You knew?"

"I guessed," She confirmed, "Spatchcock asked me to send up another rocket; this time to Mars, would you believe? Apparently, the Queen feels the need to make another statement. I was reviewing the flight plans I gave him for the 'Victoria' and discovered that I'd made a mistake; a big one: there was no way it could have made it all the way there in under a day; the whole thing had to've been a charade!"

"It would appear so," Virgil agreed with a frown, "According to an associate of my brother's, my *other* brother, Gordon is alive and being held against his will by the Americans who intend to restage the moon landing; filming the whole bally thing with one of their new-fangled moving picture cameras!"

"Edison!" Hamble exclaimed, "he's here?" She took a sip of Abdul's tea; stood up and began to pace, "All those years in father's shadow; all that time letting him take all the credit for my innovations and when I finally come clean and own up to my own substance, I'm about t'get upstaged by that Yankie charlatan!"

She slammed her hand against a wooden beam, resulting in a sudden snowstorm of accumulated dust. "Do you know where they intend to do this?"

"Not precisely," Virgil said, deciding to pass on the tea. He had drunk enough of Abdul's trademark ditch water brew to be wary of the likelihood of contracting dysentery or its ilk, "a quarry in south Wales is all I've got."

Hamble turned back to him; her eyes widening and her smile returning to brighten her face.

"Of course!" she all but snapped, "Cefngarw! It all makes sense now! That was what they wanted my weather machine for! I took it to an army training facility in a disused quarry last summer! That's where they'll be, Virgil!"

"The trouble is," Virgil said, "I have so little time if I'm to rescue him; it's three day's ride, at least! I was wondering if I might borrow one of your 'Steam Steeds' ?"

Hamble raised her left eyebrow as he had seen her do so many times before when she knew something that he did not. It had been one of the first things that had attracted him to her.

They had met back in '94, in an ante room to the operating theatre inside Buckingham palace; both having been summoned there to attend her Majesty; Virgil, as the leading surgeon in his field and Hamble as the representative of her father, the supposed inventor of the mechanical knee joint that Virgil had been hired to fit. Of course, operations such as this were still incredibly rare back then; this had been only the fourth attempted at this point, and all had been subject to the highest possible security scrutiny. It would not have done for the general public to have discovered exactly how far medical science had progressed. Life prolonging technology such as this would only ever be available to the top three percent of human society, for fear of allowing the proletariat to live long enough to cause a population problem.

Hamble's joint had been a vast improvement on previous prosthetic attempts and 'her father' had been instantly commissioned to improve on the monarch's artificial lungs. Whilst enjoying the Crown's patronage, Hamble had revealed plans for a series of replacement limbs that 'he' had been working on and so had begun a professional relationship with Virgil that had rapidly evolved into something of a more personal association.

"I'm supposed to be taking the sister ship up to St James' Park, this evening to launch it for real, but now I've got a better idea," Hamble mused, "follow me, lover boy..."

\* \* \* \* \*

"Evening, Katie,"

"Evening, yerself, Iggi,"

"Fancy meeting you here."

"Yeah, fancy, eh?"

Iggi took a measured step toward their erstwhile stalker. Something about her seemed different, but it was difficult to ascertain quite what that something might have been in the dark and from a distance, so she moved slowly and deliberately, trying not to spook the agent; the palm of her real hand gripping the hilt of the pistol at her belt all the while.

Katie wore a black leather patch over her right eye; not quite covering the extent of a very recently stitched scar that reached all the way across to the bridge of her nose. Her skin was freckled with barely healed scalds and abrasions, fanning out across her face from a deeper wound just below her missing eye. Her hair, usually long, russet and ringletted; as befitting her Celtic heritage, was matted with blood and singed and indeed missing in several places.

"We don't have to do this, you know." Iggi told her.

"Ahh, y'know, we really do." Katie assured her in turn.

"You could just tell him there wasn't enough left of me to identify."

"Nah; he wants me to bring back yer arm, so he does; they cost a bomb, these things."

She emphasised the word 'bomb', pulling back her cloak to reveal a mechanical arm, similar to Iggi's, but showing definite signs of improvements having been made since hers had been fitted.

"Useful, wouldn't ye say? Though, I really was quite attached to me previous one; as I was me eye; me breast, here, an' me higher register hearing."

"Ah," said Iggi, sheepishly; playing for time, "I really don't know what to say..."

The Agent merely shrugged her shoulders, dismissively, then; taking up a crab-like stance: arms forward; mechanical pincer whirring and flexing, she bent her knees and began to circle her colleague in a rocking, sidestepping motion, "t'be sure, it was probably nothing personal. Orders're orders, wouldn't ye say?"

Iggi shucked her coat and flexed the tendons that connected to her own prosthetic. A bolt of pain recharged her senses as she joined her fellow abused orphan in the dance of the ninja crustaceans.

It was Katie who struck the first blow, as Iggi had decided it would be. She had mutilated the poor girl only a couple of days previously, so she felt she owed her as much.

Iggi anticipated the move, blocking it with her own mechanical arm; the clash of metal on metal causing a flash of sparks that lit the road momentarily. Thankfully, Katie had her back to Tiny, who; until that moment had been hidden in the shadows, but was now revealed, not twenty yards behind the agent, attempting to aim his blunderbuss in the dark.

Iggi's eyes flared; she had expressly told him to stay out of sight, whatever the outcome of the showdown might be. She had been quite explicit on the subject. He could not shoot straight in daylight and at point blank range; he would only get in the way if he attempted to help her now and would likely cause her a distraction that she could have well done without.

Her concern for her friend's safety proved to be a novice's mistake. Without turning away from the engagement, Agent X drew a pistol from the holster on her back and fired a single shot behind her; the flash as the gunpowder ignited, lighting the glade once more so that Iggi could be certain that the shot had not gone wide.

"Y'eve gone soft, Shikiwana; that was a stupid mistake, so it was. One down; one te go."

147

For the next five minutes, Iggi met her attacker blow for blow; making no attempt to parry as she judged, through defence, her foe's current strengths and weaknesses. By rights she should still have been morphined out of her box; flat on her back on a slab back at the Ministry, wondering why she could not feel her arm. She had to be in some considerable pain, Iggi knew, yet her reflexes were still second to none.

She and Katie had known each other since childhood. They had fought each other before; in training, so knew each other's moves well enough and should have had no trouble anticipating and countering their opponent's strategies. But Katie was not completely on form. Her prosthetic; unpredictably deadly as it was, was her flaw. They may have found a way to numb the incredible pain that she must have been in so that she could be sent straight back into play, but she had not had the time to master her new weapon's full potential. It appeared lighter than Iggi's and more manoeuvrable. It also had a mean looking buzz saw blade that had already caught her upper arm, tearing through the leather sword stoppers as if they had been cotton, and inflicting a wound that was probably worse than it was likely to feel whilst the adrenalin still pumped through her system.

She was going to have to put her down; she had known as much since she had first realised who it was that had been tailing them, but if she was going to do it, then she was going to do it professionally. She was not going to let the death of her new friend make her sloppy and vulnerable.

A second lunge with the buzz saw removed all four of her artificial fingers and she began to bleed oil and, worryingly, blood, from her ruptured pipes. Iggi finally drew her pistol and swung it to cover her opponent but lost her footing and pitched forward; her world blurring and spinning as she barrelled headlong into a tree.

Unable to move or to see, she was still able to taste the blood in her mouth as the final blow came...

*****

"I call it the 'Range Roller', she revealed, proudly, showing

Virgil into an area to the rear of her workshop that had; in a previous incarnation, been the cobbled stables-cum-carriage store of the 'Kensington and Chelsea Fire Service'. Virgil's eyes bulged at the sight that greeted him. He recognised it as a variation of one of those new, novelty motor cars that one had begun to read so much about in the popular press. This one, however, was much bigger than the average toff hobbyist's automobile. Size wise, it looked more like a stagecoach; a throwback to the previous century's preferred mode of transport, though one where the horses had been dispensed with to be replaced by a bold, brass radiator and a pair of dinner plate sized, iron rimmed lamps, imbuing the vehicle; if, like him, one was prone to pareidolia, with a toothy face, locked into a permanent angry gurn. Sticking out of its roof at a backward angled diagonal, was the rocket ship 'Periwinkle', that his secret mistress had so romantically named after himself, and behind that, an enormous catapult arrangement, similar to the one used to launch the rocket's twin, but a tad smaller.

"Well?" Professor Hamble Blaise enquired, no doubt anticipating a positive response. When none came quickly enough, she ventured: "It'll do nought to ten in nine minutes and has a top speed; would you believe, of fifteen miles per hour, fully laden!"

"But that's still slower than a horse!" Virgil blustered; his major concern at this juncture being to reach his brother before his captors judged him surplus to requirement, rather than the boosting of his beau's artistic ego. Luckily for Virgil and his philandering desires of the future, Hamble was able to see past her own self aggrandising needs, calmly pointing out that:

"A horse cannot cover the required distance without need of regular rest breaks, whereas the Range Roller, need only be refuelled periodically, and will cover the distance in a straight ten hours."

When this revelation also failed to inspire him, she added: "It's the best offer you're going to get, Virgil. Now gather your things, we're going on a Yank hunt."

"Scene one, take four, aaaaand... Action!"

On Chuck's command, the two silver suited marines with the goldfish bowls wedged over their heads, stepped laboriously back into frame in front of an enormous, painted wooden flat. The painting depicted a rocket; at least three times the size of the 'Victoria', and by any layman's estimate: an extremely unlikely viability for steam age space travel. In front of the spacemen and their two-dimensional rocket; fluttering gently atop its pole in the evening breeze, flew the star-spangled banner; foreground; centre stage: lest anyone forget whose gig this actually was!

Gordon snorted as the actors edged forward; attempting to simulate weightlessness to much comedic effect, in his opinion and received an elbow to the ribs for his trouble. Above them, staked into a hillock of slag; backlit for extra effect, stood a painted cut out that was intended to represent the earth as seen from space. It wobbled as a gust of wind caught it. Top marks for research, though; Gordon conceded, silently and grudgingly, knowing that he had been fooled by less!

From his position off set; waiting in the wings; flanked by another pair of marines, Gordon was able to see his nephews on the opposite side of the arena. Each had a marine of his own to watch over him, neither of whom; it appeared, nurturing the slightest qualm about holding a pistol to a child's head.

On a cue from Chuck, the lone camera; which, Gordon had noted, was being operated by Edison himself, panned left to track the arrival of a small, cardboard cut-out of the 'Victoria', dangling on a string from a long pole, being held aloft by two burly props men. It was a nail biting few seconds for the director, whose first two takes had been scotched by their arrival in shot; pole in hand, whilst his third attempt had fared little better, due to the untimely appearance of an inquisitive pigeon, which had taken up residence on top of the 'USS Enterprise', until; that was, the General had shot it down.

Take four, on the other hand, had been on track to succeed; judging by Chuck's more upbeat reaction.

Spying the model 'Victoria', the spacemen pointed aloft, exactly as scripted; in one simple scene, ramming home the message that the Americans had arrived here ahead of him. According to said script, the camera was then due to 'wobble' as if buffeted, as the 'Victoria' crash landed off camera. It should then have tracked right to find the real 'Victoria'; steam pouring from both her exhausts and the crack in her nose cone, where she had come to rest against the lip of a manmade crater. Gordon; who by this time, was supposed to have entered his ship and been ready to throw open (the now reattached) door on a countdown from Chuck, before falling face down in a sudden feint, suddenly kicked left; taking his guards by surprise and winding one in the process. This pre planned distraction was the signal that Geoffrey and Charles had been waiting for in order to make their own move. Kicking and ducking; as their uncle had advised them earlier in the day. It was a matter of mere seconds before the boys were able to overcome their gaolers and scarper into the craggy dunes, both in opposite directions. Charles had darted forward, speeding across the set and eliciting an ear drum slicing: "CU-U-U-U-T!" from Chuck, through his brass megaphone.

"RUN!" Gordon, spat; his two keepers, now recovered, lunging for him, expecting him to attempt to join his nephews. In the ensuing panic, Letterman appeared from nowhere to jam and cock a pistol into the nape of Gordon's neck.

"You just signed the execution warrant on the last boy found." he said, twisting his gun's barrel so that it chafed the skin of Gordon's neck.

As he was led back to his cage, past the sobbing director and the makeup artist who was trying to comfort him, Gordon saw a shimmer of movement in the distance, picked out by the light of the real Moon that Chuck had been so careful to shoot away from.

'Attaboys!' he thought to himself, stealing one of his captor's own made up words, 'Attaboys!'

* * * * *

When she had told Virgil to go and collect his effects from the patiently waiting cabbie and to load them into the hold of the Range Roller, Hamble had expected Virgil to return a few moments later, laden with his portable surgery kit and perhaps an overnight bag or two. What she had definitely not expected, was to see her dogsbody and her lover, struggling to manhandle an oversized coffin between them; Virgil's principle effects balanced precariously atop it.

"Have we been grave robbing again, doctor?" she asked, sarcastically, but expecting a serious explanation, none the less. It was light hearted banter, as far as she was concerned; a regular tease of hers. She knew fully well how any allusions as to how he might have come by his superior knowledge of the inner workings of the human body were always met with a certain amount of indignation and; oftentimes, with a sudden sullen mood swing. This ought to have taught her to steer well clear of the subject, but Hamble's enquiring mind and her determination to badger a smile out of her part time sweetheart, had always brought her back to the one area of his life that he had persistently refused to share with her.

Virgil stopped suddenly, causing the much shorter Abdul; taking up the rear, to bump his head on the foot of the casket and to drop his end to the flagstones.

"I have never robbed graves," he said, obviously affronted, but managing to hold his temper in check, "It's my brother, Gerald. Come along Abdul; put your back into it," and with this, he picked up his end and continued on through the workshop toward the stables, with poor Abdul struggling to catch up.

Hamble watched him go. At twenty three years her senior, Virgil had often struggled with her sense of humour. In all other ways she felt that they were an ideal match; he was the only man whom she had ever taken a shine to who had even come close to matching her intellect, but that generational gap did keep coming back to haunt them. She was the same age as his eldest daughter, Lady Tatiana; in fact, they even shared a birthday, but Hamble was most assuredly not looking for a father figure, any more than she was looking for a husband! Their 'arrangement' suited her perfectly. Whenever he was in town on business, he would pay her a most welcome, surprise visit. She loved the spontaneity of their unspoken liaisons: the randomness of their relationship; it suited her lifestyle perfectly. She was also aware of how stringently her father would have disapproved.

Hamble gathered up the last of her things, bolted the workshop door behind her and followed the boys out to the courtyard. It was going to be a tight squeeze, if; as seemed likely, Virgil was going to insist on bringing 'Gerald' along too.

"Any reason why y'brother can't stay behind?" she asked, catching up with them at the Roller, but the look on his face as he turned around told her that there probably was.

"Once we have rescued Gordon," he explained, "he and I shall be travelling on to the family home together. It may soften the blow of losing one son if I can present my father with a son resurrected."

Hamble decided not to argue with him; she had seen that look before.

"Well, then you'll have to stick him inside the rocket," she said instead…

"Sluff," said Abdul, from behind the wheel.

"Slough," Virgil corrected, from his right hand side.

"Twenty three miles in eighty five minutes," Hamble remarked, from the driver's left, "I think we just set a new land speed record! We've also lost our tail at last…" and she paused, before adding: "So, Virgil, would you care to enlighten us as to who was following you and for why?"

"Why, pray," he responded defensively, "had they to've been following *me*?

"Because they're *always* following you," she replied, "I noticed them outside the *last* time you paid me a visit and I was only looking *that* time because my neighbour pointed them out the time before,"

She had kept her tone light; not wishing to rile him, but was intrigued none the less.

"I'm surgeon to the bally royal household," he snapped back, "I'm followed everywhere I go."

"Everywhere?" she parroted, "and why, pray, have you not mentioned this before?"

"Because I didn't consider it of particular relevance," he said, removing his Hunter from its pocket; flipping its cover and checking the time before replacing it.

"Are you telling me," she goaded, though she had vowed to herself not to do so, "that The Crown know about our... 'arrangement'?"

"I would think it highly likely," he said, as if educating a child.

"Don't take that tone with me-"

"Enough!" snapped Abdul, the vehicle's driver, from the seat between them, "I try to concentrate. It first time I drive without Brinks man in front!"

"Chepstow, three and half," Abdul said, breaking the stony silence of the previous seven hours. They had stopped three times between Slough and this point, so that he could refill the tank, but at no point had Hamble or Virgil uttered a word, either to each other or to Abdul.

It was stupid, she knew, and in the grand scheme of things it hardly mattered, but Hamble could not shake the feeling that she had somehow been undermined. She had a reputation to consider here, and not just the one that she had embarked upon this trip in order to defend; that of the inventor of the first rocket to land on the Moon, but also that of a woman in a traditionally male dominated arena such as the inventing game. If her affair with a married man were ever to come to light, then she would undoubtedly never be taken seriously again. She would become a subject of ridicule and hatred and possibly even find herself incarcerated alongside her mother!

She realised, though, that she was being unfair to Virgil to blame him for her awkward predicament. Considering the delicate nature of some of the work that she had done for the Crown, and the fact that she had herself been made to sign a secrecy disclosure form, way back when she had first helped her father to wire up the Ministry, she was probably under reasonable scrutiny herself, anyway. She had never spotted them watching her, though and she felt sure that she would have done, had they been as obvious as Virgil's shadow.

However, her train of thought was instantly derailed as Abdul suddenly slammed on the brakes and brought the 'Roller' to a slip sliding stop.

The three travellers braced themselves against the glass wind shield as the vehicle came to a halt mere feet from a portly fellow in a long coat and a bowler hat with an improbably small head, who was standing over what; at first sight, appeared to be a blood soaked corpse, lying prone in the middle of the road.

The man had his hand up, like the traffic controller on his box at Piccadilly Circus; not the action of a vagabond or a highwayman, she decided, but a fellow traveller in distress.

"Please, guv'nor," he said, loping across the road toward them; he himself obviously suffering from a wound of some kind as well, "My friend is dying! I've done all I can do, but they took her arm-"

"Drive on, Abdul," said Virgil, "It's probably a deception; there'll be more of-"

"Virgil Periwinkle, get out there and help the man!" Hamble ordered, opening the door beside her and rushing over to appraise the situation first-hand.

Virgil followed; reluctantly, pausing only to gather his medical bag from the luggage rack. Abdul, however, stayed with the car. He would later confess to his having been in agreement with Virgil's assessment of the situation.

"Virgil! Hurry it up, man! This poor girl's had her arm torn off!"

"Saints alive!" exclaimed the surgeon, "but there's a pulse!"

"What happened, here?" Hamble asked, turning to the girl's companion.

"We were attacked, miss. Tiny, by th'way... that's m'name."

"Pleased to meet you, Tiny. I'm Hamble and this is Virgil. Don't worry; Virgil, here's, a surgeon. If he can't help your friend, no one can."

With this, the man with the irreconcilable name, staggered; lost his balance and crashed to his knees in front of her.

"Be gads, man; you've been shot!" she declared, "Virgil, this man's been-"

"Then clean the wound and stem the flow, girl; I only have the one pair of hands!"

"I's jus' a scratch, miss; Iggi's more important,"

"Iggi?" asked Virgil, taking a closer look at his patient's bloodied and lacerated face, "Iggi Shikiwana!"

At Hamble's frown, Tiny interjected: "Her father was a foreigner, miss."

"No," she replied, turning back to her partner, "I mean, how do *you* know her, Virgil?"

"She's a Crown agent," he replied, "Agent Z."

"Retired," chipped in Tiny from the side.

"And she hasn't had her arm ripped off," Virgil clarified, "she's had one of your prosthetic arms *removed*... Somewhat forcibly, too."

"Well, can you do anything?"

Virgil sighed heavily before responding: "Not unless you happen to've brought a spare arm with you."

\* \* \* \* \*

# CHAPTER ELEVEN:

# THE GOOD SAMARITANS

Ollyphante had only needed one of the boys in custody for his plan to work, but then, Gordon only needed one of them at liberty for *his* plan to work, just as well. Not that it was much of a plan, not really; It was more of a general aim to cause a token hindrance, if he was honest: a futile resistance, of sorts: something to give the boys a semblance of hope in the midst of the somewhat dire situation that; through no fault of their own, they now found themselves embroiled in. But then, was it not every captured Englishman's duty; at the very least, to attempt to be a pain in the posterior of one's gloating captors?

'Always go down fighting,' had been the mantra of the great British adventurer, Egon Platypus, who had been rather a hero of Gordon's in his youth. 'As a last resort,' the great man had gone on to advise, in his much lauded memoir: 'Shout; Shout And Shout Again' (Livingstone Press, 1863); as a final titbit of advice to the novice explorer, waking to find himself stewing amid a selection of locally sourced vegetables, 'Spit in the pot, and make sure the heathens see y'do it!'

Well, Gordon had gone one better than his proxy mentor, in Swaziland, seven years ago, when; in an uncomfortably similar situation to the one described in Platypus' afterword, he had lowered his trunks and actually shat in the pot that he had been sharing with sherpa Bambot and a crop of sweet potatoes.

They had caught Charles attempting to sabotage Edison's weather manipulator and had hauled him back to be disciplined by the General, which had consisted of a typical Public school style thrashing to the bare Glutinous Maximus with the old man's swagger stick; something that Gordon expected him to be quite familiar with. Geoffrey, however, remained at large and was hopefully following the instructions set for him by his uncle.

Gordon and his nephews' misbehaviour had set the shoot back by the better part of three hours. He had been hoping for better: if Charles had been able to have stayed low until dawn, then another whole day might have been lost to the Americans, as they were apparently unable to film by day. Unable to see a way of scuppering their plans with any degree of permanence from his end, the best that Gordon could hope for was to set them back for long enough to allow either Spatchcock's suspiciously tardy assassin the time to unravel the plot and track him down, or Tiny; his Sherpa, to come bounding to his rescue, as he had heard him promise to do whilst he himself had been dangling above the smoggy streets of South London, on route; as far as he had suspected at the time, to Berlin.

Of the two possibilities, Gordon had to admit that his money was on the former likelihood. There was a chance, of course, that Tiny may have managed to overpower him/her, back in Alabaster Square, but The Crown would have merely sent another agent in their place and Tiny would have earned himself a spot at the top of that agent's kill list.

He therefore found himself in the curious position of hoping to be killed by his own countrymen, with the proviso that after doing so; hopefully quickly and relatively painlessly, they would be able to nix the American threat and in so doing, save the Empire.

He wondered idly quite why he ought still feel an allegiance to Victoria after all that had transpired, as he was imprisoned inside her eponymous rocket whilst the concert party marines mugged their way through take five of scene one...

\* \* \* \* \*

She had caught herself chuckling as she had sliced off Z's arm with her buzz saw adaptation. She had heard herself giggling maniacally as she had gathered up the bloodied abomination and secured it in her backpack for transportation back to London. She had checked herself and had spent a moment calming herself down: counting her breaths and trying to fight this sudden, inexplicable euphoria that; a few moments ago, had threatened to overwhelm her senses. There was a tune going around in her head; a familiar one, but for the life of her, she could not place it.

She had not enjoyed putting her fellow agent down; especially one whom she had known personally: it had simply been a professional undertaking; an order handed down from above; Z would have done the same had their situations have been reversed.

She had not been motivated by any kind of vengeful desire, either. Again, she considered herself a professional and would never have allowed herself to have been so distracted. The fact that Z had been the one responsible for the recent loss of several of her favourite body parts had made not the slightest difference to the way in which she had comported herself in the field. No; this was something new: something that, in all her years working for the Crown, had never happened to her before. Was she, she wondered; like Z before her, losing her touch? Had it anything to do with the dreams, she mused, or indeed, her recent mechanical upgrade? She checked the dial on her wrist that showed the level of her power reserve, chuckling again as she noted that she only had three of a possible ten joules of stored energy left in her battery before she would require a sunlight recharge. That chuckle begat a giggle, which in turn led to a guffaw and before she knew it, she was rolling around in the dirt, cackling uncontrollably to the tune in her head. In one of a few brief moments of lucidity, X remembered what that bloody surgeon had told her about probable side effects of the pain numbing drugs that he had administered at the time of her... operation. There was a small brass switch on her wrist; just beside the power dial. Crawling toward a tree, against which she propped herself; allowing her quaking body to sink into the embrace of its ancient roots, X flicked the switch once to release a dose of morphine into her system.

Within seconds she was feeling the benefit of the drug: her heart rate had slowed and her mind had begun to clear. The tune had faded away to a whisper. She made a mental note in future, to top up at the first sign of unwarranted hysteria.

With task one complete, she spent a few moments rehydrating from her field canteen whilst she re ordered her objectives. Captain Periwinkle had to be located and subdued at whatever cost and, if at all possible, returned to base alive. She wiped a bead of sweat from her brow, then choked, momentarily as a horrific image flashed across her mind. She shook her head to clear the aberration; pulling the picture of Captain Periwinkle from her breast pocket and focussing on his face. The bead became a trickle, which in turn became a flood and she was back inside her own head; sifting memories from dreams...disappearing down a rabbit hole.

Outside in the real world, her head slumped gradually forward, coming to rest against her chest; a line of dribble following its path.

Inside her head, the streets are fog bound and she is lost. Her avatar wanders aimlessly as she attempts to assert her bearings. She is only about five inches from walking into a brick wall, when its street marker hoves sharply into view. "Berners Street", she reads aloud, taking a step backwards,

"Whitechapel," she remembers... She is eighteen years old. She's been a Crown agent for almost eighteen months. She's not alone here... Agent P is with her: Agent P is her mentor... They are tracking an abscondee... It's all very 'hush hush' and P has told her very little, bar the fact that their target is a 'VIP' who has been assigned around the clock surveillance... Occasionally he slips the net and a Crown agent is sent to retrieve him... Apparently, he never strays far and is almost always found within a grid of a few dark alleyways in the vicinity of Whitechapel... Today is no exception... P spies him first, working; crouched inside the blurred circle of twilight, afforded by the gas lamp above him... She says nothing, but creeps slowly forward and; drawing a bulky syringe from her utility belt, she jabs its needle point into the side of his neck... He convulses; spasms and he drops his blooded scalpel onto his half naked victim... He falls to the cobbles himself, but she doesn't see this, nor does she see Agent P hoist his unconscious form up and onto her shoulder, no... X is transfixed by the corpse in the lamplight; her chest broken open like an egg, to reveal things that no man has any right to see... She hears P, insisting that she follow, and they return to the carriage that awaits them just around the corner... Together; in silence, they drape the man over the seat, then take the bench, opposite; P instructing their driver to return them to the Ministry at once.

In the coach, she can't help herself from staring at the prone man's blood flecked face. She knows him, or she will know him; she can't quite decide... It's Father McNulty, but it isn't Father McNulty: his lascivious grin, the first thing she sees each night when she closes her eyes to sleep. It's Captain Gordon Periwinkle, but it isn't Captain Gordon Periwinkle: the face in the picture that she knows she is holding, back in the real world... It's *the* Secretary, her controller, but again the face shifts and reforms... She sees a face above her, backlit and looming; he's smiling and telling her that everything will be alright. She's been in an altercation; she's been hurt, but she's alive: he has rebuilt her! She recognises the man; he is Doctor Virgil Periwinkle; 'The Surgeon' and, like Humpty Dumpty; the tune that she has finally identified, he has just put her back

160

together again. He is the sleeping man that she sees opposite her now; the man whom they have to protect at all costs. The same man. The same man. The same man...

*****

Gordon had been locked up more often than he had had to employ the services of a new sherpa; it was, as they say, an occupational hazard for a man in his line, but of all those occasions, incarcerated in cages; in pits; in cells; cellars or tombs, he could not recall a single time when he had not yearned for the chance to break free of his claustrophobic bonds and take his leave. Never; before today, had he craved to stay locked up and forgotten about for all time. He could hear very little extraneous noise from inside his new prison cage; ironically, the hold of The 'Victoria': the vessel that; not all that long hence, he had seen as his chance to liberate himself from the suffocating yoke of being the youngest and least worthy of the four Periwinkle brothers, and stake his claim for emancipation among the stars. 'Funny how things turn out,' he thought now, as he paced its cramped confines, contemplating the futility of everything that he had done since.

Silent films; by their very nature, were quiet affairs, but if he strained, he could still just about hear the director, Chuck, shouting in the background: attempting to cue his actors and berating his pole bearers for missing their marks. He had hoped to have been able to hear more of a commotion, by now; having dared to believe that Geoffrey might actually locate the British weather machine and throw a spanner in their captor's works, but he had heard nothing so far to suggest that his nephew had been able to find said gubbins and bring on the rains. It had been something of a long shot, after all. Disheartened and despite himself, he readied himself for his own cue. When it came, in the shape of a sudden, resounding reverberation through the ship's steel hull, as one of the director's myriad flunkies slapped its side to tell him that it was time to open up and fall out; face-first into the dust, as any useless; unheroic Englishman would be bound to do in his position, he froze. He looked around the cabin; saw the alarm lights still blinking on the dashboard: 'If only it had not all been a lie,' he thought. He would've been dead by now, having died an unusurpable hero's death and not been about to be immortalised as the first English villain in the very first American science fiction film. He considered barricading the door and refusing to come out, but he had no doubt that the General would fulfil his promise to kill Geoffrey; if and when he eventually found him, if he did not 'play ball', as they put it. A second slap to the rocket's arse jolted him from his reverie.

He sighed; resigned to his fate; after all that he had gone through, finally broken. He put his helmet over his head and he opened the door...

* * * * *

Luckily for Tiny, the bullet that had temporarily taken him out of the game, had passed cleanly through the fleshy area beneath his right shoulder blade, causing him minimal bodily damage, though considerable pain and fair loss of blood; before lodging itself in the oak, in front of which he had been standing at the time. He had lost consciousness; not due to the trauma, as one might have expected, but as his head; jolted sharply backwards by the force of the impact, had connected with the solidity of the tree's trunk.

He had apparently lain where he had fallen for some time after X's departure, awakening only a short while before seeing the lights of the approaching vehicle; whereby he had spied Iggi's body; prone in the road, and crawled toward her with the aim of dragging her from the vehicle's path.

Although awake and mentally aware when the vehicle had drawn to a halt in front of him, he had found that he remained in thrall to a concussion, which left him merely to flirt with the abilities of his senses, meaning that he caught only snippets of his helper's conversation as they alighted and worked feverishly to save his friend's life.

'A tad out of his depth' did not quite cover the way that he had felt as he had sat, whittling away at his finger nails;

watching a couple whom he had only just met, attempt to save his would-be murderer turned latter-day friend.

'Surplus to requirement' was another oft thumbed phrase that perhaps better described his post Agent X state of mind, but he had also toyed with the terms: 'spare widow at a funeral' and 'flacid member at a high society orgy', during the course of his dispirited wool gathering exercise.

He was, however, alive and for this he was grateful, and he owed this; he knew, to these convenient, public spirited Knights of the road, whom; although apparently caught at an awkward point in their own interpersonal relationship (if their raised voices and the lady's constant and free use of the vernacular had been anything to go by), had proved reassuringly professional in the deployment of their most timely and generous aid.

They had seemed an unlikely couple, at first meeting: possibly a father and daughter combination, he had considered, though they had bickered like spoilt siblings vying for a lone parent's attention. Despite this, however, they had obviously known what they had been about and so he had stepped aside and allowed them get on with the task at hand; it being, after all, none of his business, or his place to pry into the back stories of his kind hearted Samaritans.

The rather commanding lady from the improbable horseless carriage; who had introduced herself as 'Hamble', had taken instant control of the situation, directing Virgil; whom she had been keen to assure Tiny, was a highly respected practitioner of the medical arts, whilst cleaning and dressing his own wounds with quick, slick efficiency. She had then helped him up into their conveyance, where she had insisted that he rest a while, beside what appeared to have been the rocket that had sent his errant master to the Moo- to a quarry somewhere near Cardiff. Tired; traumatised and not a little confused by recent events; not to mention a little lightheaded, due to the pain and the loss of blood, the ailing sherpa had decided against argument and had slumped down into the seat as bidden, from where he could still see his friend lying, unmoving, on the road where he had found her.

Iggi came to with a jolt; instantly aware that she was moving, and automatically thrashing out both her arms either side of her for support. Her second action was actually a reaction, as she screamed in agony when her right arm connected with Tiny's face. Tiny had also been asleep, but his slumber had been natural and not enticed through the absorption of sedatives, as, he explained, had hers, following the ministrations of the kind doctor and his friend the inventor, in whose vehicle they were now travelling. Having calmed her momentarily, Tiny had then attempted to explain, both what had been happening since her duel with Agent X and why she was now in possession of a hairy, man's forearm in place of her own mechanical replacement.

Tiny related his tale to the best of his recollections; disjointed as it was, due to his admitted inability to remain entirely conscious throughout.

He told her about the doctor, who; it transpired, was the Queen's own surgeon; Virgil Periwinkle, brother to their quarry: the man who had given her the mechanical arm in the first place. He had replaced her stolen prosthetic with a 'donor' arm that; for some reason, he had just happened to have on ice, inside the rocket.

Both he and the professor, Tiny revealed, were fully cognisant of the facts pertaining to his sibling's sham voyage to the Moon and as luck would have it, they were also on their way to rescue Gordon from the clutches of the Americans, and so a pact had been forged between them; though in her absence, to watch each other's backs when the time came.

There was also a third member of the travelling ensemble; the driver. A foreigner, Tiny had informed her, who he had not heard utter a single word as yet and was wondering if he was, in fact, a mute.

Having brought her up to speed by the time they passed the 'You are now leaving Cardiff' sign, Tiny turned to her and said:

"Y'nkow, I's possible," that Agent X did us a favour, back there."

Iggi, in an extreme amount of pain and keen to speak to their 'saviours' just as soon as the noisome vehicle came to a stop, merely frowned at him.

"Well, if she 'adn't attacked us, we wouldn't 'ave met Professor Blaise," he continued, from his seat beside her, "and now that we 'ave, we know exactly where we're going!"

Iggi's expression never wavered as she punched him in the face with her good arm.

\* \* \* \* \*

The first thing that a professional Gentleman Adventurer does after stepping off the boat at Southampton; following an expedition to one of the less civilised corners of the world, is to avail himself of a copy of that morning's Times; this to devour: cover to cover, on the train journey back to London, so that by the time he reaches the bar of the Adventurers' Club, he is fully conversant with world affairs, as played out during his absence.

Gordon's return trip from 'The Moon', however, had not been embarked upon in the time-honoured fashion. For one thing, he had not expected to be coming home and had therefore given the last of his change to a beggar, before boarding the rocket in St James' Park, and secondly, his train journey back to London had been anything but conducive to the relaxing perusal of a newspaper. Since then he had spent the majority of his time being chased; shot at; locked in a cage; hung upside down like a fox's draining chicken; tortured or locked in yet another cage. The opportunity to catch up with evolving world events had therefore all but passed him by. He had been captured by the Hun and on British soil, t'boot; did that mean that London had been invaded? He had been 'liberated' by Americans; again, a militarised unit at large in the British countryside: a force, it had turned out, who were anything but the allies that they had been touted to be. Had the Empire fallen during his leave of absence or were the Empress and her cronies too busy looking outward and upward to notice what was happening in their own back garden? These and so many other questions needed answering and so in desperation, Gordon had turned to the only sympathetic soul that he had met since leaving the basement bar of the Adventurers', all that time ago: Candice, his hair and makeup artist, to fill in the gaps for him.

But politics; it would transpire, were not her strong suit.

"There's a war on?" she had answered, somewhat incredulously, when he had enquired as to the current state of play between the nation of her birth and the Hun whom her comrades had 'rescued' him from. And so it had been Gordon who had ended up explaining to Candice that which he had gleaned from his nightly tappings with the Admiral, along with what little tittle tattle he had managed to pick up via overheard conversations in the camp.

"Gee," had been her considered reply to the revelations with which he had confronted her; not quite the reaction that he had anticipated, but it had got her thinking, judging by the way that her brow had furrowed as she powdered over the shaving rash from where she had just removed his ungainly beard growth. "So these 'Hun' guys," she said; her button nose wrinkling as she spoke, "they're the guys who bombed Mr Edison's studio in New Jersey and so that's why the General brought us all here to Engerland?"

It was news of a kind, he supposed, though it explained very little that could likely have been of use to him.

"Which side do you like your parting?" she asked, flicking his floppy blonde fringe from left to right; her brow furrowing ever further and her lips pouting in indecision as if the fate of the world revolved around his answer.

Films, Gordon thought to himself, as he prepared to push open the ship's door; taking a long, deep breath and bracing himself for the slapstick pratfall that he was about to invent, should be informative, if anything; depicting sights and wonders hitherto unseen by those outside of the Adventuring community; unlike the bilge that Edison regularly churned out, such as 'Man Sneezing' or his popular pornographic: 'Couple Kissing'. It was a sad indictment on the modern world, he mused, as he screwed down his helmet, that every potentially life altering invention ever proffered, would be perverted and propagandised before its originator had even arrived home from the patent office.

He opened the door.

On Chuck's shout of: "Cue, Flash!", he stiffened and began his ersatz topple forwards, only to find himself suddenly jolted backwards when a projectile of some kind, glanced off his helmet and ricocheted into the rocket's interior. Unable to slow his downward descent; due to the weight of his brass diver's helmet, Gordon hit the deck within a second and in so doing, avoided a volley of shots that had been aimed squarely at where he had been standing. Instinctively, he rolled left, taking his body out of the line of fire and quickly released himself from his helmet. From outside he could hear the sounds of further gunshots, with bullets pinging off the hull, as if a full-scale battle were in process.

Staying low, he dragged himself along the deck plates on his chest, moving up to a crouch as he reached the forward cabin, where he risked a peak out through the starboard porthole.

There were casualties. He could see Chuck; his white shirt and jodhpurs, crimson with spilled blood, sprawled spread eagled atop his flattened director's chair; his brass megaphone still clasped in his unmoving hand. One of the two faux 'astronauts' was also down; his goldfish bowl splintered; blood pumping from what, even from this distance, Gordon could see was no mere flesh wound.

The Americans were firing wildly in the vague direction where they thought their enemy might be hiding, but had not apparently noticed that nobody was shooting back at them. It was probable, Gordon realised, that they were not the intended targets; he had, after all, been the recipient of the first shot. It seemed prudent to presume that it was an assassination attempt; that The Crown had finally found him. It was more than likely that what they were dealing with was a lone gunman. A lone gunman who knew exactly where he was.

*****

# CHAPTER TWELVE:

## CEFNGARW

"Thought I might find you lurking back here in the shadows," quipped the Secretary, materialising beside his subordinate as if he had just stepped; wraith like, through the very canvas panel behind him, "It's a bad habit, old boy," he noted; his lips twitching at the corners as if he were playing down a smile, "a bad habit, what?"

Availing himself of a flute of the '92 vintage; snaffled from a silver platter held aloft by a hovering waiter, whom he duly ignored; as social etiquette dictated, he turned to the Admiral, demanding: "Well, man; where the deuce is me rocket? I understood the timings were crucial, what? Eyes a'the world, 'n all that; eyes a'the world." Finishing his drink, he slammed the glass back down against the tray; causing the servant to perform a dextrous feat of gymnastics in order to avoid losing the remainder of his wares, "Secretary," the Admiral replied, curtly and without turning to face his superior; trying desperately not to appear in any fashion rattled, either by the man's uncanny ability to root him out wherever he chose to secrete himself or by the fact that; with less than an hour until blast off, there was still no sign of either the Blaise woman or her confounded rocket. Politeness, he had oftentimes mulled; whilst considering his on-going relationship with his social nemesis, might well cost him a degree of unseated pride once in a while, but it did at least help him to maintain a modicum of dignity: a commodity that he had always valued above all else. He was well aware that the Secretary was the architect of all that irked him about the impossible position in which he currently found himself; not to mention a very many other tiresome situations that he had been forced to endure over the course of his lifetime; he was also quite painfully aware that it would be he who would be expected to fall upon his sword, should the Secretary's plans go in any way publicly awry. Slowly and deliberately; as perfunctorily as it was within his purview to be, he added: "Everything is in hand, Sir..."

It had been at the Secretary's request that Victoria had chosen him for this posting. Their connection went way back: all the way, in fact, to the playing fields of Eton, where the fledgling Archie Spatchcock: a nestor, in his first term, had found himself in thrall to the dubious benevolence of a certain 'Montgomery Plumb-Prendergast', a sociopathic prefect (or 'God', to use proper school parlance) who had taken a shine to the Admiral's son; extending a protective wing around the terrified boy in return for certain... favours. Young Archie had been in awe of his 'god'. He was invincible; a veritable giant who none; not even the masters, dared take to task. It was as if he had been of an entirely different species, he had pondered, more than once, back then. He had learned more about the random barbarities of life in that single year than he was to experience in his entire military career and he owed it all to the man whom he would latterly come to refer to simply as 'Secretary', a hereditary appointment, by all accounts, though one that; try as he might, the Admiral had never been able to find an official record of.

The Secretary operated; as far as anybody had been prepared to admit, with a unique remit, planting himself somewhere between the government and the monarchy; flitting between the two houses, it would seem, like a double agent playing one great system against the other.

So he had found him; of course he had: he always did. This time it had been at the back of the hospitality tent on the Whitehall side of the park, from where he had hoped to have been able to spy the Secretary's entrance before he had the chance to take him unawares.

"Y'd better not let me down, again, Spatchie, old boy," he continued, his expression as unreadable as ever, "rumour has it th't the empress herself is on her way over, t'witness lift off first hand," and he paused, presumably expecting to see the Admiral's face drop at the prospect of his potential embarrassment. But Spatchcock was the very expert in disguising his emotions in situations such as this and merely nodded, formally, in quiet acknowledgement.

Unable to elicit a rise, the Secretary continued: "I see y'monkey's all present'n correct, at least."

At the furthest end of the giant marquee; erected a little way back from the enormous, steel trebuchet, for the propelling of the rocket 'Periwinkle' Marsward, a crowd of vulgarians, in cheap suits and those rather gauche bowler hats with the redundant goggles wrapped around their brims, were encircling the figure of Space Captain Harvey Haversack; their pencils spittle moistened and poised as they harangued him for a quote for the following morning's papers.

"As I believe I said, Sir; everything is in hand."

"Hmmm..." The Secretary mused, making a grab for the collar of the comforts waiter as he attempted to stray from his orbit, and dragging him back to his side, whereby he took another two flutes of Champagne; passing one to the Admiral, before clipping the hired hand around the ear and sending him on his way, "I would hope so for your sake, old boy," he continued, swallowing his drink and passing the Admiral the empty glass, "only I received word a couple of hours ago, that professor Blaise, was seen heading out of the city in a north westerly direction in that damnable motorised carriage of hers; y'r rocket strapped to the back."

\* \* \* \* \*

"As your doctor," said Virgil, reaching around from his seat in the cab of the idling Range Roller to face his recovering patient, "I would have to advise in the strongest terms that you stay in the vehicle, when we arrive. Any undue movement so close to a surgery of this kind, could cause irreparable nerve damage, not to mention the risk of infect-"

Iggi heard Tiny deliberately mistranslate into words, the glare with which she was threatening her 'benefactor':

"Ms Shikiwana," he interrupted, "would like t'thank y'f'r savin' 'er life-" but he gagged on those words as she wrenched her partner out through the vehicle's back door, pulling him on toward the scrubland beside the road, "but would politely advise," he continued, in a choked voice; the Blaise retinue merely looking on in stunned silence, "tha' if she was t'see yer again... she would quite likely rip off y-"

"Stow it, dumblewit," Iggi advised, dragging him behind her, "and follow me. Be ready for anything."

\* \* \* \* \*

"How rude!" said Abdul, cutting the Range Roller's motor; switching off its headlamps and pushing his goggles up to rest on the front of his fez.

Ignoring him, Hamble reached out through her open window and pulled up the foot plate-mounted hand brake, anchoring the vehicle to the sharp incline of the road ahead.

"Something else you're not telling me?" she asked, locking eyes with Virgil across the top of her diminutive driver's hat; in reference to both the Shikiwana woman's less than grateful attitude toward his impromptu saving of her life, but equally to the previously glossed over question of his late brother's apparent readiness as an emergency roadside limb donor.

Their constant bickering was nothing out of the ordinary; the unlikely pair having weathered more than their share of bitter disagreements over the course of their surreptitious, two year 'arrangement'. It could even have been said that it was something of a hallmark of their tempestuous affair that they argued about almost everything from hereditary titles to female emancipation and everything of even vague importance betwixt the two points. Neither were ever likely to be described as the easy going type, but then neither were either of them in denial of that inconvenient truth. In private, Hamble was happy to consider herself something of a 'stroppy bitch': a term coined by her father and frequently laid at both hers and her mother before hers, doors. It was a somewhat sexist epitaph, she knew, but one that she had chosen to own, rather than to let consume her, as it had her mother.

And so, a Stroppy Bitch she was, but a stroppy bitch who knew how to use such a condescending axiom to her best advantage.

If Virgil had a good point, then it was that he was an infinitely inventive lover; a man of boundless energy and experience in the bedroom... In the workshop... On the kitchen table.... In a harness, swinging from the rafters; even up on the roof, for god's sake, but; that said, he was still an incredibly dull and oftentimes patronising conversationalist. He was also secretive and far too easily riled: two traits that, try as she had, Hamble could not help but find herself annoyed by.

On balance, she had therefore decided that they were a bad match, a fact that; though as yet unvoiced, Hamble was certain would have been the one thing that they both would have agreed upon wholeheartedly. The trouble was, though, that they also both knew how much more fulfilling their intercourse seemed to be after a bloody good row!

"Do you think it possible," Virgil responded; flatly and after a protracted pause, "that we could reschedule this 'parlay' for a more convivial time and place? My mind is-"

But whatever the surgeon had been about to impart was suddenly lost to the backdraught, as an explosion rocked the glade that they had been parked in, lighting up the night sky and sending slate dust up and out in an arc, to rain down upon the surrounding area.

Hamble released the handbrake and replaced her hat.

"Goggles on, Abdul", she commanded, "fire her back up; it's time to take us in..."

\* \* \* \* \*

The shooting had stopped; an eerie silence, as instantly noticeable as any loud noise, taking its place as the dust settled around the set. It did not, however, last for long, as the porthole above him suddenly shattered, showering him with shards of heated glass. The single shot; fired at where the assassin obviously expected him to be, was met by a maelstrom of random artillery fire, courtesy of the panicked marines outside. He heard a new wave of competing screams from yet more casualties caught in the return fire volley.

"Captain Gordon Periwinkle, I presume?"

A girl's voice; mid-twenties; of London/Irish origin, if he was not mistaken. She was standing in the 'Victoria's doorway, dressed like some kind of stage mystic's assistant, though one who had recently lost a fight with an escaped tiger. Covering her entire left arm was a metal sleeve of some description: a weapon in and of itself, he deduced as she brought its business end to bear, aiming at the Space Captain, quivering on his knees before her; hands raised in hopeful surrender.

"Ah, no; I'm just an actor," he bluffed, affecting a stylised American accent, "we're making a film, don't y'know."

"Nice try, traitor," she breezed, "but don't worry; I'll get them too. Then I'm gunna kill the Surgeon; then the Secretary; then the Admiral and then Father McNulty-"

"That's qu-quite a l-list," Gordon commented, playing for time; the view afforded between her legs from his angle, offering him a modicum of hope, "P-paying you by the h-h-head, are they?"

"Oh, no," she said, her pout shifting to a grin as she lowered her weapon arm, "I'm only being paid for you; the rest are purely for pleas-"

"Stand down!"

It was Ollyphante's voice. Gordon had seen the group of marines sneaking up on her from behind, flanking their commanding officer. He did not rate their chances, but their fortuitous arrival had given him an idea.

The assassin smiled and turned her head to face the general and his men.

"Drup the weapon," the general ordered, "real slow, now."

"Can't," she replied defiantly, swinging it to cover them, "It's wired to my nervous system, so it is," and with that she let loose on the squad and their general, reducing them to pulp in extremely short shrift.

Realising that he was unlikely to get a better opportunity, Gordon spun on his heels; bolted for the cabin and threw himself headlong through the broken panel, slicing all four of his limbs, to varying degrees, on the jagged glass of the frame, before landing with a muscle jarring thud in the slate slag below. The rest of the split screen's toughened glass followed him down, blown out by yet another discharge from the assassin's weapon. Dazed, but still fearful for his life, Gordon rolled himself against the side of the rocket; as far as he could tell, out of her line of fire.

Which was when he felt the ground beneath him shudder; not once, but twice, followed by a pelting for both himself and his ship, of slate shrapnel and sods of airborne earth. Someone was throwing grenades.

\* \* \* \* \*

The Admiral consulted his time piece: the gold plated fob that had been presented to him by the Queen herself, to commemorate his decades of heroic service, on the occasion of his relinquishing command of the Empire's ocean borne fleet in favour of controlling its brand new star bound 'fleet'.

As he opened the case, he caught sight of a reflection in the glass: a movement on the park road up ahead of him; the royal carriage was arriving bearing his patron, Victoria Regina!

It was seventeen minutes to blast off. Speaking prior to the Moon Mission, Hamble Blaise had impressed upon him the absolute necessity for accuracy with the timing of the launch; 'one second out', she had insisted, 'and the rocket could find itself a thousand miles off target; perhaps even heading for the heart of the Sun.' Why, then, he wondered, would she cut things so finely now? Something was most assuredly amiss.

He removed his topper and ducked beneath the overhang of a leafy oak as the carriage passed him by; averting his eyes in case the monarch was to see him. If the Secretary had been correct; and there was no reason to presume his agent's information mistaken, then he had to concede, that in all likelihood, the professor was also now a prisoner of the Americans or worse still: another bally defector! 'Women!' He scolded inwardly, 'y'could never trust 'em! Soon as y'bally back was turned they'd hightail it off with the first simpering Johnny to pay 'em a compliment. Blast 'em all!' He took a moment to consider his options, such as they were. Even if she turned up within the next five minutes, they were unlikely to be able to get the rocket into its harness on the trebuchet in time not to miss their predefined launch window. He was a dead man walking; career wise, at least. The best that he could hope for now was a few minutes head start.

The Admiral crossed quickly, as soon as the monarch's Steam Steed outriders had passed. He had a flat in Portland Place; a bolt hole; strictly off the record, of course: a place 'for the entertaining of', though; sad to say, he had not had the opportunity to avail himself of that particular facility for quite some time. Although, he had not expected to find himself using it for its primary purpose again, he had kept it on just in case he ever needed to affect a tactical retreat. When one found oneself frequenting the company of men like the Secretary, it paid to keep one's options open.

"Good evening, sir,"

"Hmm? Moneypenny? What the deuce...?"

The girl blocking the path in front of him: legs akimbo; gloved fists on hips, certainly sounded like his personal secretary, but in the dusk half-light afforded him, he could not be certain. She was attired in a light absorbing matt black, figure hugging, one piece jump suit, with knee length leather boot accessory and a rather overt, hip slung, double holster to complete the somewhat fetishistic ensemble. Was his girl Friday moonlighting for 'The Gentlemen of Distinction' agency, he pondered? He hoped for the Ministry's sake that she was not! Perhaps he was mistaken.

"Agent S," the vision said, stepping into the light spill of a gas lamp so that he could see her elfin features more clearly. Unless she had a twin...

"The Secretary requests the pleasure of your company in the VIP suite, Sir."

"Secretary?" He queried, somewhat nonplussed by the situation, "which bally secretary?"

"Both of us," she replied, which he took to mean herself and 'The' Secretary; though in an abstract part of his mind, he allowed himself to imagine twin Moneypenny's in black leather jump suits with guns...

\* \* \* \* \*

"Wha' th' blue blazes w's tha'?" snapped Tiny, hitting the ground bodily and throwing his hands up over his wizened head, as a wave of slate splinters rained down upon them, embedding themselves in the moulded felt of their hats and grazing any exposed areas of skin.

Iggi was a little more circumspect. Keen not to jar her recently attached appendage any more than was strictly necessary, she had merely turned her back and bowed her head until the strafing barrage had passed.

Having left the professor and her retinue on the road above the quarry, the pair had made their way down and around the quarry's perimeter, using the wood that surrounded the lower road for cover. The two American guards on the main gate had proved but a minor inconvenience to the temporarily disadvantaged ex agent, who had despatched them swiftly; silently and one handedly, relieving them of their weapons in the process, to replace those stolen from them earlier by Agent X.

"Some twat's dropping grenades," she replied, ruffling shrapnel from her hair and pointing skyward, "Looks like we've got another stray Zeppelin to deal with." She watched a metallic object; dropped from the strangely incongruous gondola that hung beneath the silver dirigible, as it glinted in the moonlight on its terminal trajectory to earth.

"We bein' invaded?" Tiny asked, picking himself up and dusting himself down, then leaping four foot in the air to land in another heap as the German ordnance: a Stielhandgranate, that Iggi had only just managed to identify, exploded on impact with the ground, a couple of hundred yards to their left.

She was silent for a moment, listening for sounds of competing engines in the unseasonably clement Welsh summer's evening,

"I don't think so," she eventually said, "it's on its own; look," and she pointed at the squat shape of the airship as it passed overhead, circling the site, whilst its pilot and bomber tried to work out the best place to drop their next grenade.

"I di'n't know they made 'em that small," Tiny commented, seeing what Iggi had seen for the first time.

"The crest on the side would suggest they do," she replied, scrabbling for a handhold to pull herself up onto a shingle outcrop from where; thanks partly to the mini airship's cabin mounted searchlight, she could see the Americans' base of operations about a quarter of a mile due west through the dunes, "here," she called to the sherpa below, "pass me the rifle..."

\* \* \* \* \*

When the third grenade had exploded; for a split second, the resulting flash had illuminated the entire area, allowing Gordon a moment or two to gather his bearings and to begin planning a route back to the trailers. It had also afforded him a location for his would-be assassin, who had somehow managed to get herself to the top of a slate promontory, a little way off to his left, where she could be seen quite clearly picked out in silhouette, aiming a rifle at the droning blimp responsible for trying to bomb him out of existence.

A flash-blinding darkness followed just as suddenly, and Gordon used it for cover as he scurried off in the direction of the painted backdrops. What he would not have forsaken at that precise moment to have been running through a common-or-garden jungle clearing; his faithful sherpa behind him, dodging poison-tipped arrows on his behalf; a small, yellow eyed idol tucked carefully under one arm, with the protection of the British Consulate building, just the other end of that rickety old rope bridge ahead.

Oh, he was no wuss when it came to the Adventuring game, that much was recorded history; with 'escaping mortal terror' his very job description, but in such situations, Gordon generally preferred his odds to be a mite better stacked in his favour. Having fewer contemporaneous enemies on his trail would have been a reasonable start, whilst an ally or two to call upon would not have gone amiss, that, along with even an outside chance of his likely surviving the day, and everything would have been just dandy!

Gordon reached the trailers without incident. He could hear what remained of Ollyphante's troop firing wildly at shadows all around him and he silently prayed to whatever vengeful deity he must have offended as to have wrought such wrath down upon himself, that He might spare his young nephews a painful and protracted death.

In a rare example of fortuosity, the monkey cage was unguarded when he reached it, with the boy, Charles sat, hunched in the far corner, sobbing into his hands. Whilst wending his way back through the flats and various discarded film props, Gordon had relieved a corpse of his side arm and he aimed it now at the padlock on the cage door.

"Charles!" he called to the distraught boy inside, "close your eyes and cover your ears."

The boy did as he was told and Gordon released the weapon's safety catch. There followed an extremely loud bang and a lot of smoke as the cage door and a fair proportion of the trailer's wooden floor exploded in front of him. Gordon checked the pistol; not having anticipated that level of damage from a single buck shot, but quickly realised that he had been yet to pull the trigger. Turning sharply, he found himself face to face with the assassin.

"My gun's bigger than your gun," she said, coquettishly, in that North West London Brogue that he had noted earlier, and for a wistful moment, Gordon could not help but imagine himself in a different time and place; one where he may have found himself propositioning the filly before him, rather than hefting his weapon to cover her.

She chuckled, sounding every bit the psychopath that one would have expected the Crown to employ for the task of putting down innocent sherpa's on their nights' off, along with heroes of the bally Empire.

"Ah," he said, swinging, aiming and firing at near point blank range, "but I've seen a crow best an eagle on the wing. It isn't always about size, it's also about manoeuvrability...and timing."

And whilst she was reeling from the shock of being shot and desperately trying to raise her bulky gun arm in the confined space between them, Gordon shot her again and this time she went down.

Gordon tried to take a step backwards, but found himself rooted to the spot; not, as he at first presumed, due to the shock of having just killed his first human being, but because; he realised, he had an eight year old boy clamped firmly to his leg like a sexually frustrated Springer Spaniel.

"Drop the weapon," said a new arrival: the American, Letterman, flanked by four battle weary marines; one dressed as a slightly rotund astronaut, though wearing a cracked helmet through which his face was only just visible, making him look like a tooled up, futuristic take on Humpty Dumpty.

"Oh, f'Christ's s-"

\* \* \* \* \*

Not for the first time that night had Hamble wondered whether she might not have made a grave error of judgement in insisting that they stop to help the two travellers that they had found by the roadside. Of course, had she have taken Virgil's advice: leaving them to their fates; passing them by like a West end toff might disregard a starving backstreet urchin, then the pair would most certainly have died of their injuries by now and she would have spent the rest of her days blaming herself for the deaths of two 'innocents' whom she could possibly have helped. As it was; having fulfilled her conscientious duty, she now found herself wondering whether or not responsibility for the lost lives of the two quarry guards that they had just passed; slumped at their posts: their necks clearly broken, lay squarely at her own door; their murder, no doubt committed by those same two ungrateful hitchhikers who would have passed this way shortly before them.

Another flash lit up the night sky, revealing a small, grey airship, almost directly above them. The ground beneath them shuddered from the impact of the grenade that had just been thrown from it and the trio found themselves pelted with a rain of slate shards as Abdul fought to keep control of the vehicle's steering.

"That was a bloody Zeppelin!" Hamble yelped, over the aircraft's droning engines; torn from her reverie and thrust kicking and screaming back into the here and now, "We're being invaded!"

"Damn their eyes!" snapped Virgil, "It would appear that Aubrey has beaten us to it."

"Aubrey?" Hamble asked, holding onto both her hat and the door handle, as the Range Roller bumped across the crumbling dunes, its engine complaining in the most indignant of terms.

"My other brother: the barrister," Virgil explained, "Seems to've got himself mixed up with some German infiltration agent; blames Gordon for the death of his family. They were coming here to kill him!"

There were things that Hamble could have said to him at this point, but instead she just stared at him over the top of Abdul's fez, as the driver; sensing the coming of a storm, sunk down in his seat.

There were only so many times that she could raise her eyebrows quizzically and ask: 'is there something you want to tell me, Virgil?' whilst continuing to give a stray shit about the answer he might proffer. Hamble stared at him and made a decision, one that; if she were to be honest with herself, she had been toying with since she had first confronted him about his government tail, on the outskirts of London, half a day ago.

She had wasted enough time on Virgil Periwinkle. She had brought him here to help him to rescue his brother; she had done as she had promised. From here on in, he was on his own. She had her own agenda. She had risked a charge of treason in order to stop that serial plagiarist, Edison from destroying her reputation. Regardless of Virgil's deep-rooted family affiliation, she had to find him and destroy the film that he had come here to make.

Stepping out of the Range Roller, that had by this point dug itself well and truly into the shingle, almost up to the mudguards above its front wheels, Hamble was surprised to find herself thrown to the dirt by the force of the airship that they had just seen pass over their heads, as it exploded and fell to the ground as burning debris...

"-ake!"

As surreal dreamscapes went, the events of the past hour reminded Gordon of the three sweat soaked nights that he had once spent, comatose and thrashing with his unconscious mind at the mercy of a bout of Malaria fever, two adventures back, up the Congo. All that was needed now was the sudden arrival of the Harlequin character from 'Jack The Giant Killer'; the pantomime that father had insisted on taking them all to at Drury Lane, the year after mother had died, and the nightmare would have been complete! Instead, he was forced to witness the unlikely death of the Humpty astronaut, who just happened to have been standing in the wrong place, as the burning gondola that Gordon had last seen hanging beneath the incongruous Zeppelin, fell from the sky and crushed him, instantly replacing him with a memorial pyre. Once again seizing the unexpected chance offered him, Gordon quickly extricated himself from the crushing embrace of his nephew; grabbed the boy by the arm and ran in the other direction...

* * * * *

"That," said Hamble, in perfect, synchronicitous timing with the punch that she had just thrown to the side of his head, "was for Davy."

The American inventor staggered to the side; thrown by the blow, he stumbled to his knees. He had not seen her coming; she had taken him completely by surprise; his eye to the view finder of his 'movie camera' when she had appeared on his blind side, knocking him for six.

"Whereas this," she explained, giving him due warning the second time around, "Is for Joe Swan," and she kicked him hard in the kidneys with the toe of her pointy boots, forcing him to drop further and to curl himself into a ball, mumbling incoherently into the dust.

Hamble was not known for her violent tendencies. Oh, she had a vicious mouth on her; as many an unsuspecting male supremacist would attest to, but up until now she had always prided herself on her never having stooped so low as to have retorted to such base tactics as brawling.

It felt good, though; she had to admit; after all this time, and Thomas Edison was a special case after all.

There was an etiquette amongst British inventors; a convention that carried little weight, it seemed, on the other side of the pond. In England, when a British inventor unveiled his (or her) latest creation, then from that point forward; however many improvements may ultimately be made to it, and by however many individual inventors to come, the originator's name would be the name by which that thing would always be known. Thomas Edison; the man whom she now kicked quite hard in the testicles, had claimed the patent for the electric light bulb in 1877, even though Humphry Davy, a British scientist, had demonstrated a much cruder, but yet still workable example of said bulb, seventy seven years earlier! Joseph Swan, a contemporary of her father's, had improved upon Davy's earlier work, unveiling his own, more sustainable version in 1860, the template; incidentally, which Edison had 'borrowed' for his own improvement, a few years later. Yet neither man had the American credited when he had sought the patent for 'his' light bulb.

This second kick; the gonad buster, Hamble had dedicated to the Lumiere brothers of France, whose moving picture technology; many in the circles in which she corresponded, was believed to have been the basis for Edison's own 'movie camera'.

"And this," she said, wrenching the cover from the camera that protected the film and exposing it to the light of the burning airship, "Is for me!"

A sudden crack of thunder made her look up, followed by a few odd spots of rain which very quickly became a drizzle. Somebody, she realised, had found her weather machine...

\* \* \* \* \*

A sudden flash of forked lightning rent the sky, followed in quick succession by a sonorous clap of thunder; the interval between the two meteorological events informing Gordon that the brewing storm was indeed, directly overhead. It also told him something else:

"Geoffrey!" he started, startling even himself, "Charles; it's Geoffrey! He's alive and he's found the other weather machine! Better late than-"

He jumped, mid-sentence: a second flash of lightning revealing a cadaverous figure standing just ahead of them on the path in a chasm formed between two piles of dolomite. It was a hideous pastiche of a human being; distorted and disfigured and steaming where the rain fell on its blistering skin.

"I don't bally believe this!" Gordon groaned, halting in his tracks and turning an exasperated circle, "how is it even possible to make so many enemies in such a short time anyway, and then what would the odds have to be that they'd all turn up in the same place at the same bally time?"

"Gordon... Pervi... Vinkle!" the abomination spat, "Ve meet... again!"

"Seriously?" Gordon asked, of the many gods whom he was now convinced he had offended in recent years, with his systematic purloinment of so many of their revered idols. He held out his hands; palms upturned; eyes to the heavens, "Alright, I'm sorry! I won't do it again!" but he received no reply from any of the possible supernatural rulers of the universe.

"You... und I, ...ve haf... unfinished... buziness," the corpse-like apparition droned on. His cape was on fire, but he did not seem to have noticed, though considering the state of the rest of him, this was the very least of his worries. Oberst Vienna had been burned beyond visible recognition. One of his legs seemed somehow shorter and wider than its compatriot. The only thing identifying the vengeful monstrosity before them was his voice and his pointy helmet. He moved with the stiffness of gait of a reanimated corpse, such as Gordon had fought in Haiti on his last adventure before blasting off to the Moon. He pulled a Luger from its holster as he lumbered toward them with the most awkward of all limps.

"You vill pay-" the Austrian continued, stopping mid rant to look down at the foil that had just begun to erupt from beneath his ribs. It withdrew through his body as quickly as it had appeared and he dropped to his knees, blood bubbling from behind his teeth and dribbling onto his chin. He made one last attempt to threaten Gordon before his head exploded and the remainder of his body slumped forward, finally dead.

Standing where he had been was yet another face that Gordon recognised: the other assassin, the one whom he had last seen outside his brother Aubrey's house in Battersea, before he was winched away to meet with Vienna. Her left arm was in a sling, but in her right she held the foil that had pierced the Oberst's organs.

"I give up," said Gordon, raising his arms; the mute Charles beside him following his uncle's lead.

"Capt'in!"

"Tiny?"

"S'good t'see yer! We're 'ere t'rescue yer. This is Iggi."

"Iggi?"

"Yeah, 'er father w's a foreigner,"

Iggi thrust forward her good hand for the captain to shake.

"And we found this wandering by that ridge over there. He says he's your nephew."

"Geoffrey! Thank god! Or gods..."

\* \* \* \* \*

# CHAPTER THIRTEEN:

## CONSEQUENCES

In the years following the death of Mirabeau, the second of Octavian Periwinkle's three wives and the mother of his four sons: Virgil; Gerald; Aubrey and Gordon, his Lordship had become an increasingly difficult man to please. Never a particularly doting nor tactile father to begin with, his approach to parenting had tended toward the fashionable method of the time; a system that the upper echelons of ordered society tended to think on as 'tough love'. He had never been short of encouragement for his boys; consistently communicating his support for their endeavours; if, of course, they had been in the areas where he had noted their natural talents, but in the field of positive endorsement: praise for a challenge well met, he had always believed it a more productive tactic to play one son's achievements against another's, in order; he would argue, to instil a sense of healthy competition among his spawn.

As the eldest, Virgil felt that he was more keenly aware of their father's paternal failings than were his brothers. He had failed to save his mother's life and the old man had never let him forget it. Aubrey; he was fond of telling him, would be a member of parliament by the time he was thirty; whilst Gerald, he was in no doubt, was destined to become the youngest ever Archbishop of Canterbury. Gordon had already discovered him a lost city and he had been willing to bet that the family's Adventurer son would one day achieve the ultimate and become the first man to set foot on the Moon!

Of course, each of them would have been beaten with a different version of that same stick; Virgil was well aware of that, and it was possible, he also knew, that each of them may have felt as guilty for their lack of achievement as the next, but this presumption still did nothing to lift his own spirits. He wanted to find Gordon; he needed to find Gordon; not quite for the reason that he had told Hamble, but in order to prove to the old goat that Gordon never had been the first man to walk on the Moon!

But it was dark; it was also pouring with rain and he was completely lost, stumbling around among the dunes; occasionally hearing a moan or a cry or a burst of gunfire in the distance.

He had been wandering for what seemed like an age when he came upon the wreckage of the gondola. It had still been smouldering, but the rain had all but doused its fire.

"Is... Is someone th-there?" he heard; a smoke addled croak from a survivor, emanating from the ruined gondola itself.

185

"Keep talking," Virgil replied, "I can follow the sound of your voice."

"V-Virgil?" the injured man replied, "Virgil, is that you, bwother?"

"Aubrey?"

"C-c-cold, Virgil; s-so c-cold..."

"I'm coming, Aubrey,"

"C-can't feel me bally legs..."

Aubrey was trapped under a twisted steel girder. From Virgil's initial assessment, the prognosis was not good, but it was too dark to be certain, and Aubrey was right: it was cold. If he were to save him, then he had to get him to shelter and quickly...

\* \* \* \* \*

"On behalf of her illustrious majesty: Queen Victoria of England; Empress to fully one quarter of the world's population, in all her colonies; dominions and mandates around the globe (including the Moon), I have been hereby authorised to inform you, 'Fleet Admiral' Sir Archibald Spatchcock, 'OBE'... that She is not amused; 'not'; I would take pains to emphasise, 'amused'. Do I make myself clear, Archie?"

The term 'Not Amused', was not merely an expression of the Queen's negative state of mind at any given moment in time, moreover, it was a 'code' to be acted upon with immediate effect. If issued in response to a threat levelled by some upstart foreign power or other, then it was to be considered an urgent call-to-arms: a standing order to batten down the hatches and to let loose the dogs of war. If; as in the Admiral's case, it had been directed toward an individual, then it was to be accepted as a 'dressing down' in the strongest possible terms. Anybody receiving such a dismissal was expected to remove oneself from polite society with due expediency and to retire from sight, never to show their face on imperial soil again.

The Admiral, whose head had remained bowed ever since he had been ushered into the room by his former secretary,

Moneypenny; now revealed to be deep cover Crown Agent 'S', lifted his chin and locked eyes with the man whom he had both hated and revered since his first day at school. The Secretary stared back at him across the desk, not showing the slightest hint of either amusement or satisfaction at having passed the buck for his own mismanagement of the situation.

The Admiral smiled; the penny finally dropping. It was only at times like this that one seemed able to see one's situation from a neutral perspective. For all this time he had mistakenly presumed himself to have been of some importance in the grand scheme of things; to have been a reasonably large cog in Victoria's great empirical machine, but he had been wrong; so wrong, it now transpired. He had merely been a pawn on the Secretary's game board. The man no doubt had many more useful 'pieces' like the Admiral in play at any one moment; nurtured and manoeuvred over the years; expediently positioned until such time as their sacrifice was required.

Archibald Spatchcock was always going to be an admiral; perhaps not a 'Fleet' admiral, that was; after all, a promotion requiring connections, but he saw now what Montgomery Plumb-Prendergast had seen during that first day drubbing at the old school and he knew that there was nothing else to be said...

\* \* \* \* \*

"What d'you think you're doing?" Hamble asked, arriving back at the Range Roller; Edison's 'moving picture' camera, thrown nonchalantly over one shoulder, to find Abdul helping Virgil to heft another body into her rocket.

"A little help, perhaps?" her lover replied, sharply. He was as yet unaware of his relegated status to 'ex'. "It's my brother, Aubrey," he elucidated, adding: "he needs warmth and shelter. Quickly."

Hamble had no idea whether he was telling the truth or not, but as usual, she was a sucker for a casualty, regardless of its heritage, "thought you said he was a traitor?"

"A little misguided, perhaps," Virgil apologised for his kin, "but I think I can help him with that."

"That's rich; isn't it?" interjected a newcomer to the conversation, "from you, of all people…Jack," the figure tailed.

She was standing a little away from the party, leaning heavily on an upturned rifle, using its butt as an underarm support. The barrel ended in a requisitioned shoe, presumably in order to stop it from sinking into the ground. Hamble could see that the stranger had originally been dressed in all black, but owing to the sheer number of open wounds that currently peppered her body, she appeared like walking Swiss cheese, though one attired in all scarlet. Hamble had seen the figure approaching and had initially assumed it to be the Shikiwana woman until, that was, she had spoken.

Virgil attempted to hurry Abdul, but the stunted Egyptian was having a great deal of difficulty in squeezing his end of the prone Aubrey through the rocket's door.

"Why do you say that?" Hamble asked, positioning herself between the interloper and her servant's back.

"Ah… You're the adulteress, ain't ya,"

"Some may see it that way, I suppose."

"We've been watching you. We had a bet on; so we did, back at the Ministry, as to whether you knew or not,"

"Knew what?" asked Hamble, finally recognising the woman for who and what she was, "that he was being followed?"

The Crown agent raised her weapon arm and attempted to shoot through her, but her weapon arm failed to respond.

"Hmmm," said Hamble, pulling a disappointed face, "Looks like I'm going to have to rethink the whole 'solar power' thing."

"By the fact that you're prepared to protect him, I'm going te have te concede that I was wrong, and that Agent S was right,"

"Right about what?" asked Hamble, irritated now as Abdul closed and spun the door lock, then jumped down from the rocket, pulling a pistol to bear on the agent.

"Y'man, Virgil, there," she said, "He's Jack th'bleedin' Ripper!"

Hamble absorbed the allegation but said nothing.

"Ye didn't know; did ye? Jasus; I had a week's wages on the fact that ye did!"

The rain had stopped. It had probably stopped a little while ago, but Hamble had only just noticed. The world around her seemed somehow sharper, pulled into focus as if she had been living in a fug for the past couple of years. Virgil was Jack the Ripper; of course he was. How had she not even suspected the possibility? It made sense of a lot of things; hell, it made sense of everything!

She passed the camera to Abdul, who accepted it whilst keeping the agent covered with his gun.

"You thought I knew?" she said, stepping toward the agent; as miffed at the suggestion that she had been covering for the most depraved mass murderer of the age as she was at discovering that she had been sleeping with the most depraved mass murderer of the age, "Well this says that I most certainly did n-" but she checked herself at the last minute; having drawn back her arm in readiness to punch the already mortally wounded agent into the afterlife. She stopped, having had an idea.

She pulled a chart from her pocket, memorising the co-ordinates that she had scribbled onto it earlier. She checked her fob, then moved toward the array of levers, dials and ratchets on the left hand side of the mobile catapult that the rocket 'Periwinkle' was harnessed to in the back of her motorised vehicle. She made a few adjustments to the angle, lifting the rocket to face directly upwards toward the now clearly visible Moon, far above them. As the rocket's nose cone, rose she heard Virgil and his unsecured brother Aubrey, slide down the deck to land in a heap at the bottom of the ship. Trapped, presumably between Gerald's corpse and Aubrey's bulk, Virgil began hammering on the door, shouting for help.

Satisfied that her calculations were correct this time, Hamble began ratcheting the catapult back to its tightest notched setting: the one marked 'escape velocity' and, without due ceremony, she pressed the 'release' button.

* * * * *

"So this is it, then," said Tiny, pulling up a tea chest and parking himself down with a weary sigh beside the others, "this is where y'were when we all thought yer was on the Moon?"

The Periwinkle party had decided to decamp to Gordon's old cave in order to shelter from the storm whilst they worked through their onward options. He found it much as he had left it when he had stepped outside to die, that fateful day; albeit ransacked for supplies by the Americans, and a little damper, due to their having returned the door to the rocket so that Edison could make his film. As luck would have it; whilst a tad wet, the generator had still been working, and could still be used to boil the kettle. The first thing that Gordon did was to head for the Assam. Thankfully, the Americans seemed to have ignored his tea stash, on the hunt; he had to presume, for that rather nasty tasting 'coffee' stuff, that they seemed to prefer.

"If I could just point out," he replied, to Tiny, though his explanation was not exclusively aimed at his sherpa, "I was just as convinced as everyone else that I was, in fact, on the Moon." and he relit the shag pipe that he had found amongst his plundered effects and took a deep drag. It had been too long; far too long.

The general consensus seemed to be that they believed him, which was a stroke of luck, because he really felt that his will to fight had finally been sapped. They had swapped stories as they had traversed the quarry, filling each other in on their adventures so far. He had at first found himself reluctant to trust Iggi; the former Crown agent who had, after all, been dispatched with an order to kill him; an act for which she adamantly refused to apologise. 'Would he apologise for deceiving the entire world?' She had asked in return; not unreasonably, he felt; 'for not dying for his country as he had been paid well so to do?' No, he would not.

She had, however, apologised for killing Gerald, admitting that his brother's death had probably not been entirely necessary. Gordon had found himself admiring her veracity and respecting her all the more for having the courage to admit to her failings without attempting to fudge an excuse. 'Quite a game gal', he concluded, exhaling into the low-ceilinged cavern; 'in other circumstances…'

Breaking his reverie, Tiny added credence to Iggi's cause by insisting that she had paid her penance by helping to find him, and in that moment, an understanding had been reached between the three of them.

"'Ere y'go, Capt'in: nice cup a'tea for ya'."

Gordon smiled, accepting the steaming mug gratefully whilst perching himself on the lip of one of a number of upturned, wooden tea chests, previously containing his adventuring equipment, but which the Americans had either pilfered or discarded around the cave.

"Thank you, Tiny; much appreciated," he said with a heavy sigh.

"Pleasure, sir, t'finally 'ave th'chance t'make y'one."

"The first of many, I hope," said Gordon and he lifted his mug in salute before taking a much needed sip of the ol' nectar of life.

"If I's not an impert'nant obsa'vation, sir," Tiny went on, passing a sloshed out bean tin alternative to Iggi and taking another for himself; Gordon having packed only the one mug for the Moon mission, "y'do seem a little glum f'someone what's jus' bin rescued from sev'ral mortal enemies all at once."

Gordon smiled sincerely, replying: "Not at all, my good man: on both counts! It's just that, well," he faltered, unsure exactly how to phrase the line that he had been mulling, "we do seem to have done the Admiral's work for him."

"How so?" asked Iggi; former assassin, now freelance bounty hunter, frowning into her tin of tea.

"Well," Gordon began, taking a long gulp of his own. He stood up in readiness to pace to his monologue, "when I left here: a week; a month, however long ago it was; I do seem to have lost track of the days, somewhat, but when I finally worked out that I'd been duped and affected my escape, I had fully intended to tell the world all about Victoria's little scam. Y'see, I can't shake the feeling that the courses of all our lives were perverted that day; sent off in directions that they were never intended to go. What I'm trying to say here is," he went on, pausing in his pacing to face his newly made friends, "would we three have even met otherwise?" He pondered this point for a moment, looking each of his rescuers in the eye as he did so, "if the 'Moon Landing' had never occurred," he said, "would any of those people out there have died today; had the British Establishment not conspired to concoct this... pantomime in order to bolster its reputation as the world's greatest power?"

"I see y'point," Tiny answered, with a subtle sideways glance toward Iggi.

"It's changed us," Gordon explained, "irreparably. The trouble is, if I had succumbed to either the Hun or the Yanks' plans, then the world's course would have altered once again and; who knows, possibly, even, for the worse." He renewed his pacing, this time heading toward the cave's entrance as he spoke, "If any nation should revel in the standing born of a faked conquest of the Moon, then it ought really be the British, wouldn't you say?"

Tiny nodded, thoughtfully in response, but Iggi merely carried on frowning.

"I mean to say," Gordon pressed on regardless, turning to look back at them, "can either of you imagine a world in hock to the Hun, or the Americans, for that matter, should either of them have been able to've laid a similar claim?"

Tiny's eyes widened as he released an elongated exhalation.

"Trouble is," Gordon said, resting a hand each on Geoffrey and Charles' shoulders, "either way, I have to die."

"It's stopped raining, Uncle Gordon," Charles interjected, from just inside the entrance to the cave.

"Geoffrey?" he asked, staring out at the bleak, grey quarry beyond the cave mouth, now silent except for the odd drop of water, dripping into a puddle from the lip above the entrance, "you said you found the professor's weather machine at the far edge of the site, yes?"

"I did, uncle," Geoffrey replied, "it'd been hidden under a net."

"Hmm," Gordon mused, "So that I wouldn't find it and have it give the game away…" he deduced, "So it's unlikely that anybody else would have found it, which means that whoever's still alive out there has probably just reactivated the American's weather machine.

"Okay team, looks like we might be better to ship out tonight, rather than wai-"

"Gordon Periwinkle!"

Once this was all over, Gordon mused, he was seriously going to have to consider changing his name!

"Langtree Letterman," Gordon replied, sardonically, "what a pleasant surprise. I take it this is a social visit? Can I get you a cup of tea, at all? 'Fraid we're out of biscuits, though-"

"Enough of the English crap," snapped the American, waving his revolver in the explorer's face, "this isn't over yet. You've caused me a great deal of trouble," and he moved his weapon toward the terrified Charles' head. Another figure stepped into focus, slightly shorter than his compatriot, less confident in his gait and quite obviously out of his depth. He cocked his own pistol and pointed it at Geoffrey's head. Gordon recognised the man as the dresser whom he had met when he had first been brought back here. The fact that Letterman had enlisted a civilian as his backup told Gordon that it was probable that they were the last two Americans left.

"Oh, what is it with you Yanks and guns?" Gordon spluttered, campily waving his arms about him in an attempt to focus the American's attention on himself, "you're obsessed! Where are all your mates with the bigger guns, eh? Got us staked out have you?"

Behind him; on either side of the hollowed-out passage, Tiny and Iggi had taken up position in the dark; their own weapons poised. Gordon had seen them moving out of the corner of his eye but was banking on the fact that the two Americans had not.

193

"It isn't about the size of the gun," Letterman began, "or even how many we have," inadvertently answering Gordon's unasked question, "all that matters is that we *have* guns and you don't."

Gordon stepped forward a pace and dropped to his haunches in front of the boys, spreading his arms and pulling them in toward him.

"Oh, don't worry," said Letterman, obviously mistaking his action for acceptance of his fate and presuming him to be about to say his goodbyes, "the kids are coming too. They'll be useful leverage."

Ignoring him, Gordon broke into a whisper: "Do you trust me?" he asked of them and both boys nodded firmly, "Good. Now when I say 'drop' I want you to hit the deck; close your eyes and cover your ears; got it?" They both nodded again, "Good. Now DROP!"

The boys obeyed and Gordon followed suit, giving Iggi and Tiny a clear aim with which to take their captors down.

The former agent and the sherpa did not disappoint.

"You're getting good at this," said Iggi, turning to clap Tiny on the shoulder as the dust began to settle. He yelped; it had been his wounded shoulder.

"Nicely don-"

Gordon's congratulation was cut short, and the expletive with which he replaced it drowned out, as the rumble of a not too distant engine became a roar; with a large and improbable motorised vehicle suddenly appearing and blocking their exit.

"Do any of you know First Aid?" asked a woman, as she stepped from the vehicle's cab, removing both her goggles and her gloves.

"Miss Blaise?"

"*Professor* Blaise," she corrected, as she shook out her curls to remove the drizzle, reminding him of one of father's Labradors after a cooling dip in the lake, though he checked himself before saying as much.

"I thought-"

"Wrongly," she finished for him, "but it doesn't matter, not for the moment, anyway. What does matter, however, is getting both our reputations back on track. Now, you come with me and you two," she said, indicating with a flap of her gloves toward Tiny and Iggi, "see what you can do for our mutual friend on the back seat."

* * * * *

"B't she tried to kill yer," said Tiny to Iggi, as they gently laid the paralysed body of Agent X, down onto Gordon's camp bed. Geoffrey filled a tin mug with water from his uncle's flask and passed it to Iggi, who pressed it to the lips of her fallen comrade.

"We do what we're ordered to do," Iggi replied, wiping a strand of damp hair from her patient's brow, "it's what we're trained to do; besides, I did try to kill her first, if you remember."

"But you w's... colleagues-"

"We were more than that," Iggi went on, smoothing her old friend's hair. 'Friend', she thought. She had never actually thought of their relationship in that way before. The nuns had always discouraged the orphans from forming close bonds with one another. They had a deal with a certain 'fixer' within the government; a shadowy 'mandarin' who bought the girls from the orphanage and put them to work either as 'agents of The Crown' or as 'concessions' for foreign diplomats; dependant on their natural attributes.

Katie had a scar; it was impossible to see it now: her entire body was either scar tissue or seeping wound, but it was there: between her lip and her earlobe, on the left-hand side of her face. Iggi knew because she had been the one to have put it to there. She had slit her open with a piece of flint when her victim had been just thirteen. Thirteen had been the age when the decision was made by Father McNulty and the Superior: the decision as to which girls went for military training and which became closer associated with the priest. Katie had been lucky, ultimately. She had confided in the somewhat plainer Iggi, after only her second night of 'concession indoctrination' and Iggi; with the help of a sharpened stone, had helped her to be transferred to the 'agent' programme instead.

Permanent facial scarring was not generally the kind of thing that a friend did to a friend, but under the circumstances, it was the kind of thing only a real friend would do.

"Iggi?"

"Right here, Irish."

Katie tried to smile at Iggi's use of her childhood nickname, but the effort was too much for her and a rivulet of blood ran out from the side of her mouth.

"Rip-Ripper," Katie forced; blood spraying with the sibilant, "G... Got him," she eventually managed to croak.

Tiny frowned; quite nonplussed, but Iggi smiled, despite herself.

"Good girl!" she said, "One last act of defiance, eh?"

Katie coughed again, this time spraying blood across both of the twins, who had been hovering a little too closely, apparently having never watched a person die before, they would explain to Iggi later.

"McNul... Mc... McNult... ty..." she whispered, with her dying breath, living just long enough to hear Iggi vow to 'wet the bastard'.

\* \* \* \* \*

With Abdul operating the winch, Hamble and Gordon had managed to manoeuvre the 'Victoria' up from the quarry floor and into the firing harness on the back of the Range Roller. She had then secured Gordon into the pilot's seat; screwing his helmet back into place, before climbing up onto the nose cone to hammer a couple of copper plates; purloined from the deck, over each of the windows that had lost its glass. As soon as she was happy, she slid down to terra firma and began to align her invention as per her target calculations. She adjusted the angle at which the 'Victoria' sat in its harness, then swivelled the whole kit and caboodle on its axis so that it was facing roughly South Easterly. Finally, and with Abdul's help, she ratchetted back the firing spring to the proscribed tautness to achieve the required speed for the journey.

"See you on the other side!" she shouted; though she doubted that he would have heard her, before releasing the firing pin, thus launching the 'Victoria' on its final voyage.

* * * * *

# CHAPTER FOURTEEN:

# RETURN OF THE MAN ON THE MOON

Given the option, this would not have been the way that the Admiral would have chosen to bow out. He had been hoping for a modest do, in recognition of his many years of service; perhaps a hundred or so of his peers and their better halves in attendance; a carriage clock for the mantelpiece, perchance, followed by a by-line in The Times and a generous pension that would have seen him comfortably into old age. But, in a strange; some might even have suggested 'masochistic' way, he actually felt quite relieved as he considered the ultimate inevitability of that which had been wrought upon him. He indulged a smile as he strolled along The Mall in the early morning half-light; his personal effects gathered inside a brown paper parcel tied up with string chucked under one arm, whilst he listened to the birds tuning up in readiness for the dawn chorus in the trees of St James' park to starboard.

He knew what was to come, of course. They would send an agent; most likely Moneypenny, or whoever she really was. It would be professional; he consoled himself with that fact: clean, efficient and quick. She would probably be watching him now: keeping her distance; waiting for him to get closer to the river or to enter a dark alleyway where witnesses would be few and far between at this hour of the day.

Archibald Spatchcock's life had not been as easy as had often been speculated by those for whom his was the final word.

Although always destined for a position of command, he had still had to work hard to reach such giddying heights. The chances of anybody; despite their heraldic ties, making it from Blue Admiral, through White and all the way up to Red, was really quite unlikely, as post-captaincy promotions tended to be 'lifetime appointments'; meaning that one had either to await the man above's retirement or his eventual death before assuming his lofty post. Many an experienced admiral had wasted his final years in anticipation of the position that Archibald had managed to secure; some of whom might even have made a better fist of the job than he. For it was a role of great responsibility: the ability to juggle the obligations toward those who served beneath one, with the accountability toward those who stood in judgement above. He had never realised before now, the true extent to which that workplace worry had marred him as an individual within the chain of command. Many would have thought his ultimate rank one of comfort; of power and influence: a rank to aspire to if one coveted the 'cushy life', and to a certain degree they would have been right, but it was a also a posting of immense psychological pressure, the likes of which; few, bar those who had witnessed at first hand, the stresses and strains that came with such a vocation, could ever truly appreciate.

He would have been fifty-five, next birthday. He had done better than the majority of his predecessors, he knew; many of whom had befallen 'accidents' the like of which he was about to encounter, much earlier in life than this.

He felt sorry for his wife, Sarah and their daughter, Davina, but he felt assured that the payment with which the Crown would compensate their loss would be more than adequate to help them through the grieving process.

He was feeling remarkably stoic, he noted; for a man walking blithely to his own death. On some level, he found himself welcoming the finality of it all: a decisive end to the one sided relationship that he had endured all these years with the Secretary and the chance finally to put to bed the 'what ifs' of his unfairly curtailed relationship with his beloved, 'Beau'. But there was one thing still riling him about this whole 'Moon' affair; one thing that he would have liked to have seen resolved before the curtain came down, and that was the blatant treachery of Messrs Periwinkle and Blaise, whose self-serving actions and traitorous deceit had brought this premature end upon him.

He was mulling this regrettable turn when his attention was suddenly drawn to an object in the sky directly ahead of him. Already bold, it seemed to grow larger by the second, therefore; logic decreed, it must have been getting closer by the moment. His first thoughts were that it was a Zeppelin; one that had slipped through the coastal defence net in order to deliver a blow to the very heart of Victoria's Empire, but the object was surely travelling too fast to have been an airship.

There were people too, tracking its progress from ground level, following at a run, beside and beneath it, like disciples chasing a falling star in the hope of finding a messiah... 'Yes,' he thought to himself, 'exactly like that!'.

Realising that he was directly in the closing object's path, he quickly sidestepped onto the pavement, mere seconds before the thing hit the road with a steel rending clang and set to gouging a scar in the earth with its brass tail-fin as it fought the inertia that took it forward toward the gates of the palace. It ground to a halt only feet from the bebusbyed guards who; at a loss as to any more practical a response, brought their rifles to bear and covered what Archibald was now able to identify as the rocket 'Victoria', apparently returned from its trip to the Moon.

Archibald held his position as the rabble reached the crash site, others joining them from numerous directions at once; several of whom he recognised as opprobrious gentlemen of the press. He smiled as he noted that the incident had not gone unnoticed by those inside the 'big house', either.

"I wouldn't, if I were you," he said to Moneypenny; sensing her appearance behind him, and guessing that she would already have drawn her knife, with the intention of carrying out her orders and using the crowd as a distraction, "not just for the moment, anyway. I think they may well be needing me alive after all."

Though he would not be admitting as much in the soon to be published accounts of his outer space exploits; only a few short hours ago, Gordon had surprised himself by entertaining a brief dalliance with the thought of taking his own life. Thankfully, this unwelcome notion had been as fleeting as had his inappropriate attraction to the assassin who had been dispatched with orders to dispatch him: the girl whom; in an act of impromptu self-defence, he had himself been obliged to execute. He had, however, quashed both these momentary aberrations of the mind, like a Tory lord would an underclass uprising, by puffing out his chest, denying the facts to hand and merely blustering forth; a lesson learned from his father, many moons past. As a result, he now felt magnificent; revitalised; reborn, even and ready to greet his public as the untouchable hero that they expected. It would have been too easy for him to have submitted to the coward's resort, he mused, though many in his situation would have done so, but 'twas not the preserve of a man who had stared bloodcurdling death in the face as often as he; fighting with vigour and efficacy on every occasion for his right to live to quip another day. His narrative would be bold and fearless, he decided; there and then, and without vacillation of any kind. It would tell a tale of unbounded courage when faced with certain extinction and of his peerless ingenuity which had resulted in his safe return to terra firma, having cobbled together an adhoc trebuchet, using nothing more than his own wits and wood culled from the equipment cases that he had taken with him.

This would be the official story; this would be his legend, but in truth; up until a few hours ago, the mortal course had, indeed, seemed the most viable of Gordon's long-term options. That was, of course before 'she' had breezed into his life; she being Professor Hamble Blaise: the woman with a plan so audacious in its simplicity that he could not now believe how close he had come to throwing in the towel.

They had already met, of course; briefly; shortly before the first launch of the 'Victoria', though at that time; so preoccupied had he been with his attempts to assimilate the many instructions that she had been doling out, that he had scant noticed that she had even been a woman, let alone the mind responsible for sending a man to the stars!

It was the weirdest of feelings which assaulted him now: a rare blending of hope; prowess and belief in his own hyperbole, as he unspun the hatch and stepped from the returned rocket to be met by a cacophony of journalists and flag waving well-wishers, all keen to welcome home the hero of the bally Empire.

But it had been all her doing; he would never forget that: Hamble's great plan to reinstate his honour. Having sent him on his way with a vigorous, rubbery slap to the arse end of his battered rocket ship; a pre prepared explanation for his unanticipated return on the tip of his tongue, she had sent word to the capital's press offices; via her vehicle's mobile Morse-Tapper, in order that his arrival in London and subsequent debriefing be intercepted by the hacks and the word catchers before the mandarins of officialdom had their chance to intervene. Theirs would be the official line, this time, and none would be able to debunk them.

As his eyes gradually adjusted, following their sudden flash blinding courtesy of the city's gathered press corps, Gordon was surprised to find Admiral Spatchcock standing beside him. He was smiling. The Admiral: the man at whose door ultimate blame for all that had befallen him could squarely be laid; the man; how could he forget, who had set not one, but two killer agents on his trail, thereby causing the unnecessary death of his brother, Gerald; the man; let's not beat around the proverbial bush here, who had knowingly duped him into giving his life for a lie!

The Admiral said nothing as Gordon answered the slew of questions that were duly thrown his way. Only after the questions had started to become hackneyed and platitudinous, did he hail them both a SteamSteed with the intent of whisking them on to the Ministry.

"The truth?" the Admiral asked; again with that smile, as the driver circumvented Trafalgar Square; 'asked', Gordon noted, not 'demanded', and so he told him, making sure to add a blow by painful blow account of his very real trials at the hands of enemy agents. It had been Professor Blaise, he would insist; albeit, ably abetted by sherpa Tiny, who had concocted the plan to rescue him in this way, thus causing her to miss the Mars launch. (Hamble had been keen for him to shoehorn this point in at his earliest convenience and well before she attempted to make her own dramatic reappearance.)

As agreed between the survivors back in the cave; when asked by the Admiral as to the fates of Agents X and Z, Gordon would relate the tale told to him by Tiny, of Agent X's attack on the Chepstow road and of Z's mortal injury at the hands of her comrade. With a theatrical flourish, he then pulled her prosthetic arm from his knapsack to prove that Z had indeed been killed in the line of duty and explained how X had died later from her own injuries.

He was surprised at how well the Admiral received his statement; shonky as it so obviously was, in fact, he was just as surprised at how amiable the old man was being toward him, considering their history, but the Admiral had merely continued to smile, as if proud of him, nodding as Gordon had told his tale, in something of an avuncular manner, he thought, as if the ludicrously unlikely tale had been something of a relief to him.

Upon the pair's arrival at the Ministry, they were immediately ushered into the company of the man whom, it seemed, went by no other name than simply 'The Secretary'.

One of four.

He had been one of four before, of course: usually the fourth of four. He was used to being the fourth of four: the last in line; the little one on the end, but this was different. This was not one of father's Sunday morning inspections: 'line up in order of seniority; the boy with the least shiny shoes wins the thrashing', No. This was the day that he had been interviewed for the Moon Mission; this had been the day when he had made the great leap from fourth place, all the way up to first!

He remembered it well; it was one of those pivotal moments in a chap's life, on which everything from that point forward would hinge.

Initially, there had been some four hundred of them, with applicants hailing from all four corners of the British Empire. They had been whittled down: evaluated by a list of criteria, not altogether transparent to the applicants themselves.

Proof of heritage seemed to be the board's keenest concern; the vexed question of whether or not an individual was, in fact, a bonafide Englishman; for it was all very well being the first nation to put a man on the Moon, but if that man was later revealed to have been of 'foreign extraction', then the whole exercise would become somewhat moot. Free movement within the bounds of the Empire, along with the introduction of both a common tongue and a system of shared beliefs; courtesy of the army of Christian missionaries that followed in every professional Adventurer's wake, all combined to make Johnny Foreigner that much harder to pull from a line up, these days. It was becoming increasingly difficult to tell a man's lineage in this homogenised modern world, and Gordon remembered thinking this to himself as he had sat silently in that Whitehall ante room, surreptitiously assessing his cohorts by their set; their accents and the way that they drank their tea.

He had been the last of his quartet to be called. He had seen more medals and braid adorning the three naval types to precede him than one would have expected to find in a Portsmouth pawn shop between the wars and so he had not seriously anticipated his chances of winning the role. This, set against the fact that he was a whole half Welsh on his mother's side, had made him doubt that he would even rate as a viable consolation if all three of the decorated mariners to be seen ahead of him were to contract some fatal ailment within the time frame for the launch. Sat alone, expecting at any moment to be given the old 'heave ho', Gordon had been surprised to find himself ushered into the self-same office that the other three had entered, but from whence none had returned.

It was here that he had first met Archibald Spatchcock, bedecked in his finest naval dress uniform and the russet faced bearer of the most ridiculous set of silver mutton chops that Gordon had ever seen. He had been standing mutely beside an enormous, cherry wood desk, so shiny that Gordon fancied he saw the further reddening of the Admiral's skin reflected back in it before he noticed the effect on the man himself.

Behind said desk; perched upon a throne-like chair to match it, loomed a spider, Gordon was to speculate: the living enigma known so cryptically as 'The Secretary'

He was tall, Gordon recalled, though by no means a giant; well fed, but not unduly portly and endowed with a natural confidence, rarely found outside of the royal line. His most striking feature, however, was the size of his face. If Gordon had been asked to describe the man in ten words or fewer, then he would simply have said that he had been 'built to a different scale to most'.

"Take a seat, Mr Periwinkle," the man had suggested, apparently innocuously, but at the same time; probably due to his size, with a stentorian boom that would have made a lullaby read as an order, "I have some rather splendid news to impart…"

With the Admiral at his back, Gordon related his woeful tale of torture and foreign incursion once more; this time for the benefit of the Secretary, who said nothing until his rendition reached its climax.

The man then thanked him kindly, pressed a button on his desk and then excused Gordon into the company of a footman, who showed him to a room that he presumed to be the more usual haunt of cabinet ministers; military bigwigs and their ilk. Here he was introduced to 'Kandy', a young lady whom he would come to know quite well over the course of the next two hours, as she would strip; bathe; rub down; oil; massage; fully service; dress his wounds and then re dress in a new purple and gold braided uniform and boots, before dismissing him and sending him to re-join the Admiral and the Secretary, who; whilst he had been away enjoying the gratuitous comforts of Kandy, had received and no doubt debriefed Hamble and Tiny, and were now waiting for him to join them all for dinner. Gordon felt himself blush as his eyes locked with Hamble's; she, in return, offering him something of a coquettish smile, he noted, as they passed along the corridor and into an ornate, Jacobean style dining room where they were shown to their seats by a pair of waiting waiters.

The atmosphere in the room was a little tense, he felt, as they awaited the arrival of the Prime Minister himself, but Lord Salisbury did not keep them thumb twiddling for very long. Acknowledging both the Secretary and the Admiral with a pair of firm, congratulatory handshakes; Hamble with a bow and a kiss to the back of her silk gloved hand and Tiny with a nod and a polite smile, he broke with received protocol on reaching Gordon's side: clasping him by the shoulders and then hugging him manfully to his breast.

By the time that dinner was eventually served, Gordon had told his tale a total of four separate times, though each had been slightly different as the story became entrenched. He was ravenous and the feast in front of him bountiful, but he restrained himself from gorging like a savage on a side of Wildebeest or an orphan picnicking from the bins behind The Ritz. He calmed himself; tempering his excitement at the prospect of all that was to come and fought down the adrenalin surge by considering the gruesome fate of his brother Gerald; murdered at Iggi's hand, and wondered how he might explain the tragedy later to his father and to his other brothers, Aubrey and Virgil.

"If I were wearing a hat," the conspicuously hatless Secretary proclaimed, to those with whom he had just shared a rather indulgent, gout inciting meal, but who were now gathered on the platform of 'Downing Street Station': a secret subterranean shuttle stop, way down in the lowest basement, beneath the Prime Minister's official London residence, "then I dare say I might remove it; briefly, in your collective honour," and he smiled in a way that he obviously intended to appear collusive, but which; due in part to his somewhat imposing stature and in another, to the fact that he was probably not used to having his hand forced in such a way, Gordon found really quite sinister.

On entering the cavern, the man; whom even Lord Salisbury seemed a trifle wary of, had stepped ahead of both his ranking cohorts, thus creating a spearhead formation, in order; Gordon felt, to attempt to delineate a hierarchy within this newly founded cabal. Gordon was given the distinct impression that Hamble, Tiny and himself were being threatened, albeit in a genteel and rather impotent way, for the reputations and indeed the futures of all six of those present; not to mention the fate of Victoria's entire Empire, rested on the ability of each one of them to keep to the agreed script from this point forward. It was a stalemate, and all concerned knew as much; one that had appeared to suit the Admiral just as much as it had Gordon and his friends, if the old man's atypical joviality at dinner was anything to go by.

There were, of course, four others still at large, each bearing first-hand knowledge of what had actually transpired in Cefngarw quarry that day: Agent Z; whom the titled three believed dead and who would by now be enjoying a quiet retirement somewhere well outside of the Empire's borders; Gordon's two nephews, Charles and Geoffrey; whom he had been informed during dinner, were currently undergoing some kind of 'treatment' to help them to 'come to terms' with what they had witnessed, and finally Hamble's driver, Abdul, who of course was a foreigner and so of no credible threat to their deception whatsoever.

Still smiling, the Secretary stepped past them and bent to open the doors of an awaiting carriage; ushering them forward to take their places on the shuttle. The Admiral moved to join them, leaving only the Prime Minister and the Secretary behind on the platform; the former apparently none too excited by the prospect, judging by the sudden change in his set.

"Admiral Spatchcock will enlighten you as to royal protocols on route," the Secretary informed them, "but suffice it to say," and he paused, leaning in a little closer toward the palace bound quartet, "Her Majesty can be spared the sordid details."

They watched the Secretary move down toward the end of the platform and release the locking mechanism on a huge metal wheel that was affixed to the brickwork by four iron bolts. Around the wheel was coiled a heavy, greased chain, one end of which; Gordon had noted upon their arrival, was connected to the shuttle's coupling, with another on the corresponding coupling at the other end of the shuttle, pulled taught and disappearing into the gloom of the underground railway tunnel that they were about to be pulled along.

"Enjoy your moment," the Secretary declared with a mocking salute, closing the door of the carriage, "Speak only when spoken to; don't look her in the eye and never turn your back on her," he added, smiling once again as the shuttle slowly began to depart the platform, bound for a similar gas lit cavern; no doubt, beneath Buckingham Palace.

"I don't trust him," declared Gordon, as the slow-moving carriage was suddenly plunged into total darkness.

"And you'd be wise not to," said the Admiral from his seat opposite, "in fact, Captain Periwinkle," he continued, with a frankness that Gordon would not previously have expected of him, "you would do well to make a mantra of that statement from this point forward."

"I still don't understand who he is," said Hamble, from Gordon's left-hand side.

"And that, my dear," the Admiral said with a wry chuckle, "is how it should remain. We are lucky," he went on as the shuttle bounced over a connection in the track, "that we are all still alive, but never forget that we remain so at the whim of that man. Now, heads up and look lively: you have an appointment with the sharp end of Victoria's sword!"

\* \* \* \* \*

# EPILOGUE

Iggi had never been one for pomp and pageantry. Growing up within the confines of a pious Order, she had seen enough 'ceremony for its own sake' to last her several lifetimes and as for blind patriotism: the religion of the masses, her imposed career path had seen her privy to far too much of what went on behind the velvet curtain of state, to find her puffing out her chest at the sight of the red, white and blue or throwing herself, prostrate into the path of an oncoming marching band.

Ordinarily she would have avoided an event such as this, in the same way that she had always managed to avoid emotional attachment of any kind, but today; she had told herself, today... well, today was different. She was different. Events of the past couple of weeks had changed her perspective, altering the way that she would previously have acted and reacted to things; quite possibly, she conceded, for the better. She owed this change to the people whom she had come to pay her respects to. Because of them, she had a chance to begin her life anew. She owed them her freedom; she owed them that new perspective, and so she did this for them, even in the certain knowledge that they would never know that she had done so.

Watching from her cramped vantage point; shoulder to stinking shoulder with the entire population of proletariat London, Iggi pondered the wisdom of such an egotistical display. The only practical use that she could imagine for parading VIPs around in a public space like this was to make an easy target of them for an opportunistic assassin. It was a security nightmare, but not; she reminded herself, as she felt herself bumped from behind by someone trying to gain themselves a better view of proceedings, any problem of hers. Not anymore, anyway.

With the aid of her trusty spyglass, Iggi could quite clearly make out the figures of Spatchcock; Blaise and Periwinkle, decked out in their finest; the two men wearing what appeared to be fancy breed chickens on their heads and Hamble, regally appointed in a floor length, black lace dress; not dissimilar, from the waist down, to the Queen's mournful ensemble, though with a rather courageous red satin and lace corset adorning it that would most definitely not have met with the monarch's approval. The trio were waving to the crowds from the prow of the Royal Barge as it sailed past Somerset House, heading down river toward Greenwich. Victoria herself she could also see clearly perched atop a raised throne amidships; flanked on the one side by her son, the Prince of Wales and on the other, by Lord Salisbury, the Prime Minister, looking on mutely with that vaguely bemused expression that she tended to employ for dull occasions of state.

And there was her friend, Tiny; lumbered with Nanny duties to Gordon's twin nephews, languishing in the stern, amid an assortment of courtiers; guards and what looked like the leader of the opposition, deep in conversation with the Secretary. Iggi smiled despite herself, happy for Tiny; the first sherpa to be awarded royal recognition, and comforted to know that both Gordon and Hamble had taken on the system and won, against the greatest of all odds. She saluted as they passed; knowing full well the futility of the gesture, then turned and vanished into the crowd.

She should have been miles away by now, as had been her intention when she had parted company with Hamble at Mermaid dock. Within minutes she had made a few discreet enquiries and found herself a ship with a spare berth and a captain whose blind eye seemed to her to be a blessing rather than a disability. The boat, however, had not been due to sail until the evening tide and so Iggi had found herself with a little time to kill, hence the detour to catch a glimpse of the 'Heroes of The Empire' parade and; of course, the other little matter that she still had to deal with.

She had made a promise to Katie as she had lain dying in the cave: a promise that she had also made to herself some years ago. She was not intending to return to England after tonight and so if she was ever to fulfil those promises then it would be now or never.

There was a faint tingling sensation in the fingers of her new hand. She removed her sling and tested its strength; chewing down on one of Tiny's leaves as she did so. It was already less painful than that damned prosthetic had been, but she had not forgotten what Virgil had told her about the risk of infection and the possibility of permanent nerve damage if she was too quick to use it. This put her at a temporary disadvantage, should she find herself needing to defend herself, but for the task that she had in mind, she did not see it as a particular problem.

Leaving the main drag, Iggi slipped into Parson's Passage: a featureless, narrow alleyway that linked the Embankment with a small courtyard that was overshadowed by the looming buildings all around it. The brick corridor had presumably been considered at a time when the average priest cut a far more frugal figure than his modern day counterpart and would have been able to have passed its length unhindered. Although able to move quite freely herself, she noted a lighter colouration to the brickwork, in a band at the point between the average shoulder and elbow and her mind was briefly taken back to laundry day at the orphanage and the relentless scrubbing of soiled cassocks.

At the centre of the courtyard sat the crumbling edifice of St Barrabus, the brazen: the ecclesiastic fiefdom of one Father Seamus McNulty, and behind it; skulking in its shadow like a dark and guilty secret, her former home: St Barrabus Academy for Stray Girls.

It was a long time since Iggi had been inside the church, but still she found herself bowing in automatic liturgy before an effigy of the Holy Mother and crossing herself whilst summoning the words 'forgive me, fath-' before reminding herself that she was no longer under the catholic spell.

She had kept an eye on the corpulent nun worrier ever since leaving the orphanage. She had always hoped that she would have the chance to be his reaper. The only reason that he was still free to defile his vulnerable charges was that; like Jack the bloody Ripper, he was under Crown protection.

Pulling aside the hessian curtain, Iggi took her seat in the confessional, recoiling as a sharp object entered her left buttock.

"If you're looking for fat priest," said the figure on the other side of the gauze curtain, whilst she felt the seat beneath her and found the tip of a nail protruding through the wooden slats, "you just missed him."

The voice was heavily accented and she knew that she recognised it, having heard it only recently, though for the life of her she could not place it. The pain in her backside was exquisite and she felt her head beginning to swim. She had been poisoned. Instinctively her hand went to her holster, but she knew before she alighted upon it that it would be empty.

"If you looking for this," the voice continued from beside her, as she struggled to stand, "I took it from you down by river. Very sloppy," he chastised, "unworthy of Crown agent's demarcation."

She thought she heard the distinctive whirring and clicking of an armoured limb, but could not be certain. Her head was spinning now and she could easily have been mistaken.

"Anyway, I saved you bother and emptied both barrels into priest for you. You see, like you, he's become something of liability."

Iggi slumped forward, her forehead connecting with the wooden panel of the box. She could feel neither her hands nor her feet and had lost the ability to control her tongue.

"Things are changing," she heard the interloper say, from somewhere in the middle distance, "world has changed," as Iggi's vision began to blur,

"British Empire is entering new phase, Agent Z; out with old, in with new. Sure you understand need to keep house tidy?"

These were the last words that she heard before her head connected with the floor...

*  *  *  *  *

He was smiling as he stepped out of the confessional and pulled back the curtain on the sinner's side to confirm the hit. He kicked at the mark's body to test for a reaction and chuckled to himself when he saw none. He pressed a button on the wrist of his artificial hand and released a small, hinged ariel which he extended upwards and tapped out a message to his controller using the mobile Morse tapper embedded into his palm. Once completed, the agent smiled; chuckled to himself and, turning back to the scene of the crime, bent toward the body; removed his fez and placed it on Iggi's head...

# POST EPILOGUE

If, over the course of the past nine months, someone had asked Alyce what she least expected to see through her window on any given shift, she seriously doubted she would have found herself describing this. How could she have done; it was not even supposed to have been possible! However, she was now one hundred percent certain that what was currently playing out before her eyes, was indeed the very last thing that she would have expected. Alyce gagged on her Muesli; soggy cereal and milk catching in her throat as the thing hove slowly across the flat grey plain on the other side of the glass, decelerating gradually as its rear fin dragged in the dust, gouging a channel to mark its course from left to right. She dropped the book that she had been reading and put down her bowl, sloshing milk onto the control panel beside her. There was a spark and a flash, followed by a thin wisp of smoke from behind the bulb that she had just shorted. The cabin lights dimmed momentarily, but recovered as the emergency fuse reset kicked in. Lights were flashing all across her boards, but Alyce was too busy choking on her breakfast to acknowledge them. "Knackers!" she cussed, in a language that was definitely not English; finally dislodging the raisin that had gone down the wrong way. Wafting away the smoke with her left hand, she began frantically stabbing at buttons with her other, until she was left with only a single blinking red bulb. There was a sudden burst of static from the oval speaker grille at the top of the control board and Alyce swore again just before the base commander's voice warbled through.

"Watch Officer, Troll?" she asked, formally, before shifting her tone, "Is everything alright up there, Alyce?"

Alyce pressed the 'speak' button and replied: "Er, you might want to come up here and have a look at this, Commander," She dabbed at the milk residue on the control panel with her sleeve and flicked a nut behind the desk, "We've got... company," she added, warily. After a quick tidy around; slipping both her bowl and the book that she had been engrossed in before everything had gone haywire, back into her satchel, Alyce activated her viewing screen and had a proper look at the unidentified object from the various angles afforded her by the base's exterior cameras. It was as she had first thought: a space rocket, though an extremely primitive one. Could it really have come from the planet below? Conventional wisdom had it that the humans were at least another six of their decades away from reaching their moon. Was it perhaps another of Bartley's practical jokes, she wondered; something he had cooked up out of spare parts down in the maintenance bay? She certainly would not have put it past him. He did that sort of thing to alleviate the boredom, she knew. Keeping watch over a planet whose inhabitants were yet to discover every life form on their own world, let alone realise that they were not the only 'intelligent' life in the system, was a tedious business at best; you had to get your kicks where you could. Something caught her eye on one of the camera views. She toggled the zoom and saw what she presumed to be a nameplate bolted to the object's side. On Mars, Alyce had trained as a linguist; she had therefore, found it relatively easy to understand the various primitive languages most commonly spoken on the planet below, by listening to recordings made of life on the surface. It helped to pass the time. Her job was to watch the boards and to report any anomalous readings, up the chain of command. In the whole nine months of this; her first off world posting, she had reported precisely nothing, until now. The script may have been alien, but; she considered it was quite beautiful in its simplicity. 'VR PERIWINKLE', it said; not that she had the first idea what that meant.

# THANK YOU

Thanks to Donna Ray (obviously); Darren Laws of Caffeine Nights Publishing (for taking the chance); Colin Edmonds: a great inspiration; Tabitha Daniels-Moss for all the mathematics involved; Fay Roberts for Welsh translation; Jonathan Lambton who introduced me to the concept of both Steampunk Literature and music (and was responsible for photographing the Victoria), and to Chris Cracknell (the doktar) for building her.

This book was written to the accompanying sounds of, 'The Men Who Will Not Be Blamed For Nothing' so, many thanks should also go to them.

# ABOUT THE AUTHOR

In 1984 a journalist writing for The Watford Observer dubbed 'wannabe enigmatic pop star' Paul 'Eccentric' because he refused to give his surname during an interview. It stuck. For the past thirty years he has been writing, directing and performing under this ridiculous moniker, but at least it got him noticed.

He is a published songwriter, poet, playwright and novelist.

His debut novel: 'Down Among The Ordinaries' was published by United Press in 2004. He then spent the next few years writing and directing for stage and radio, which culminated in his first Edinburgh Fringe run with his play 'The Sorry People'.

In 2009; along with Ian Newman and Donna Daniels-Moss, Paul co-founded Rhythmical Ravings and Rants (RRRANTS), a poetry, song writing, comedy and storytelling collective. Their first in-house publication was Paul's poetry collection; 'The Kult Of The Kazoo' at the end of 2009.

In 2010 he published a self-help guide to performing, based on his performance workshops and coaching classes entitled, 'Quaking In Me Stackheels'. He followed this in 2013 with 'Rrrantanory Little Stories', a collection of bedtime stories for adults; both for DesertHearts Publishing. In 2015 he wrote, 'The Edinburgh Fringe In A Nutshell' which was published by Burning Eye Books; a guide to taking your first show to the biggest arts festival in the world.

He has written numerous plays and stories as well as documentaries and articles for radio and has had his poetry featured in various newspapers, magazines and anthology books.

He is probably best known as the mouthy half of dyslexic poetry duo 'The Antipoet': the beatrantin' rhythm'n views act that currently takes up most of his life.

He has been fronting The Odd Eccentric since 1984; albeit with a break during the mid-1990s, and The Senti-Mentals; on and off since 1996, along with several other bands: Polkabilly

Circus, Sly Quip & The Quickwits, SLOB and The Rocketeers.

When not writing or performing, he is Artistic Director, and one third of the triumvirate behind The RRRANTS Collective, helping to promote and disseminate independent poets, songwriters and storytellers. He is available for compering duties, events hosting and after dinner speaking if you're very, very brave.

His passions include The BARDAID Initiative, (of which he is the founder); Doctor Who, vegetable growing; punk rock; animals; the countryside and Donna.

He has no truck with bigots; supermarkets; the gentry, and animal killers.

He is a committed anarchist, atheist and vegetarian and a keeper of cats, ducks, goats, chickens and Samantha the tortoise. He continues to sponsor various donkeys, sheep, dogs, Alpacas and most recently a herd of reindeer.

He lives with his wife, Donna in Aston Clinton, Buckinghamshire.

Pauleccentric.co.uk